SHADOWS ON

An Alternative

Foreword

This novel explores what might have been if Richard III had won the battle of Bosworth and defeated Henry Tudor. This is an historical romance which has very little to do with the 'real' history of the time, being a 'what if' story. Richard has defeated one enemy, but there are others who oppose his reign and will work to overthrow him. He has the continued support of his new young queen, Isabella of Spain, but most of all the unwavering friendship of Francis Lovell, his most trusted and beloved friend. In the ten years following the battle, Richard works to bring peace to his country. But conspiracies continue, and one enemy in particular strikes where he is most vulnerable.

Acknowledgments

You can blame Covid-19 for this! Writing it helped keep me sane during the long months of lockdown.

Thanks are due: -- to Kathy, who loved the opening sequence so much that she felt compelled to nag at me to carry on and offered encouragement when I flagged.

To Terence, and Chris and all those who read the manuscript, pointed out the errors, and made suggestions.

For the beautiful cover photograph Linsey Williams.

And to my computer guru Patrick!

1. Richard Redux

Bosworth 1485

He was bone weary, weary unto death. Every muscle, every fibre of his body ached, a symphony of pain that made his breath catch at every grace-note. He could not get a deep enough breath – his chest, constrained as it was by his cuirass, by breast- and backplate, struggled for air, and he was gasping like a landed fish. What air he did get was foul with battlefield stench of burst bowels and spilt blood. Blood caked his gauntleted hands, his arms to the shoulder, clammy on his skin where it had seeped under metal and padded jupon, sticky and glistening on the bright steel of his armour. His surcoat with the royal arms was ripped and sodden.

“Dickon?” Francis Lovell’s voice, hoarse. “Dickon? Your Grace?”

He managed to croak an acknowledgement. “Francis. White Surrey…”

His beautiful destrier, pride of his stables, staunch battle-companion par excellence… So much carrion, now. Cut down in the final charge.

“Tudor,” he said. “Francis. Where is Tudor?”

“Someone look to the king!” Francis shouted over his shoulder, making him wince. “Dickon. You took a blow to the head. Tudor is dead. You killed him yourself.”

Someone was offering a flask – water? No, barley-spirit. He gestured it aside. Tudor, dead? He found a brief jewel-clear memory – a white face, upturned, mouth gaping, eyes wide with terror. And the axe swinging down almost of its own volition to cut the man off from life and breath. “Yes,” he said. “It’s over, then…Deo gratias…”

Someone – his squire? – was lifting the sallet helm from his head, and the mail coif settled around his shoulders. The arming cap had matted his hair into a sweaty felted mass. The air felt good. The fever-heat of the previous night had gone, sweated out, he guessed, by the exertion of battle. Francis had an arm around his shoulders, leading him through the carnage to his tent. He roused himself to issue the necessary orders, because that was what a king did.

"Tudor's body to the Greyfriars, for public viewing. Then he must be embalmed, to make him seemly before taking him to London. When we have the numbers of his surviving army, we will decide what is to be done. The Stanley brothers – I should never have trusted them, Francis, you were right – do they live?"

"They do, your Grace." That was faithful Rob Brackenbury, going to one knee to salute his king.

"They are in your charge, Rob. The Tower, then trial for treason." Hands were stripping his arming jacket, his plate armour, leaving him in his sodden shirt and hose. "Lady Margaret..." He thought briefly of her grief at the loss of husband and son, but also how she had repaid his generosity with the most heinous treachery. "She is to be immured in a convent. Bermondsey, I think."

"Dickon!" An objection from Francis.

"I do not make war on women." There was wine, and water, and fresh clothing. "Now, I want a Mass of Thanksgiving as soon as possible. And send word to Sheriff Hutton. The children must be reassured. And, Francis – "

"Your Grace?"

"I want White Surrey buried fittingly. He was faithful and most valiant to the end."

There were tears standing in Francis' eyes. "I'll see to it, Sire."

There was another message to be sent. "And to the Duchess, ma mere. Tell her – " and he smiled, "Tell her 'Richard liveth yet.'"

*****

The road back to Leicester was crowded – carts for the wounded and dead, and people gathering at the roadside for news of the battle. A ragged cheer began, gathering strength as they saw the White Boar banner. "God save King Richard!" and "God be praised!" Word ran ahead like a river of rumour, and more folk crowded forward, waving their White Boar bannerets, so that the herald, Blanc Sanglier, had to force a way through the press. The horse the king rode was unused to this kind of crush, was jibbing and dancing – Francis, riding close, used his own mount to control the crabbing sidewise gait. Richard, however, sat like a rock. He acknowledged the cheers, nodding to right and left – accepted a garland of white roses from a worshipful girl-child – but as soon as the door of the White Boar Inn closed behind him, he accepted the support of Francis' shoulder, and submitted to the ministration of Hobbes, the royal physician, and the surgeon in his train.

"What word of our losses, Francis?" He grimaced as the skilled fingers checked the bruises already purpling on his body, and leeches were applied. He hated leeches.

"It can wait, Dickon, surely..."

"Now, Francis." And it was the king who spoke.

"Richard Radcliffe... Rob Percy, also. And your niece's husband, Lord Scrope-- " It was a rollcall of nobility, of the men who had ridden to battle with their king. And the commons, too, though names would come later.

"They will not be forgotten," he vowed.

"You must rest, your Grace," Hobbes advised. "You were fevered last night. The fever has left you, but its effects are still with you. Rest!" It had the force of a command, and Richard knew better than to argue. Besides, he longed for the oblivion of sleep.

Hobbes and the surgeon left, after seeing the king to his bed, and after making certain that everything was in order, Francis bade the king goodnight. "God's peace, your Grace. I'll be outside the door."

"Thank you, Francis. I shall do very well. Get some sleep yourself. We have done ten men's work this day."

"That we have, Dickon!" Francis agreed, with a chuckle, and left him alone.

Richard lay back, carefully, against the heaped pillows of his travelling-bed, wincing as the battle-injuries made themselves felt again. God be thanked, there was nothing that would not mend. The surgeon had left some pain-deadening potion, but he ignored it. The wine was good, and he cut it with water, the better to quench the thirst that still plagued him. The sickness, the feverish weakness that had plagued him the previous night, was eased. The light of the solitary candle Francis had left flickered on the walls, on the dark timbers with their vermilion vines – not for the simple inn of Leicester the luxuries of tapestry – and the silence rang in his head like a bell, echoing with the ghost-cries of battle.

Yes. He was remembering details now. The sickening instant when he realised that the Stanleys had turned their coats again – the rage that surged through him, and the ice-cold realisation that he must risk all now on one throw of the dice. *Alea jacta est*. Had he actually spoken that aloud? And valiant little Salazar, bloody from head to foot, clutching at his stirrup, entreating him to fly the field, to regroup and live to fight again. But no. *As God sees me, if I die, I will die like a king!*

He clapped his heels to White Surrey's sides, felt the power in the destrier's loins, bunching under him, the willingness for the charge, and they were flying down the flanks of the hill, he and the Household, arrow-straight for the knot of soldiers around the Red Dragon banner. Smashed into them like a hammer-blow, mowing them down like grass under the scythe, and the gigantic figure of Sir John Chenye loomed in front of him for just an instant before his axe found the man's life and then he swung the blade round to cut Brandon down, and the banner fell with him, and there – there – was the Tudor! A pale face, eyes stretched in terror, mouth gaping, and he struck, the jar of the blow as the blade scythed though flesh and bone…

"God forgive me," he whispered, and ignoring the pain struggled from the bed to kneel at the *prie-dieu* beneath the figure of the crucified Christ. He signed himself, bent his head on his folded hands. He murmured the *Te Deum*. "*In te Domine, speravi…*"

Tomorrow he would make confession, and hear Mass, and receive his Saviour. Until then, he must trust himself and all he loved to the Hands of God. And surely he had been in God's hands this day, Who had delivered him the victory.

As it was, the king spent three days in the town, recovering from his injuries – which, thanks be to God, were not serious. On the second morning, he went to where Tudor's body was displayed, as was the custom, and then to the church, where he ordered Requiem Masses to be said for all the dead.

He had Catesby, his Lord Chancellor, compile lists of names – those who had supported him, and died for it. And those who had supported Tudor, and survived. Rhys ap Thomas, who had taken oath that the invader would pass 'only over his body', and had broken that oath. John de Vere, Earl of Oxford. Reginald Bray. Jasper Tudor, the usurper's uncle, was reported killed. As was Edward Woodville. Of the others, he must decide who would be indicted for treason. The Stanleys, certainly. He had been too trusting.

But it went against the grain to be vindictive. He could consult with his advisers, and listen to them, this time, but those who sued for mercy would be heard. The French mercenaries would be shipped back to whichever gutter they came from…

*****

London was London – stinking like a privy in the late summer heat, raucous; but they cheered him through the streets, their Good King Richard, and Parliament sent a deputation to congratulate him on his victory. Westminster Hall, where he met them, was heavy with the mingled reek of many sweating bodies. They called for his justice on the traitor Stanleys, and it was swiftly decided. Sir William and Sir Thomas would go to the block. Their families to be attainted. Their lands, titles, and goods all forfeited to the crown. Parliament approved, as did his Privy Council.

"It is little enough," Norfolk growled. "Their treason could have cost you the crown, Sire."

"God's mercy that it did not," he agreed. "We have lost too many loyal men… Master Secretary Kendall is to grant pensions to the families of those killed in my service."

"Your Grace is generous." The Speaker of the House, Sir William Catesby, cleared his throat. "On another matter, your grace – I am constrained by your lords and loyal commons to beg your indulgence…" He cleared his throat again, shifting in his seat. "On the subject of your Grace's marriage…"

Richard closed his eyes briefly. The pain of that loss was still raw in his heart. "What of it?" he said steadily. "Name of God, my queen has been dead scarce half a year, and you would force another wife on me?"

Sir William looked even more uncomfortable. "My lord King, your Grace, we mourn the loss of the gracious Queen Anne, of course we do, and the whole country shares in your sorrow, but..."

He sighed. "I know, I know, I must needs have an heir of my body. Do you reassure my lords and commons that I am aware of this, and I thank them for their concern." He got to his feet. "You are dismissed."

Outside, the August heat pressed down like a hot weight. "Francis, I am for Berkhamsted. Will you ride with me?"

"With a good will, your Grace!"

The country air was sweeter than the city stinks, and Richard felt his spirits rise. The sun was warm on his shoulders, and he pulled off his velvet cap to let the breeze cool his face and head, lifting his hair from his neck. "Francis, should I cut my hair?" he said idly. "A shorter crop is the fashion now, is it not?"

"It is. If you were ever a follower of fashion." Francis gave his quirking grin. "It is cooler, I can tell you." His own mouse-fair hair was cropped short, and tended to stick up in spikes, like a hedgehog.

"I will give it due consideration." He smiled at his friend, and signalled his escort. "Gentlemen – " And he urged his horse into a canter.

The Duchess' manor of Berkhamsted was a rich one, and in good order, as he would have expected, knowing his mother's insistence in overseeing her holdings. She had had the training of Anne, her daughter-in-law, and Anne had run Middleham with ease and grace. Anne… He could think of her now with less of the intense anguish of the past months. It was so short a while since she had left him.

He drew rein, letting his horse breathe, and patted the sweaty neck, and let the grooms lead the animal away. His mother's household steward hastened to bend the knee to him.

"My lord king…"

"Is the Duchess receiving, Michael? Announce me, if you will."

She had been known as Proud Cis, and the Rose of Raby, and that legendary beauty was still evident in the fine bone structure of the face framed by the starched white wimple of a religious. She was in stark Benedictine black and white, but, as befitted her status as mother of the king, the stuffs were of the finest. The rosary in her hand was of ivory and gold, a gift, Richard knew, from his father after Edward's birth.

She rose from her chair as her steward announced him. "My lord King…" she murmured, dropping into a deep curtsey, and then smiled up at him. "My most dear son."

"*Maman*," he raised her, returning her smile. And kissed the cheek she offered him.

"Come, sit. Michael, some wine, if you would. Dickon, you look peaked." She sat down, arranging her skirts, and he took the stool at her knee as if he were not king but just the beloved last-borne son. "Are you well? There was some talk that you were taken sick."

"Aye, before the battle. A fever, but mercifully brief. I had a battle to fight, sick or well, and the Tudor would not wait. You got my message."

"Indeed. 'Richard liveth yet'. I have had masses said in thanksgiving ever since. I think I near wore out my knees praying for your victory."

"God had me in His hands that day." He signed himself automatically. "Is it over now, do you think? This Civil War that has killed so many. My father, my brothers – "

"We must trust in God, my dear, that those lives were not spent in vain. Tell me, the Beaufort woman – you have not left her free to spread yet more of her poison?"

He grimaced. "I was a fool, before. I was warned, but I thought to be merciful. No, my lady Scorpion is immured in Bermondsey Abbey, for her lifetime. With her son and husband both dead, she has no affinity left to call on. Oh, she'll be fairly treated – I make no war on women. But she'll not breathe free air again."

"It is better than she deserves," Cecily said grimly. "And her son?"

"He will be buried as befits his blood, be sure. He was Richmond at one time, and of noble blood."

"Yes, you will do all rightly, that I know. Now," And she settled herself more firmly in her chair, her hands on the carved lions of the arm-rests. "There is the matter of your marriage."

He winced. "*Ma mere*, Anne has been gone scarce half a year..."

"I know, my son, and I know how dear she was to you. To all of us. Next month, on the sixteenth of September, you will hold her Month-Mind. But after that, you must think of another bride." She fixed him with a gaze that held compassion and determination both. "Is it the Portuguese match that you are considering?"

"It has the benefit of a double match, since we know Dom Manuel is desirous of taking Elizabeth."

"A good point. That would scotch those foolish rumours once and for all. But consider this, Richard. The Princess Joanna is – not young. Her chances of conceiving and bearing even one healthy child diminish as she ages. Sir Edward is well aware of this. He has made sure you are neither pledged nor promised. A younger bride would be better. The Infanta Isabella, of the House of Trastamara – "

"She is a child."

"She is a woman, and of an age to wed, or her parents would not have considered it. Send a copy of your portrait to her. No," She held up a hand to forestall his objections, "It does not commit you to either one. The agreements are *de futura*. The succession is paramount, my dear. You wed for love once – as did I. Now you must wed for policy."

He bowed his head, and after a moment, felt her hand on his hair in a caress. "Dear son," she murmured. "God be thanked that of all my sons, he has left me the finest. Will you join me in my chapel to hear mass?"

Richard chose to spend the night at his mother's house rather than make the journey back to London, and asked Francis to join him for a cup of the Duchess's excellent wine before retiring.

"I must send to Margaret in Burgundy," he said, filling their cups and dismissing the hovering page. "Get some rest, Piers, I will not need your services tonight. Francis, will you go to Burgundy for me?"

"As you command, Dickon. Of course."

"You and the good Brackenbury. My most trusted friends..." He smiled, raising his cup in salute. "And you can enjoy the fleshpots of my sister's court. She and my dear brother had much in common. Save an infestation of Woodvilles, that is!"

Francis snorted into his winecup, and his brown eyes sparkled. "So I have your leave, Dickon, to ...indulge myself?"

"So long as you make confession on your return! Father Dominic will set you a ...suitable penance, I am sure." They grinned at each other. It felt so good to be able to relax, to be as they used to be, two boys at Middleham.

It was in a sombre mood that Richard rode back to London and the cares of his kingship. He knew that his mother the Duchess was right. She had never steered him wrong.

*****

The embalmed body of Henry Tudor was sent to the Benedictines at Lancaster Priory, to be buried there without undue ceremony. There was none to mourn him. Richard paid the Mass Penny himself, and instructed that masses be said for the dead rebel's immortal soul. Privately he wondered if he would have received like courtesy if Tudor had won the day...

He had already decided that John of Gloucester, bastard but beloved of his father, should be confirmed as Captain of Calais – that should be put in train. Katherine, his daughter, was too young for marriage yet, but she would have a place at court. He decided that Francis would replace deVere as Lord Chamberlain and Master of the Household. And there were land grants to be given out, and judicial matters to be heard and settled before he could leave the reek of London behind and head north.

But at last, rejoicing, he was able to ride north to York. His entry through the Micklegate.found that city, city of his heart, was *en fete*, delirious with joy, welcoming their favourite son with cheering crowds, with flowers and garlands and overwhelming love. The sunlit air quivered with the cacophony of bells, as if every church vied to outdo its neighbour in rejoicing. From the scarlet and red of the assembled Aldermen and city dignitaries, foursquare Thomas Wrangwysh, grinning so widely as to threaten his ears, stepped forward and proudly presented his king with a gilt cup brimming with gold.

"We thank you, Sir Thomas," Richard smiled at him, accepting it.

"Nay, your grace." Flustered, the man sought to correct the mistake without angering his king. "Plain Tom Wrangwysh I am..."

"*Sir* Tom, from this day. Note it, all. But take back your gold. I desire only your loving hearts."

The cheer that went up resounded off the city walls.

*****

He had summoned the Council of the North, his northern lords and affinities, who had served him so well in the battle, to meet him at St Mary's Abbey. He had trusted Northumberland – and against all expectation, Percy had not let him down. Without his support, the battle might so easily have gone another way. He deserved reward, as did so many others. Folk said he preferred the north over London and the south, and it was true. How not? He had spent his boyhood at Middleham – had brought Anne there after their wedding. And they had been happy there. His son had been born there, was buried at Sheriff Hutton. What had London and the south given him save intrigue and sorrow and death?

And the crown.

A burden, an obligation that he did not want, but knew he must accept, or plunge the country into more years of vicious civil war. He had been a good king, and he knew he had it in him to be better yet. He would set in train the ideas that had been crowded out by the invading Tudor.

He should have expected that the first item for discussion, as in London, was his remarriage. Catesby, his Chancellor, and Francis, as Lord Chamberlain, had prepared him. “She is no beauty,” Francis said, regarding the portrait of the princess Joanna. “And her age is against her, Dickon.”

“I am no stripling youth, either,” Richard pointed out.

“But you do not have to bear living sons,” Catesby said bluntly. “Just sow the seed. She is thirty and three, sire. Old, for a first bearing.”

Richard winced inwardly. It was true. Yet, did he have a choice? He took his seat at the head of the table in the Council Chamber. He knew what was to come. The Council said unanimously that the succession was of paramount importance.

“The Princess and her brother Dom Manuel have been invited to visit us for our Christmas Court, my lords. I can make no decision until then.” At least that gave him some breathing space.

“I understand that the Princess is a most pious lady,” That was the Archbishop of York. Pompous old raven...

"Well and good," Catesby said dryly. "But it is not piety that will give us a Prince of Wales."

"True enough," one of the Northern lords chuckled. "Not so much time on her knees as on her back, eh, lad?"

Richard's lips compressed. He was used to the blunt northern humour, but this was approaching a step too far, and the Council knew it. Luckily the Council could not read his mind. He was hard put to keep a straight face. But John Kendall his secretary stepped in smoothly to intercede.

"Your Grace, you may wish to consult with Sir Edward Brampton. There is the other possible match, with the House of Trastamara. The eldest daughter of Queen Isabella and King Ferdinand, the Infanta Isabella? Their Majesties are anxious for a closer alliance with England."

"I have been informed of this. Sir Edward has taken my portraits to both courts." *For all the good it may do,* he added silently to himself. "I have sent Sir James Tyrell to Sheriff Hutton, to escort the children here. Now that the immediate danger is past, it is time they took their places at court. I am tasked, also, in finding suitable marriages for my brother's daughters, as I promised. There is a possible suitor in Dom Manuel of Portugal for Elizabeth -- or Cecily, now that she is widowed. Their husbands must be gentlemen born, of good character and sufficient wealth to keep my nieces in style. And I will not force them into marriage. We saw enough of that with Dame Grey foisting her relatives on anyone with wealth, or power, or noble blood, and we all know what came of it."

"Ah, well, there's time enough," Lord Dacre said comfortably. "The Lady Elizabeth is but eighteen..."

Eighteen, and fair as a wild rose...

Sir James Tyrell escorted the children from Sheriff Hutton to York where they lodged at the Archbishop's Palace, and told them, grinning, that the king would come to visit them shortly. There was a bustle of making ready, the nurses and governors in a panic lest they and their charges be found wanting. It was for Elizabeth, like a centre of calm in the midst of a storm, to get everyone settled.

"Cecily – stop primping. You look pretty enough. Anne, Catherine – can you stop those boys fighting?"

"It's only in play, sister!" Catherine said. She was flushed with excitement, and her silky fair hair, under the gold mesh cap, was coming down. It never held a curl.

"I know, but they'll start throwing muck at each other… John! Can you control them?"

John of Gloucester strode to the two combatants, Edward of Warwick (who should have known better) and the pageboy Rufus -- took a scruff in each hand, and separated them with an admonitory shake. He was a handsome lad, the oldest of the Sheriff Hutton group, and very like his father the king. And like the king, he wore an air of authority, and wore it well. The boys, rather dusty and rumpled, were delivered, chastened, to their governor.

"Anything else I can do, cousin?" He gave her a smile. The murrey-and-blue of the York colours suited him well. She smiled back.

"It's like herding cats," she sighed. "Oh, Lord, we'll never be ready…"

"Ready for what?" queried a familiar male voice, and she whirled, seeing the king in the doorway. Everyone bowed or curtseyed – the king gave his quirking little smile. "You are all looking well. Very well. Was the journey good?"

"It was, your Grace." John straightened up, and returned his father's grin. He was already the taller. "The weather was dry, thanks be to God."

"Indeed. Cecily – Mary – Catherine." Each dropped in a deep curtsey. There was less formality from the ten-year old young Earl of Warwick, who escaped his governor's hand and skidded to a halt in front of his uncle. And bowed sketchily.

"H'llo, Uncle Richard. I need a new pony."

"Do you, indeed. We must look into it, Ned. You have grown."

"We are all rejoiced to see your Grace," Elizabeth spoke for them all. "And we thanked God for your victory."

"Non nobis," the king said, bowing his head. "To Him the Glory…" Then he lifted his head. "Elizabeth, will you walk with me?"

The little enclosed garden was redolent with the scents of lavender and thyme, brought to sweetness by the August sun. He paused by a bed of sage, plucked a leaf to crush in his fingers. "I must talk to you, niece."

"I am your Grace's to command," she murmured, and sank in a deep obeisance, her blue skirts spread around her like the petals of a flower of which she was the heart.

"Rise, Bessie," he said gently, using the affectionate little nickname they had grown used to using between them from her childhood. She took his offered hand, and came to her feet – standing, she was his height to the inch. But both her parents had been tall. *My Rose of England,* he thought fondly. *True daughter of York – a white rose, indeed, new-come to full blooming.*

He kissed her brow, and then the lips offered to him so trustingly.

"I am so glad, Uncle," she said softly. "I don't have to wed the Tudor now. I never wanted to. If I'd had a choice, I'd have chosen – someone else." Her eyes dropped. He knew the wish in her heart, and berated himself for not discouraging it – though it had been thought a necessary ploy, to thwart

Tudor's ambition by casting doubt on her purity. It had misfired, sadly, and he'd had to deny the rumours publicly.

"That was never to be, dearling," he told her. "I was at fault, for true. But my queen and I – we saw you as the daughter we would never have. I loved you – I still love you – as a daughter. "

"Oh, I know." She sighed, and he took her hand, tucking it into the crook of his arm as they walked together. "I suppose I must think on the Portuguese match now…"

"As must I." He paused. "Dearest, it is the lot of princes to marry for reasons of state. To marry for love – as your father did – is rare. Negotiations are now in place for the visit of the Portuguese princess and of her brother. I have little choice in the matter – it seems the lady is not uncomely, if a little over-pious. But she could have a face like a pig, and manners to match, I must still wed her, or another, and get heirs of my body. You, on the other hand – Bess, if you see him, and you think you can come to love him, then good. If you cannot like him, I will not force you to his bed. My word as your kin, and as your king. There are princes enough in Christendom who would go on their knees praising God for a smile from my Rose…"

She gave him that smile, a little tremulous. "I understand, Uncle, and I thank you for all your kindnesses to me and to my sisters…"

"Would God things were different," he said, heartfelt. "But until I have sons, you and your siblings are the last Children of York, my dear. When my queen died, so soon after my boy – God assoil them both! – I despaired of having an heir. I needed a man tried in battle, and John of Lincoln is a worthy knight, so for now he must carry that burden."

"There will be more fighting?" she asked, her brow creasing.

"Inevitably, dearest. The Scots will ever be a thorn in our flesh. So I shall invest him as Lieutenant General of the North, as I was before my brother's death."

"Until you have sons to inherit. What of my brothers?"

He smiled. "My lords Bastard are over-young for high office, Bess, do you not think? Ned can be Lieutenant of Ireland, perhaps. In a few years. And think, if you wed Manuel, you will be a Duchess of Portugal."

She nodded, silent for a moment. Then, with a flash of mischief: "Or he can wed Cecily. She is ripe for it, Uncle! And she would so adore to be a duchess!"

His eyebrows rose. "Indeed? And what of you, my Rose?"

She looked down, not meeting his eyes. "Is the Grand Cham of Tartary yet unwed, do you think, Uncle?"

"I will make enquiry," he said gravely. "And I believe the Prince of Hungary, Matthias Corvinus, is a widower. His ambassador was at court last Martinmass. Or there is the king of Moldavia, Stephen the Third. Or the Grand Prince of the Rus, Ivan..."

He was laughing at her, she realised. "Given my choice," she said carefully, "I would rather wed a good Englishman."

"Given my choice, I would that you could. See Manuel, first. You may find him much to your liking. Tell me, is little Bridget still set on a convent?"

"She is over-young, I think, but insists she has a true vocation."

"Well, her dowry will serve for a corrody..."

They were interrupted, then, by the arrival of a messenger, dishevelled and dusty from the road. He dropped to one knee, held out a letter. “From her Grace the Dowager of Burgundy, sire.”

“Thank you. Go and refresh yourself.” He turned to Elizabeth, smiling. “This will be word of your brothers, now it is safe for them to come home.” He broke the seal, and was silent as he read. She saw his face go sallow-grey under the tan. “Oh, dear God…”

“Uncle…?”

*****

Elizabeth Grey, once Queen of England, twice wed and twice widowed, lived in comfortable retirement at the manor home of Sir John Nesfield. Richard had offered her a place at court, but understood that she would see it as a humiliation – to be plain Dame Grey where once she had been Edward’s gilt-haired queen. He had settled an annuity on her, and Sir John had been instructed that whatever she desired (within reason) she should have.

She had never corresponded with him, even to thank him. He knew that she resented him, that she had been a part of the conspiracy to topple him – but understandably she had wanted her boy to succeed his father, to be crowned as Edward V. He remembered the temper-storm when the news of the bigamous marriage came to light, bastardising her children, and barring her boy from the throne. To give her credit, he did not think she had known of Edward’s previous marriage. If she had, it might have made a difference. Or not. Edward’s lust had been matched by her cunning, her lust for power. She had wanted Edward as much as he had wanted her. Her grief at his death had been genuine, if short-lived. Then her Woodville kin had taken control, ready to dare anything to get their puppet-king on the throne. When those plans had come to nothing, she had backed the Tudor, baiting him with the offer of her daughter

Well, it had all come to naught. But he felt no ill-will toward her now – and indeed, he pitied her. No mother would bear with equanimity what he must now tell her…

Sir John greeted him fulsomely, but seeing his grave expression, merely escorted him to the solar where Elizabeth sat, desultorily working on a piece of embroidery. As he was announced, she stuck her needle through the fabric, got unhurriedly to her feet, and dropped him a deep formal curtsey.

"Your Grace…" she murmured. Richard gestured to her to rise, stepped forward, and gave her the kiss of kindred on her cool cheek.

"Sister Elizabeth," he said, and kept his hands on her shoulders, seeing confusion in her fine grey eyes. "Sister. I have news from Burgundy. You should sit."

She groped for her chair, her eyes never leaving him. The sunlight from the oriel window fell full on her face – pitiless, it showed the marks of her age, undisguised now by the clever lotions and creams she had used as queen. The skin around her eyes was pleated, the lines bracketing her mouth scored deep. The beauty that had snared a king was gone. He had a moment of realisation – that was another reason she shunned his court. Never would she welcome comparisons between her and her daughter. Her pride, her vanity, would not allow it. The silver-gilt hair that had been her chief pride was coiled in a loose knot at her nape. Her plain linen cap did not hide the first ashy strands of grey at her brow.

"I know that you suspected me of the basest murder when your boys vanished from the royal residence at the Tower. I could not tell you – or anyone – that they had been sent secretly out of the country, on my orders, to my sister in Burgundy."

"Why? Why was I not told? I am their mother!"

"And you were in correspondence with Margaret Beaufort, Lady Stanley. Could you have kept that secret from her? Here they were in danger of death from Tudor's people – Margaret Beaufort tried more than once to breach the measures I had put in place at the Tower, to keep them safe. Men said they had not been seen for months – I was pressured to show them forth, to deny the rumours that I had done away with them. I could not, nor could I say why. They were in the safest place I could contrive – incognito, at my sister's court, in Burgundy. I could not risk Tudor or any of his affinity discovering them. I gave you what proofs I could without betraying their location – and you agreed to leave Sanctuary with the girls and trust to my care. Your sons I arranged to stay with their aunt until all threat was gone."

"Then – " Her hands flew to her throat, her eyes blazing. "Tudor is dead – they can come home!"

He turned and made a summoning gesture to someone hovering on the threshold. She saw a young page come hesitantly forward, then push back his crimson hood. A tall stripling, gangly as a colt, but with the grey eyes and barley-blond hair of her second royal son, Richard of Shrewsbury.

She let out a sob of pure joy, opening her arms. "Dickon, oh, Dickon, my boy, my heart's darling…"

Richard would have given them a moment for their reunion, but she looked over her son's head. "And Edward…? Is he here too?"

"No, Madam." Richard drew a breath. "Sister, Edward is dead."

She gave a great choking wail, clutching her younger son to her. “Oh, God, merciful God, no, no, no, it cannot be…”

“It was the Sweating Sickness, my sister writes. He was well at supper, but by dawn he was deathly ill, and by sunset he was dead, God rest his innocent soul. Dickon succumbed that same day, but fought off the infection. Sister, I grieve with you. My court is in mourning for him. I have given orders that he is to be buried at Windsor, with his father.”

Francis would see to it. He had escorted the younger boy home from Burgundy, and brought the chested body of his brother with him. It had taken some negotiation, as sea-folk disliked carrying corpses, even those of the Blood Royal.

Richard wasn’t sure she even heard him. She was rocking back and forth, keening, her face glazed with tears. Young Dickon clung like a limpet, choking. For once she did not care that his tears spotted her grey silk. Richard stood uncomfortably watching her. Then: “Madam, by your leave…” She made a gesture of dismissal, gulping, and he left mother and son to their anguish.

There was wine waiting below. He poured a full cup and drank it down. And a second. The steward silently brought more wine, and manchet bread and sheeps-cheese, but he could not eat.

There was some commotion outside. A few minutes later, another visitor arrived -- the newcomer, travel-stained from the road, halted in mid-stride and they stared at each other. Thomas Grey, Marquess of Dorset, was newly returned from exile in Brittany, as his mother had requested. Well, at least Dame Grey would have another son to ease her grief.

Dorset dropped to one knee. "My lord King... Your pardon, I did not expect..."

"My lord Dorset." Wearily, Richard gestured to him to rise. "I could have wished you a happier homecoming. Go to your lady mother, my lord, and comfort her. She is in sore need of it."

*****

The court was once again in mourning. It seemed that there would never be a time when the dull colours, the dark blues of royal mourning, the blacks, the greys, the purples would be put off and replaced by the splendours of the Royal Wardrobe. Not that Richard had ever been one for the rich crimsons, scarlets, cloths of silver and gold, and the ermine trims and linings.

It was a different matter when he summoned his Parliament to Westminster Hall, lords and commons, and when they had settled, like a flock of ravens in their dark robes, he rose to address them. At times, in past meetings, the heavy and sumptuous Parliament robes had seemed almost to overwhelm his slight figure. Now, he invested them with the full power of majesty.

“My loyal lords and commons, I have asked you here for one purpose. There were rumours, not long after I took the throne, that my brother’s sons had been imprisoned in the Tower, and indeed, that they had been put to death, and by my order.” There was a murmur of disquiet from the assembly, and he stilled it with a raised hand. “It was suggested that I produce them, that they should be seen at Court. I did not do this, and for a good reason. The Lords Bastard were no longer in England.

“There had been attempts, by treacherous persons – by the Duke of Buckingham, by Margaret Beaufort Lady Stanley, and those of the Grey affinity, to take the boys from the Royal Residence at the Tower, and for what purpose we may imagine. To safeguard their lives, therefore, in fulfilment of my oath to protect them, I sent them by secret ways to my strongholds in the north, and thence to my sister Margaret in Burgundy.

"I trusted her to keep their secret, and to keep them safe. And this she did. When Henry Tudor was overthrown, I deemed the threat past. And I sent emissaries to bring them home. Alas, for young Edward, it was too late. But let his brother, Lord Richard, speak of that."

And he gestured at the boy standing beside the dais, bringing him forward to his side, a hand on his shoulder. There was a stunned silence, then a rising buzz of comment and question. Richard let them settle into silence. "Dickon? If you will, tell of what happened when Sir Edward came to you in the Tower."

It was no short tale, and the boy's voice was heard in absolute silence. When he came to tell of his brother's death, though, his voice cracked.

"It was the Sweating Sickness. There had been an outbreak in the town, but Aunt Margaret had forbidden any of her household to venture out, or to let anyone in. Ned and I, though – we disobeyed her. We escaped our governors, and went into the town. It was the next day that Ned sickened. I cannot tell of that, for I was stricken just hours later. And when I recovered, they told me... they told me that Ned was d-dead..." The young face was streaked with tears. "It was my fault, I persuaded him, I wanted to go to the market... And he died."

There was a murmur of sympathy. Richard laid a hand on his shoulder.

"All the Children of York, the true Plantagenet Blood, will have their place at my Court. I value their love and loyalty above my crown. I charge you, my lords and councillors, to pledge your allegiance to the House of York, as you did at my coronation – to renew that oath, as I renew my oath to you and to this our England; to give good lordship and fair dealing to all my people, be they the most puissant lord or the meanest peasant."

The shout of approbation echoed off the high vaulted roof. He laid a hand on young Dickon's shoulder, smiling into the boy's eyes. "They trusted your father, and God grant I also prove worthy of their trust, lad. Come now, I want to make you known to our people."

*****

Much though he loved his mother, young Richard was soon desperate to escape Sir John's estate and his mother's smothering attentions. She did not want to hear of the Burgundian Court, nor Aunt Margaret's kindness, but only over and over again to have him tell of his brother.

"We were not close friends, *Maman*, we hardly knew each other, with him at Ludlow learning to be king."

"You should have been with him," she said. "That was your right."

"Oh, when he stopped bemoaning the loss of his crown---"

"And well he might, for it should have been his. Your uncle ---" She stopped abruptly.

"I could wish you would come to Court, *Maman*. The girls are very happy. The king would welcome you, you know. My cousin Warwick and I do well. We share a tutor."

His mother's eyes were wet. She embraced him convulsively. "I am glad you are content, dearling. But I cannot bring myself to come to Court." *To be Dame Grey again, no longer the fabled gilt-haired queen… No.* "Not yet, sweet boy.

Maybe when the court is out of mourning, though I shall grieve life-long for your dear father and your brother."

He put a consoling arm around her shoulders, and she leaned against him.

"My brother Dorset returns to London shortly," the young man said. "I am minded to go with him. By your leave, of course."

"I cannot prevent you." She sniffed, and blotted her eyes on her kerchief. "Of course, you must go. But come back soon. You are all I have, now..."

*****

"He's a fine boy," Lovell remarked, watching young Richard and Edward of Warwick in the courtyard, riding at the ring, with John of Lincoln in attendance. The late afternoon summer sun was warm on their shoulders.

"He is. He'll be a better man than his late brother – God assoil him! – when he's grown. He and young Warwick will be an ornament and a bulwark to my Court, as well as my loyal kin." He was looking thoughtful. "In a few years, maybe..."

"Dickon?" Francis shot a glance at him. "You're not thinking what I think you're thinking?"

"And what might that be?" Richard said, not looking at him.

"You're not thinking of legitimising him? And the girls?"

"And thereby reversing *Titulus Regius?* Do you think me such a fool, Francis?"

Francis grunted. “No, Dickon. But I’m talking to the fool who trusted the Stanleys, who pardoned m’lady Viper, so who knows what you’ll get it into your head to do next?”

“Your point is taken, my friend. No, I was thinking of Wales.”

“Wales.” Francis repeated, nonplussed.

“Indeed. I have long thought that our Welsh cousins – for so they are, Francis, our line being descended from the Welsh prince Llewellyn ap Iowerth -- have been treated ill. I want all loyal Welshmen to have the same rights as English. I can appoint young Dickon as Lord Governor of Wales and the Marches. Next year he can go to Ludlow and have his seat of administration there.”

“Dickon. Ludlow is the seat of the Prince of Wales.”

“Ah. Indeed. Chepstow, then. He and Warwick can keep company with each other, since it’s hard enough to keep them apart.” He turned to face his friend. “Francis, I am minded to move the Court to York on a more permanent basis.”

Francis gaped. Recovered himself, shaking his head.

“Why am I surprised… Dickon, we should go inside. You’ve had too much sun, it’s turned your brain.”

Richard gave his rare laugh. “Maybe. But Parliament must needs be where the king is. Not *vice versa*. Edward the First made York his temporary capital when he warred against the Scots, did he not? So there is precedent aplenty. I have little love for London, you know that. And York is – has ever been – the city I love best. My Council of the North meets at St Mary’s. We may investigate Clifford’s Tower as an alternative site for now. I’ll leave it to Catesby to look into it.”

*****

Peace with Scotland was high on the King's agenda. Warfare beggared both countries, and he thought that the Scottish treasury must be as depleted as his own, and it behoved him to broker peace. He invited some of the Scottish lords to attend as an embassy. Among them was one of King James' bastards, who had been ennobled and given the honour and title of Rothesay.

Along with the other maidens at court, her sisters Cecily and Cathy in particular, Elizabeth of York was intrigued by these exotic lords, with their plaids and broad accents. One in particular took her fancy when they were introduced at the Court, in York.

The young Duke of Rothesay was taller than she was, lanky and lean, but, by all accounts, a proven warrior. He was tawny-blond, with a soft beard beginning to shadow cheeks and chin. He had bright grey eyes, and a charming smile, and an endearing smatter of freckles across the bridge of his nose. He bent over her hand, brushing it with his lips, and the grey eyes laughed up at her. "My Lady Elizabeth," he murmured. "I am enchanted."

"My lord Duke." She gave him the small curtsey his rank demanded, smiling into his eyes. She was in apple-green that day, and knew it suited her well.

"Will you walk with me, Lady? And tell me about this fair city."

He gave her his hand, and she took it. They walked the pretty knot-garden with its scented herbs and damask roses perfuming the air, and found much that they liked in each other. She told him of York and the manifold beauties of Westminster. He painted for her a romantic word-picture of Scotland. It was inevitable that Elizbeth, denied her first choice of husband, should look elsewhere – and somewhere she could not be constantly reminded of her loss. Such as Scotland.

She wasted no time, going to the king at her first opportunity.

"Uncle," she said as she rose from her curtsey, "I know who I want for my husband." Her eyes were dancing, she had a pretty flush.

"Indeed, my Bess?" He raised an eyebrow. "You are rejecting the Grand Duke of the Rus? He will be disappointed."

"Oh, Uncle, you know that was not to be!" She pouted prettily. Richard smiled.

"So, dearling, who has stolen your heart?"

She turned, and the young man who had been hovering in the doorway came to her side. She took his hand. "This is 'Xander, Uncle."

Alexander Stuart, royal bastard, bent the knee before the man his Borderers had known for many years as 'that bluidy little reiver'. Who was now King of England. And guardian uncle to the lovely Lady Elizabeth.

"Your Grace."

"Rothesay." Richard acknowledged. It would serve, he thought. Wed to him, Elizabeth might never be a queen – as her mother no doubt still wished. But the rank of Duchess would give her status which otherwise might elude her. Yes, it would serve very well. "Bess, I would speak with the young Duke alone, if you will."

She made a deep curtsey, flashed a dimpling smile, and left. Richard poured wine into two cups, indicated that the man should sit, and offered him one. “It would seem you have made a conquest, Rothesay.”

A flush stained the high cheekbones as he took the cup. “Sire – your Grace – although we have but lately met, the Lady Elizabeth and I have come to esteem each other…”

“So it seems.”

“And as you are her guardian, your Grace, I ask you to look with favour on my suit, and allow us to be betrothed. My father would welcome the match, you may be sure.”

“For all that the lady is baseborn?” Richard raised an eyebrow, saw the flush deepen.

“Sire, whatever the circumstances of her birth, the Lady Elizabeth is of royal Plantagenet blood. And I am baseborn myself, though I have my father’s favour.”

“Very well. God forbid I should stand in the way of a true love match… We will write to your father. And the wedding will be arranged as soon as may be. We will write to the pope and investigate any need for a dispensation. If there is that necessity, I have no doubt it will be granted.”

*****

There had been a time when he had thought he could not bear to visit Middleham again. But time had dulled the keen edge of grief, and there were so many good memories of the place that had known him from his boyhood. With the sweet clean air of Yorkshire to flush London’s stink from his lungs, it was a homecoming.

And there was leisure, too, between all the necessary administrative duties. Riding out on the moors with his friends, with his great white gerfalcon Frost and his austringer Hodge, and his favourite hounds running ahead and the scent breast high, the day cold and bright—oh, that was joy! Clad like the others in plain hunting leathers, a thick wool cloak around his shoulders against the keenness of the wind, he was Richard Lord of the North again. Frost brought down a heron, and the party paused for the falconer to split the bird's breast and feed the liver to Frost.

It was Hector, the brindled wolfhound, who first spotted the man scuttling from cover to cover, and led the huntsmen to bring him to bay. Richard looked him over. “Your name, man, and why you are trespassing on Royal land?”
”

“Robin,” the man muttered. “Robin of Niddesdale.” Surrounded by horsemen and huntsmen, with the great hounds eyeing him as if he was rightful prey, he shrank into himself, shivering.

“He's an outlaw, sire, a wolfshead,” one of the huntsmen said scornfully. “Shall we take him in charge?”

“No, not yet.” Richard leaned forward in the saddle. “We will speak to him first. So,” he addressed the trespasser. “You call yourself Robin. Robin of Niddesdale.” He turned to John of Lincoln. “What is it about that name, do you think?”

“Invoking the outlaw legend, perhaps, sire.”

“Indeed. And do you steal from the rich and give to the poor? For certain, you do not seem to enrich yourself.” The outlaw was a ragged sight, indeed, threadbare wool and badly-cured hides in a patchwork motley. “Well, sirrah?”

“Answer my lord, varlet!” Lincoln's command was sharp. Richard raised a hand.

“Hold, John. We asked you a question, Robin.”

"We gives what we can, to those in most need." It was a mumbled response in dialect so thick that it might have been a foreign language. But the king nodded.

"Go on. And who is your paymaster? It was my lord of Warwick who funded Robin Mend-All. He used Middleham as his power-base, John, as I did when I was Lord of the North... It was Neville country. Still is, to a degree."

"Nowt pays us owt," the outlaw growled. "Lord, is it? No lords hereabouts. Not any as'll listen to us common folk. No law runs here."

"Indeed?. But the King's Law prevails, throughout the land, Master – what name was given you at your birth? For sure it was not Robin."

"'arry," he said, and stood straighter. "'Arry Ramsden."

"So, Master Ramsden. Come to Middleham in two days' time, and I swear to you, you shall be heard. If you have complaints about the lordship in these lawless parts, then list them."

"Oh aye?"

"Aye. Word of –" Richard paused. "Word of the lord of these parts."

"'E'll not listen,"

"Oh, I think he will. In fact, I guarantee it. Fare thee well, Master Ramsden."

The Great Hall of Middleham Castle had seen many similar courts. Richard was making it clear, to lords and commons alike, that the rule of Law would run throughout all his kingdom. The Ramsden case, alas, was nothing new.

Harry Ramsden gazed about him, greasy cap clutched in both hands, staring in wonder at the gilded company, at the slight figure seated on the dais. And dropped to his knees, gulping.

"Your pardon, m'lord – sire – lord king – I din't know you…"

Richard raised an eyebrow. "Indeed, and how should you? Master Ramsden, I have heard from the Percy steward, and I would have you tell me yourself, in your own words, why you have turned wolfshead. State your grievances to the court."

The Ramsdens had been sheep-farmers, in a small way, father to son, until one of the Percy stewards had decided that the grazing land should be put to better use, and the Ramsdens had lost their livelihood, and turned, perforce, to outlawry.

Quite clearly, they had not been very good at it.

"…me mam died, the first winter. Tom 'n' Alfie, me brothers, took sick frum hunger. There were nowt to eat. I was a shepherd, me, like me old da. I din't know owt about 'untin' game. Snared a few coneys, but there weren't more'n' a pick of meat on 'em." He sniffled, wiping his nose on his ragged sleeve. "Winter were the worst. No shelter, see. Went to earth, then, like foxes…"

There was a silence. And quietly, Richard got to his feet. "We have heard this case," he announced. "Stand, Master Ramsden We find for the plaintiff. Investigation has revealed that monies changed hands in bribes. We find that the Percy steward acted unlawfully and without consulting his master. Restitution must and shall be made. Master Ramsden, my clerk will see to it. Within thirty days the Percy estate will provide you with a decent living, a fair wage. You and your father were shepherds – it is an honourable trade." He smiled, suddenly. “What is it the country folk say ‘I thank God, and ever shall, it is the sheep hath paid for all’.”

“Aye, Lord King. Can us go back to bein’ shepherds, then? God bless you, sire!”

His knees hit the floor again, and tears cut trails through the grime on his face. Richard stepped down from the dais.

“On your feet, man. And take my hand.” The filthy paw was wiped hastily on the ragged jerkin, and Richard took it in both of his. “Word of a king, Harry Ramsden. We shall amend where we can. Francis, a purse. There is enough here to feed you and your family until you can provide for yourself.”

*****

Richard loved his Middleham stud, established there when he had been awarded the Lordship of the North, and brought his bride to Wensleydale. Here, among the folk he knew best, he could set aside the cares of kingship for a little while. Here, he had overseen the breeding of his famous ‘Syrie’ line, of whom the late-lamented White Surrey had been the best.

He was a born horseman, loved the beasts and understood them, and enjoyed schooling them when he had the time. The animal being exercised, a grey barb of White Surrey’s getting, showed all the qualities he looked for in a warhorse. Whether it could replace White Surrey remained to be seen. Sir James Tyrell, as Master of Horse, was doubtful. They leaned together on the fence, watching a groom put the animal through its paces in the thin sunshine.

“I don’t know, Dickon,” Sir James said candidly. “Looks aren’t everything. He’s a pretty enough creature, I grant you, but he’s had young George off twice. And me, once.”

The king was silent, thoughtful. Then he pushed the gate open and walked into the ring. "George – if you please…" He took the lunge-rein and walked slowly towards the horse. Which stood with ears pricked and a wary intelligence in the dark eyes. "Oh, th'art a beauty, lad, for true." Richard said softly, slipping unconsciously into the dialect of his northern realm. "Coom up, then, my 'andsome. *Douce*, now. Softly…" He was close enough to reach up and run a hand down the silky nose. "What do they call you, hey?" He found a salted crust in his pouch, and offered it. Velvet-soft lips took the treat, and quested over his palm for more. "Pegasus, I think, would be a good name for you, my beauty…" Still talking, his voice a croon, he stroked up to the stallion-crest, down the arched neck, feeling the sweat wet on his hand, and the twitching of nerves. Gathering the lunge-rein up, he grasped the base of the mane, took a step and swung himself astride the bare back. It was a manoeuvre taught in knightly training, and he had practised it assiduously, in armour and out of it, to overcome any awkwardness. A saddle helped, the high front and back providing support, but he had ridden bareback almost before he could walk. He felt the horse – Pegasus – shift under him, and adjusted his seat. "Easy, lad. Easy…" And Pegasus, perhaps recognising the expertise of the man on his back, responded to knee and heel and the gentle hands on the rein. Totally involved in his empathy with the powerful animal, Richard felt the surging muscles beneath him answer to his will. "*'Hast thou given the horse strength?'*" he thought, rejoicing. "*'Hast thou clothed his neck with thunder?'*" So had White Surrey been – *'he mocketh at fear, and is not affrighted; neither turneth he back from the sword. He saith among the trumpets, Ha, ha; and he smelleth the battle afar off, the thunder of the captains, and the shouting…'*

Would Pegasus be another such?

He put Pegasus through the necessary paces, had him to a smooth canter, and then backing, turning, and a canter again. The horse was arching his neck, almost dancing, but responding to the slightest shift of balance, the near-invisible aids the expert horsemen uses.

Yes. This would be a horse in a thousand, and a credit to his mighty sire.

Richard reined him to a halt, patting the glossy neck. The watchers stirred, their awed silence more than applause. He swung his right leg over the withers, slid to the ground – and there, as Proverbs put it, Pride goeth before a fall. Because his foot slipped under him, and he had to catch himself by the horse's mane, pain knifing through his back like a blade. He managed to straighten, wincing, and Tyrell came hurriedly to his side.

"Dickon – your Grace –"

"Give me your shoulder, James," Richard grated, holding on. It would never do for the king to crumple in a heap. It was all he could do to mount the stair to his Privy Chamber, where he subsided with a groan. "It's all right," he managed, seeing Sir James' face curd-white under the countryman's tan. "I've just pulled a muscle. It'll be fine."

"Aye, and pigs have wings," Francis Lovell said, striding in with a face like thunder. "I'm sending for Hobbes."

"Absolutely not. It'll be the leeches again, and you know I cannot abide them." He tried to sit up, but fell back. "Help me off with the jerkin, will you?" So acting as chamber groom, Francis did as ordered, pulled off the fine Spanish leather boots, unlaced the neck of the cambric shirt, soaked with the sweat of pain.

A page pushed open the door, stood gaping in surprise, then gathered his wits. "Your Grace – Sir Edward Brampton is without..."

The king's "Admit him," and Francis' "Later!" came together.

"Admit him," the king repeated firmly.

Sir Edward's beam of pleasure changed to consternation as he regarded his lord. "Your Grace..."

"A minor indisposition," Richard said. "What news, Sir Edward?"

"Portugal is still havering, Sire, but the Princess has been persuaded to visit –your Christmas Court..." He broke off. "Forgive me, but there is someone I would like you to see, Sire."

"Not now, Sir Edward!" Francis objected, but Richard, unwilling to be dictated to, even by Francis, overruled him with a gesture.

And the man Sir Edward escorted into the royal bedchamber a short while later was tall, dark complected, and possessed of a neat little beard and moustache. His long gown was a dark red figured damask, furred with squirrel, and he wore a black velvet skullcap on his greying black curls. His eyes were unnervingly keen, Francis thought.

"Your Grace, this is Doctor Hussey," Sir Edward explained.

"I thank you for your concern, Sir Edward," Richard got out. He was chalk-white, and sweating. "But if I need a doctor, I have Master Hobbes."

Hussey took no heed, stepping to the bedside, and with a murmured "By your leave, my prince," took hold of the king's wrist. After a minute, he said "No fever. Good. But much pain. How is this happening? A slip, a fall? No matter. I can amend." He moved around the bed. "The shirt...?"

Francis, completely at a loss, eased the fine fabric up, exposing Richard's torso.

If the doctor was shocked by the sight of the sadly twisted back, he gave no sign. He was murmuring something under his breath, his fingers delicately touching, working downward – then, with a small grunt of discovery, pressing. "There is the problem..."

Richard, grimacing, gave a harsh bark of a laugh, then winced. "It's been a problem for twenty years!"

"No, no, not the deformity, my prince... But you were not born so? This comes later, as you grow?"

"You trained too hard," Francis said, then bit his tongue.

"Yes, and I am paying the price, am I not?" Then Richard gave a sharp yelp of pain as the clever exploring hands manipulating his spine did something Francis did not see, and the doctor gave a grunt of satisfaction. There was a look of quite comical surprise on the king's face. The pain was clearly lessened. "What did you do?"

"There was – how do you say? – a misalignment. More than before. I – amend."

"Good Christ, it's a miracle." Richard tried to push himself up, but found himself restrained by the hands that had so cleverly eased his pain.

"You must be still, my prince. Inside, there is bruising, swelling. Soreness. It will pass, but you must rest."

"I'm the king, I can't rest. Tell him, Francis. I am grateful, Doctor Hussey, and you will be rewarded, but –"

"But the kingdom can trot on by itself quite well, for a while, without your hand on the rein," Francis said firmly. "Do as you're told, Dickon."

"Jesu, who's king here!"

"You know well, and you made me your Chamberlain, and I'm telling you there is nothing that cannot wait. I'll send for some wine..."

"Tch." The doctor, engaged in positioning pillows to support his patient, shook his head. "Wine, no. Willow bark tea, if you have it. Much better."

Richard made a face. "Tastes like horse-piss."

Francis snickered. He was so relieved to see that his friend was no longer in the excruciating pain, it was making him light-headed. "I wouldn't know, but if you say so."

"And extract of valerian. For relax," Hussey ordered. "For the back, I have an unguent of my own making that will help." And, amazingly, it did, the tight-spasmed muscles warmed and loosened under the clever hands.

Leaving Richard to follow the command to rest, Francis drew the doctor aside as they exited.

"All right, Doctor Hussey," Francis faced him. "Just who exactly are you?"

The doctor made a graceful gesture, touching brow, lips, and breast as he bowed. "I am Husayn Ibn Yusuf. Of Cordoba. In Al-Andalus. In Spain."

"Yes, I know where Cordoba is," Francis said impatiently.

"So. I am trained there. I am a physician and chirugeon. I come with my friend Sir Edward. He tell me there is much need of good doctors here."

"It's true, Francis. He cured me of the Tertian Ague when old Hobbes had told me there was nothing to be done," Brampton cut in.

If, as it seemed, the man had some arcane skills to ease Richard's condition, Francis was all for it. As Chamberlain, he had the authority to order the Household. He would see to it that this man joined the Royal entourage.

"Perhaps, Doctor Hussey – if that is how we should address you? – you might join the king's household for a while? You will be amply rewarded."

Again that graceful gesture. "I shall be pleased, Lord Francis."

"Good. Sir Edward will see to your quartering…."

Richard, being Richard, found inactivity almost unbearable. His mind, at least, was under no restriction, and while he was under orders to rest, he began to formulate an idea that had been in the back of his mind ever since his encounter with the dispossessed shepherd. He had done what he could to amend that injustice, but he felt there were wider issues to consider. He began to put together a plan. He would bring it before his next parliament, he decided – which would have to be soon, before Christmas, as the Royal Treasury was in no good state. He would need to return to London, though, as soon as he could comfortably make the journey.

It took longer than he would have liked, as Francis and Dr. Hussey were insistent that he travel by easy stages. In a way, it became a kind of informal Progress, stopping for a night here or there at various manors and castles, some of whom were hard put to host their king at short notice. Francis would send a messenger ahead, an advance warning of maybe a day or two, of the king's imminent arrival. At least that cut down on the usual extravagant banquets and festivities.

At each halt, Francis would bespeak a bath for the king, which the doctor approved, and certainly it seemed to help, and Richard enjoyed the luxury of having hot herb-scented water to relax into. "Good God," he commented at one halt, the best inn at Stony Stratford. "Sage, rosemary, hyssop, woodruff, and – what's this?"

"Basil," Francis said, gesturing for the young pages to have more hot water brought. "Sovereign against muscle aches."

"Do you tell me." Richard murmured. "Am I to bathe in this –pottage – or am I to stew in it?" He lowered himself into the steaming water with a small groan of pleasure.

"It's better than the leeches, is it not?"

"Anything is better than the leeches," Richard agreed, closing his eyes. "Send a messenger post to Westminster, and inform the lords and commons that they should hold themselves in readiness for our next parliament within the month."

It was a well-attended Parliament, as Lords and Commons alike had been given enough advance notice. Also, the weather remained fair, enabling easy travel. Richard was feeling the benefit of Dr. Hussey's advice and treatments. There was no remedy on earth for the spinal deformity itself, but the discomfort was lessened considerably. So it was that Richard donned the weighty Royal robes appropriate to address the Three Estates in the Great Hall of Westminster. He took his seat on the King's Bench, and the Speaker called the assembly to order.

Taxes were high on the agenda – he had no wish to increase the burden, but it was clearly becoming necessary – as was the recurrent urging for him to choose a bride. There at least he could satisfy the curious.

"I have two options, my lords. Joanna of Portugal, and Isabella of Spain. My portrait has been sent to both. The Portuguese princess has agreed to visit for our Christmas court, along with her brother Manuel. Sir Edward Brampton is acting as our ambassador. Be assured, therefore, that we can hope to welcome a new queen within the year.

"But there is another matter close to our heart. In spite of the law reforms enacted by our previous parliaments, we find there is still injustice. We intend to remedy that. We shall introduce a new court, to be held at need here in Westminster. This will supplement the judicial activities of both common-law and equity courts, and we intend that it will guarantee the fair enforcement of law against those people of such high standing that ordinary courts might hesitate to convict."

There was a silence, then a buzz of talk. He halted it with a raised hand. "The lord Speaker, Sir William Catesby, will see to all details. If you have questions, then you may address him."

"I have located a suitable room, sire," Catesby told him later, as he and Secretary Kendall dealt with the work that had accumulated during his absence. Divested of the heavy parliament robes, Richard was comfortable in a doublet of grey velvet, clasped with silver frogs, over a white lawn shirt. "It is here in the Palace, and commodious enough for the purpose. And pleasant in aspect. The ceiling is decorated with stars."

"I like it. We can call it our Star Chamber, then. Good work, Will. Better arrange for our Cardinal Archbishop to bless and dedicate it for use. And how stands your web, Will? I think we may have need of it."

Sir William smiled thinly. In his plain black gown and the flat cap, unadorned, he might have been any of the lawyers in the Inns of Court. Richard had raised him to the post of Speaker of the House in Parliament, and employed him more secretly as his Spymaster – a nondescript-seeming spider at the heart of his web. He had feelers out in every corner of the realm, gathering information for his king. Anything in any way suspicious was brought to his notice. There were always rumours, of course, and some could be discounted – but the most concerning came from the west, from Wales. Sir William employed several native-speakers in that area, his best being the man he called the invisible Welshman, Miles Bluett, whose agents were ever on alert in that area. There were whispers still, following Tudor's defeat – unrest bubbled up, died down, rose again. Yes, Wales would bear watching.

"The Red Dragon is not dead, sire. And there are those who would rejoice should it rise again."

"Yes," Richard agreed, frowning. "Cast your web wide, Sir William. I think you are right, and we may yet see trouble from that quarter..."

*****

December 1485

Joanna, Princess of Portugal, and her brother Manuel, arrived with an entourage that settled like a flock of crows on the Christmas court. Most of them favoured black in their clothing. What they thought of their reception and the festivities was anyone's guess, as few of them spoke English, and the interpreters tended to rely on a scant knowledge fattened by Latin. The formalities were observed, and the principals bowed before the throne. Richard could see immediately that Manuel was clearly taken by the York girls, with Cecily to the fore. He was a handsome lad, with his sister's colouring – tawny as a dog-fox. And from the look of it, Cecily was equally smitten.

Joanna, though was, as he had guessed from her portrait, no beauty. She was tall, with tawny-fox hair – the little that showed under her coif – and fox-brown eyes. She was dressed all in unrelieved black velvet. Her skin was good, alabaster-pale. She curtseyed deeply to him, head bent, murmuring "*Alteza*..."

"Rise, Princess." He stood, extending a hand to assist her. "You are most welcome to our Court."

The interpreter translated rapidly. Then: "*A Princesa* speak the Latin tongue, your Grace."

"That is good. *Quod bonum est.*" He saw her smile. Her teeth were not good, some missing and what were left uneven and discoloured. Her hand was cold, limp in his. He drew her to his side, made the introductions to the Household and to his nieces and nephews. She bent her head in acknowledgement to each.

"She smells funny," muttered the young Warwick, and was hushed by his tutor. Not speaking any English, she was unaware of the comment -- but it was unfortunately true. Under the expensive scents of musk and amber, there was a thick odour of unwashed female.

Richard, himself fastidious about personal cleanliness, did not show his distaste. But Sir Edward Brampton, doing his office as ambassador, was at Richard's elbow, and must have sensed his master's mind. "The Princess is deeply religious, sire." he murmured. "Her women tell me that she wears a hairshirt next the skin."

That would explain it. Richard knew then that this lady, whatever admirable qualities she might possess, was not suited to be his queen. And he thought she knew it, and was not sorry. But the formalities must be observed. There was dancing, and Richard led the Princess out for the stately basse dance. It was clear that she had no love for dancing. Every step was precise, but she showed no enjoyment in it. By contrast, her brother Dom Manuel was all courtesy, leading out Elizabeth, and then Cecily. Then Cecily again. The Princess declined another dance, however. Nor did she care for music, though the King's musicians were the finest in the realm. Worldly things were clearly far from her mind.

He had that confirmed when he dined alone with her that evening. She ate sparingly, took no wine, and responded only politely to his efforts at conversation. It could hardly be called courtship. Conversing in Latin did not help.

At last, when the servers had brought the last course of wafers and hippocras and preserved fruits, none of which she touched, she clasped her hands in her lap. "I tell you in honesty, highness, that I have no heart for this proposed marriage. I have rejected other matches, as you may know. I am here only to satisfy my brother. My only desire, since childhood, is to join a religious house." She gave a small shrug. "He has promised that he will no longer stand in my way, if I remain of the same mind. So I agree to come here, to see and speak to you, and to tell you – to tell you of my reasons for refusing your offer of marriage. I know, none better, that I am not fitted to bear children. But more important, I am called by God to become a Bride of Christ."

A small part of Richard sang hosannas. But he kept his face grave. "I cannot offer you a higher match than that, Princess. How can I, a mere earthly king, contest with the King of Heaven?"

She nodded agreement, pleased at his understanding. "There is another thing I must tell you, highness. I have told my brother. I had a vision. When I agreed to come here, I prayed to God for guidance, and that night, God sent me a vision. An angel stood before me, and his face was sorrowful. If I agreed to wed you, he said, I would be a widow before I could conceive a child."

So, my death is foretold. Well, no man lives forever.

"Further, my lord, he told me that you are fated to die in battle." She let her eyes close. "God be my witness; it pains me to speak of this."

"That is in God's hands, Princess."

"Yes. And God grant it be far from this day! For I see that you are a noble and a Christian King." She got to her feet, curtseyed. "I am wearied by this day, highness. I will withdraw, and pray for you."

When she had gone, Richard sent for Kendal, his Master Secretary. "Reassure me, John, that the betrothal of the Princess and myself was *de futura?*"

"It was, your Grace." Kendal looked slightly puzzled. "Is aught amiss?"

"The lady has rejected my suit. Jilted, by God." Far from looking the disappointed bridegroom, the king had a small smile playing around his mouth. "And the Infanta Isabella?"

"*De futura*, also, your Grace. As her parents required."

"And His Holiness has agreed a dispensation."

"Since both ladies are deemed to be within the bounds of consanguinity – and it exists also for Dom Manuel and the Lady…" he paused. "For whichever of the daughters of York, your Grace."

"Cecily, then. Has the young man shown a preference? Never mind. Take a letter." He sat back in his chair, picked up a slice of candied quince, bit into it. "To the Most Christian Kings, Ferdinand and Isabella, etcetera etcetera, it is our Royal wish that the match proposed between myself and your eldest daughter the Infanta Isabella be regarded now as *de praesenti,* etcetera, etcetera..."

"If you will forgive me, your Grace... This will please your Councillors. And content your people."

"And so it should. We need the alliance with Spain against the threat of France. Sir Edward can stand proxy for me, and we'll see how soon the princess can get here."

*****

The Easter festival was later this year, in April, with Spring already tentatively putting forth shoots of green. The previous year had seen the feast-day still in the chill grip of winter, frosts hoary and treacherous. It was not something Francis cared to remember.

Because the queen was dead.

And the king moved through his days like a puppet, a shell of the living man. Francis had made sure to be wherever he might be needed, through the Maundy ritual, the Good Friday masses, where Richard had crept agonisingly to the Cross. And the darkness of Tenebrae, when the light of the world was extinguished. Come Easter morning, with a thin sun struggling through cloud, and the celebration was for Christ Risen, Francis had seen only an unremitting anguish on his friend's face. The skin was sallow-grey, eyes sunk in dark sockets as if smudged by a sooty finger. Francis thought he could see the skull beneath the skin, as if the king was already with his queen in the grave

He had scant hope this year would be any better. The memory was still too raw.

This day, the Royal party processed to the Minster, where thirty-three paupers awaited the King, one for each year of his life. Privately, Francis thought Richard might have been spared the ceremonies, might have contented the beggars with the customary dole. But equally, he knew Richard.

Stripped of all finery, clad in a simple shirt and hose, the king knelt before each man, laved and dried the foot, bent to kiss the instep. The choir sang the Maundy anthem, *"Mandatum novum do vobis"*, and each man accepted his dole of towel and gold angel before mumbling a thanks and blessing the king's name.

It seemed an interminable time before Richard completed his act of humility. Francis brought him a loose gown of purple velvet trimmed with sable and a woollen shirt – the air in the Minster was chill – and stood ready to offer bread and wine in the quiet of the vestry.

"Thank you, Francis," he smiled, "but I will fast today."

Small use to object, to hope that Richard would accept at least a few mouthfuls. Francis replaced the winecup with exaggerated care, tight-lipped. "Dickon," he said quietly, "to my certain knowledge you have eaten nothing for three days, and taken scarce more than a sip of water in that time. You have been shrived, you have heard mass, and yesterday you touched a score of the afflicted for the Evil. Other than nailing yourself to the Cross, how else will you punish yourself? Do not you talk to me of duty, dammit! You are no anchorite, to spend yourself in prayer and fasting! You are king of this realm, and with God's help you will be wed before midsummer!"

Richard stared at him. "Anne –" he began.

"—Has been dead a year, Dickon!"

"Do you think I do not know that?" Raw pain in his voice. "She wanted me to marry Elizabeth, do you know that? My niece, of all people! My poor sweet love begged me to marry the girl, though she was out of her senses by then with pain and weakness. And I had to deny her wish and make public that denial!"

"You could do no other," Francis assured him. "Dickon, hear me now. You know I am your friend, and want naught but good for you. But unless you take better care of yourself, you may well have to travel to meet your bride by litter like Lancaster Harry instead of riding like the king you are. She will be here in but a matter of weeks. So, in God's name, eat something!"

Richard looked at him. "I hate it when you talk sense, Francis. I will eat, though stockfish is hardly to my taste…"

"Come Sunday, we can indulge in more dainty fare! Certainly not stockfish!"

Richard's rare smile lit his face, and he clapped his friend on the shoulder. "I do not know how you put up with me, sometimes."

"Neither do I. I'll order a posset, with egg beaten in. Maybe a crumble of cheese as well and you can eat a few sops of this manchet bread…"

It wasn't Lenten fare, but when pages brought the posset, Richard obeyed his friend and managed to eat. He wondered how they kept the Holy Season in Spain. Since both her parents were deeply Christian, it would be a certainty that his princess would be equally strong in her faith.

And he would be meeting her within weeks…

2. Isabella By the Grace of God

Spain 1486
Midsummer

Midsummer, and the sun was a brazen hammer on the anvil that was Spain. Granada sweltered, but the courts of the Alhambra palace were cooled by the endless play of fountains.

Isabella of Aragon and Castile, Princess of Asturias, eldest daughter of the Most Christian Kings, dabbled a hand in the limpid waters, dreamily. For ten of her sixteen years, she had been educated by the nuns of Sancta Maria, trained in all the ways that she would need to run a household and administer a great estate – but now she had been sent for by her mother, the Queen of Castile. She had not been told the reason for the summons, but guessed it was to do with her marriage. She had little idea who her prospective groom might be. An alliance with neighbouring Portugal was a strong possibility. She favoured that choice, it not being so far from home. But it would ultimately be her parents who made the decision.

So now, she sat idly beside the pool in the palace court, glad for once to have shed the austere costume of the convent, and enjoying the cool freedom of the light silks of Court dress. She closed her eyes, liking the drift of fountain spray as the breeze caught it. It was so good to be alone, to be idle and not tied to the endless regimen of the canonical hours. She was free to let her mind wander. What would he be like, her intended? Would he be young? Beautiful as a prince in a story? She painted a picture of him in her mind – tall, with dark hair and eyes, elegant and educated, smiling…

"Infanta, *querida*, where are you?"

Isabella sighed, hearing the voice of her former nurse and now her *duenna.* Dona Lucia was amply proportioned, with a love of sweetmeats that were evidenced by her curves. Isabella loved her deeply.

"I am here," she said, and stood up, shaking out her skirts.

"The queen your mother is asking for you, *muneca."*

Isabella felt a little frisson of anticipation, and walked to join Dona Lucia. The corridors that led to the Royal apartments were lined with gorgeous mosaics, marble underfoot that whispered the tread of her kid slippers. The doorway into the queen's rooms was guarded by two tall black slaves, who saluted her as she halted, and one announced her arrival with her full titles. It had been a while since she had been addressed so. The convent's discipline discouraged vainglory. "The Infanta Isabella, princess of Asturias, your Grace."

And then, even before she could perform her curtsey, her mother was there, taking her in strong arms and kissing her. "Ah, *hija mia!* It is joy to my heart to see you again!" The queen was much as her daughter remembered her, tall, impeccably regal. "Come, come see your newest sister!"

Catalina was still in the charge of nursemaids, but she beamed gummily at the new arrival. Isabela crouched down and held out her hands, and the little girl staggered towards the offered haven, crowing.

"She is much as you were at that age," her mother said dotingly.

"She is adorable," Isabella said, lifting her sister into her arms and cuddling her. Catalina promptly grabbed at a loose lock of Isabelle's auburn hair and tried to eat it. Thwarted of this aim, she squalled annoyance, and Isabella reluctantly relinquished her into the care of her nurse, who carried her away. The queen drew Isabella aside.

"I imagine you have guessed why you were sent for, *hija mia.* Tell me, how goes your study of languages?"

"As you required, *madre mia*. I have a grasp of French, and some German, and English, though my Latin is better."

"As it should be." The queen nodded. "I sent you the best tutors in the land. You must be a fit consort for the prince we have chosen for you."

Isabella drew a breath. *They had chosen, then? Who would it be?*

"Some years ago," her mother went on, "My hand was offered to a king newly come to his throne. However, it seemed that he had gone against all his advisors, and already wed in secret. Let us just say that I was angered at this rejection, but it was as well, as your father and I were destined by God to marry, to fight for Spain and to unite the country."

"Thanks be to God," Isabella said piously, and crossed herself. She knew, all the world knew, that the warrior queen had led armies against the heathen Moors, that she was as skilled in warfare as in ruling. Aragon, Castile and all of Spain were blessed in her parents.

"We thank Him indeed, daily." She paused. "Now. You are of an age to be wed, and to bear children. Look on this portrait."

Against a crimson damask background, a kingly face. Dark hair to the shoulder, slightly waving. Level brows, a straight if somewhat abstracted gaze, a firm jaw. He was clad in black velvet, a livery collar about his shoulders. His black velvet cap was ornamented by a great jewel. His hands were slender, long-fingered – he wore only three rings.

But he was certainly not the prince of her dreams.

"He is Richard Plantagenet, King of England," her mother said. "We have received his ambassador, Sir Edward Brampton, and his master asks for your hand in marriage."

Isabella had been expecting this news, but still she felt a little dizzy, looking at the man in the portrait. Richard. King of England. The queen was still talking. "You will go with a dowry of sixty thousand pounds in gold, and an appropriate entourage for an Infanta of Spain…"

"*Perdon, madre*," Isabella said faintly. "What is he like, this king?"

The queen smiled at her, patting her shoulder. "Of course, child, you wish to know more of your betrothed! You may ask what you will – I will ask if Sir Edward will attend on you. He knows the king well." She clapped her hands sharply, issuing brisk orders. "In the Fountain Court. Dona Lucia will accompany you."

With the duenna nearby but out of earshot she waited, sitting on the rim of one of the fountain pools, while the falling water made a soft plashing music behind her. Her hands were gripped tight in her lap, and she made herself relax. A tall man approached her, made a deep bow, and kissed the hand she extended. "Infanta." he said. "I thank you for seeing me." He was clearly a gentleman, an *hidalgo*. He was impeccably dressed in sober stuffs, dark grey satin trimmed with silver. His black hair was cut very short, and he wore a pendant pearl in one ear. His eyes, in a face dark-tanned, were also black, and she thought he looked kind.

"Don Edwardo." She bent her head in acknowledgement. "Please, sit."

"*Con permiso*, Infanta."

“You may withdraw, Dona Lucia,” Isabelle told her. “Now, Don Edwardo, you come with an offer of marriage from your king. I would know more of him.”

“Of course.” He gave her a reassuring smile. “Let me say, first, that he will not be disappointed in you—”

“No courtly flattery, please.” His Spanish was excellent, she thought. “Tell me, is he like his portrait? Artists lie to please their clients. How old is he?”

“He has seen thirty-four summers come this October, Infanta. I do not think the portrait does him justice, myself. And though he has not the height or build of his late brother, who overtopped even me, he is very much a proper man.” He paused. “A warrior-prince from his boyhood – he fought in his brother’s battles, to secure the throne. He was made Lord of the North, and ruled there well and wisely. When his brother of blessed memory died untimely, he left his realm in Richard’s hands. It was not a light burden.”

“So my mother says. But duty over all.”

“Just so. He took the throne, but endured great sorrow. The death of his beloved wife, and their son…then, just last year, he defeated the usurper who sought to depose him in battle. Ah, *princesa*, you should have seen him! Just when it seemed that all was lost – for the enemy were many -- he led his Household in a final magnificent charge, and routed them! Reaped them like grain at harvest-time!” Don Edwardo’s eyes shone at the memory. “But let me tell you what our England has endured for so many years…” He gave a concise description of the terrible civil war that had devastated the country until King Richard had ended it and brought a much-needed peace…

“And England itself,” Isabelle prompted, as he paused. “It is not like Spain, I think.”

"Indeed not!" He grinned. "It is a green land, a fertile land rich in all good things – though you would not find oranges there! I was born in Portugal, but my home is in England now."

"You love it."

"I do. As will you, my Infanta. And the people will love you. As will my lord the King, I am sure."

"Thank you, Don Edwardo." She got to her feet. "I may have more questions..."

"I am at your disposal, Infanta, always." He bowed again and kissed her hand.

At the proxy ceremony, where Sir Edward stood in for his king, he and the Infanta recited the vows which bound the bride and groom in holy matrimony. Rings were exchanged -- Sir Edward gave Isabella a ring with a great diamond set in gold, and in turn she presented him with one with the arms of her House done in enamel. Documents were signed, seals affixed, and it was done. "My Queen," Sir Edward saluted her on one knee, with a smile. "For so you are, now."

She was a queen, of equal rank to her mother. It was all a little unreal. The machinery of the Court was set in motion – she was to select those ladies who would accompany her to her new home, to approve the selection of other servants, her Mistress of Robes, her Master of Horse. Too many, she thought privately, and resolved to send most of them home once she had found her feet. If she was to be Queen of England, it would be better if she were served by Englishmen and women.

*****

England 1487
(early spring)

Though among the finest of the Spanish fleet, the *Esperanza* was like a cockleshell on the bosom of the wild Atlantic. Spring gales had whipped the waves into froth as if white horses rode the wave-tops, and the ship wallowed in the troughs, plowing into the walls of water and breasting the peaks before dropping again into the maelstrom. Used more to the relatively calmer waters of the Mediterranean, the Spanish ladies thought themselves in hell, or on their way there, and told their beads constantly when they weren't retching.

Only Isabella and Dona Lucia were not sick, and perforce had to minister to the others in their party. Sir Edward, however, seemed unaffected by the storm. "I am a shipmaster, my ladies, and this, as they say in Bristol, is naught but a 'bit of a blow'."

"Indeed, Don Edwardo." Isabella flinched as another roll brought a cascade of salt water sluicing down from the hatch above. She pushed a sodden lock of hair back from her brow. Every stitch she wore was soaking wet. She almost envied the sailors, who could go about in just shirt and slops. Sir Edward was little better dressed, save for an oiled leather cape. Gone was the elegant courtier diplomat – this was a man in his element and enjoying it.

"Weather's on the change, madam. The wind's coming southerly. It'll blow us into harbour sweet as you please."

He was right. As the *Esperanza* sailed from storm into calm, the sun showed itself, welcome and warming, and a breeze replaced yesterday's gales, a breeze that carried the scents of land. They rounded an island – "The Isle of Wight, madam," and a river estuary brought them into the bustling port city of Southampton. There were her horses waiting, and the rest of her train, and they were able to set themselves to rights before they rode to meet the royal party assembled to greet them.

*****

Her portrait had been a standard Court painting, and had shown him nothing but a bland fair face – what hair showed at her brows and temples was a bright red-gold, however, and the eyes were a deep and startling shade of blue. True Trastamara blue, indigo blue, dark and mysterious as sapphires. Her mouth was a little too wide for fashion. Her chin showed strength and self-determination.

Richard sat and regarded the picture while Francis picked up and discarded the clothes that the Master of the Wardrobe had brought for the king's choice.

"The scarlet cloth of gold...?" He held it up for consideration. Richard glanced at it and gave a most unkingly snort.

"Hardly. I'm no popinjay, Francis, as you know well. I'll wear the dark red."

It was sumptuous deep crimson velvet, however, powdered with white roses picked out in silver and pearls, trimmed with ermine. Under it he wore a white silk shirt, and a doublet of quilted silver satin. The effect, Francis saw with approval, was of restrained but regal elegance. Tom Naseby, the King's current Groom of the Bedchamber, gave a small nod of satisfaction.

"No popinjay, Dickon. Every inch a king." Francis told him. "Remember Louis in his leathers, looking like the meanest kennelman?"

Richard grinned. "Covered in dog-hair and slobber." He looked wryly at where his two favourite hounds luxuriated in a welcome pool of warmth and sunlight. "Tom, have the new dog-boy take Caesar and Hector out for a good long run, and then well-brushed." The two dogs, hearing their names, lifted their shaggy heads. "Good lads," said the king, and crossed to fondle the silky ears. "Young Harry'll run the legs off you. Maybe we'll get to ride out and hunt tomorrow, hey? I tell you, Francis, there is little leisure in being king, and no time at all for honest enjoyment."

"Your Royal brother found time to play," Francis pointed out.

"My Royal brother, may God grant him rest, was the best warrior since Alexander, and the finest man you could ever meet, but he left the kingdom to the rule of lesser men. And Woodvilles. And their idea of administration was to line their own pockets. I have good men around me now, but there is still enough work to crush the spirit." He stood, settling the weight of the robe, and let Francis fasten the great gold-and-gemmed livery collar of suns and roses around his shoulders. "The yoke of kingship, Francis ..."

"You wear it well, your Grace."

But what would she see, this young princess of Spain? He had never been one to prink in front of a mirror. So – hair a mid-brown. Eyes – Anne had always said his eyes were like changeable taffeta, blue-grey one minute, hazel-brown the next. A man of middling height, though the twist of his spine took inches off him. A man approaching his middle years, also, with the map of his life writ clear on his face. Not uncomely, at least, with character clear in the set of mouth and jaw. And she – she was very young, gently bred, shipped to a foreign country for policy.

Mary, pity women!

Not for the first time, he thanked God that he was a man.

*****

Isabella's train was if anything more numerous than that of Portugal. The outriders flaunted banners with the arms of the Spanish royal house, of the kingdom of Asturias, of Castile and Aragon, and the ladies either rode in bedizened litters or went pillion behind their lords. All save one, the Infanta herself. Trumpets blared a Royal welcome as she urged her mount forward, a beautiful Arabian bay, barded in scarlet and gold. She herself was sumptuously dressed in sable-furred gold brocade, and veiled after the Spanish fashion. She was not tall, but neither dwarfish in stature – a petite and slender figure from what could be told beneath a wealth of figured velvet and fur. She was assisted from her mount at the castle gateway by Sir Edward Brampton. "Your Grace, I have the honour to present to you the Infanta Isabella..." She went down in a deep curtsey.

"You are most welcome to our Court, Infanta." Richard extended a hand to raise her to her feet.

"I thank your Grace." Her voice was soft, with an attractive accent.

"Highness," he bent his head in greeting, "Will it please you to lift your veil?"

"It is not a custom in our country," her senior lady - the duenna? – said quickly.

"But you are in England, now," he countered, smiling. "Infanta? If it please you?"

She shot a quick look at the duenna, and with a gesture that was part mischief and part pride, she lifted the heavy lace and drew it aside. Her hair revealed was the colour of red-gold, confined by a golden fillet which held a single pearl pendant.

She was, he thought, not conventionally beautiful. But she had good bones, a prettiness, a charm, that was clear in the bright eyes and the rather tremulous smile. He was quick to put her at her ease, giving her the kiss of kindred, a mere brush of his lips across her cheek. He was pleased to sense no maquillage, just the freshness of young skin.

"Have you travelled well, Infanta?"

She made a small grimace. "The crossing of la Manche – it was very rough. Some of my ladies – they were unwell."

There were a few of her attendants who had a greenish tinge to their faces still. One of them was the duenna. The sooner they were settled in the Infanta's rooms, the better.

"Tonight, ladies, we will spend here in Southampton, for you to rest and refresh yourselves. Tomorrow we will travel to Winchester, and thence to London, where you will be lodged at our castle at Windsor. It is in the country, and more healthful than the city." The whole troop of them curtseyed again. He was pleased to note that the young Infanta did not replace her veil, and as he offered her his hand to lead her within, she took it with an instinctive trust.

"We shall be very happy to see more of your so beautiful country, your Grace," she confided.

"You speak the English tongue very well, Highness," he told her, bringing her into the great hall. It was something of a surprise. He'd been expecting to speak French to her, it being somewhat of the *lingua franca* of the courts of Europe.

"My Mother was insistent that I learn, your Grace." she confided. "Also, Latin and Greek. She says that women should have education. Royal women doubly so."

"She is wise, your mother! And it is good that we can speak together."

"I knew I must learn to speak the language of the country where I am to be the queen consort. Don Edwardo was a great help to me. You must tell me if I make the mistakes, your Grace."

"As you wish, Infanta. And I think – I would like it if you would call me Richard."

She smiled at him. She had dimples. His heart gave an absurd little skip. *I think we will do well together, although she is very young,* he thought. *My marriage to Anne was arranged long before we wed, and though I loved her heart-whole for her life, this is a marriage I must make. For England.*

Her introduction to the Royal Court was an unqualified success. The family took to her almost immediately. She was received firstly by the Duchesss Cecily, the King's Mother, at Baynard's Castle, her London house, and in her tapestry-hung Privy Chamber, where the spring sun streamed through the windows in warm splashes on the floor, Isabella gave her the deep curtsey she might have made to a queen. The Duchess was clad in her usual black, but the fabric was rich damask, and there were brilliants scattered over her headdress and veiling, interspersed with rare black pearls.

"No ceremony, child," the Duchess said kindly. "You are very welcome to England." She extended a hand to bring the girl to her feet. The shrewd grey eyes evaluated her. No flaunting arrogant queen like the Woodville. A child, no, a young woman, to be moulded into the position she must inevitably hold as wife to the king, and, please God, the mother of kings to come.

"I bring you greetings from my mother," Isabella said in her accented English. "She asks that you accept these poor gifts as a token of her esteem." A page brought forward a bale of fabric, revealing embossed black velvet and embroidered silk, jetty black on black, entirely appropriate to the Duchess's widowed status.

"I shall write to thank her," And she leaned forward to plant a kiss on Isabella's brow. "I ask only one thing of you, my daughter – for so you are now! – make my dear son happy. He has known much sorrow – it is time he knew joy again."

"I will try, madam. To the best of my ability." Her eyes sparkled with tears, and the Duchess kissed her again.

The Duchess, she had learned, held a prominent place at court when she attended, though that less often now. She was retreating into the religious life more and more. For important events, she would make the effort to attend—otherwise she was more and more content to rule at Berkhamsted. Now it was for the Duchess, as senior Royal lady, to make the introductions to the rest of the immediate family.

The daughters of York all made their deepest curtseys – young Warwick seemed quite smitten – the Infanta was younger than he had expected. He and John of Gloucester and Richard of Shrewsbury performed perfect Court bows, and kissed the hand she held out to them.

"If it is permitted," she said, looking at the Duchess, "I have some gifts for my new family?"

Thought had gone into the choices. For young Warwick there was a bright-feathered bird in a cage that to his amazement and delight 'talked like a Christian!' "His name," the Infanta said, smiling, "is Pedro." At which the bird shrieked and repeated the name, clambering about his cage in excitement. Warwick was speechless.

"Oh, my lady -- my princess, I mean – Thank you!"

The girls were given ells of the finest Spanish silks and lace, and even Elizabeth had to admire the exquisite workmanship. Little Katherine Plantagenet, the King's natural-born daughter, exclaimed her pleasure. "And now we have a queen again, we can make merry!" She could hardly wait to show herself in her new finery. "Look, Lizzie, this green damask is perfect for you! And Anne, the scarlet! Ceci, the lilac! With the silver embroidery!"

For John of Gloucester, a slender dagger in fine Toledo steel, with belt and scabbard of tooled leather, and the same for young Richard of Shrewsbury.

The king had made a quiet entrance, and stood smiling, watching them. The Duchess beckoned him forward, and he forestalled the bows and curtseys with a gesture. He kissed his mother's cheek. "Well, *ma mere*?"

"Very well, my dear."

"The wedding will be in the Abbey. Will you honour us with your presence?"

"Forgive me, dear son, but this wedding is the Infanta's day, and I would not overshadow her. Bring her to me at Berkhamstead. I would like the leisure to get to know her better."

"As you please, *ma mere."* He kissed the hand she extended to him before he took his leave.

"That was well-done, Princess," Richard said quietly, a little later. "You have conquered my family entirely."

"I have a gift for you, also, your Grace -- Richard." She signed for a page to bring a silk-wrapped reliquary, chased in gold and crystal, holding a fingerbone of St. James. "Santiago. He has a most beautiful cathedral in Compostela."

Much moved, Richard kissed the golden casing reverently, and kissed the donor on the brow. "This is a treasure beyond price. I shall have it placed in our private chapel, at Middleham."

His wedding to Anne had been a quiet and very private affair, for all Edward's wish to make it a great celebration. The required dispensation had not arrived, after all, but they did not want to wait. The king himself had escorted her to the altar, his big golden bulk dwarfing her fragility. St. Stephen's Chapel had been lit by pale spring sunshine, picking out the diamonds trembling in Anne's hair and the wash of tears trembling in her eyes. Her hand had been so cold in his, and she had been shivering, for all the wealth of furs he had wrapped her in. She had been wed to Edouard of Lancaster, by her father's command and that of Marguerite of Anjou. That had not been a successful marriage. He had vowed that she would know only happiness as Duchess of Gloucester. He thought he had fulfilled that vow.

Now the Abbey would see his wedding.

As was his custom, he went to his private chapel, and asked his chaplain Father Dominic to hear his confession. Signing himself, he knelt as the priest vested himself.

"*Peccavi*," he murmured. "Bless me, father, for I have sinned."

"In what way, my son?"

"I must wed, I know that, for the good of the realm. But my heart fails me, Father. She is very young, gently raised, and innocent. And I have so many regrets, so many… Aye, what man does not? But regrets for mistakes made… A king's errors are the worse for the people suffer by them. So I have regrets, for things I did, for actions taken. But they were necessary, in most part – not for my good, for surely my soul is stained black by them, but for the good of the Realm. My brother, God assoil him, was a wanton. A great leader, a fearless warrior, but addicted to the pleasures of the flesh. A glutton at table, a whoremonger…" He flinched. "He was king. None said him nay. And there were those who encouraged him… His dearest friend, Lord Hastings… I blamed him for Edward's untimely death, perhaps unjustly, but I could not forgive him. When I uncovered what I thought was a plot against me, I had him executed. I regret that. But it was necessary… Buckingham, my cousin, played me false. The Stanley brothers, also. It is a sin to take life, and I have erred on the side of mercy – oh, and regretted that, for the lives lost because I was foolish and trusted them…" The priest sat silent and listening. "So if I have been harder of heart, I have good reason. It was necessary. My brother George… I wept blood for him, I begged Edward to spare him, but I knew he deserved his death. I was complicit in that, as I was at the death of King Henry, but I must trust in God that my atonement is penance enough. But my greatest regret, Father, is that I took the throne that should have been young Edward's. Would have been, had he not been bastard. Men say I feared his Woodville family, that he had been corrupted by their counselling. Yes, he was half Woodville – but he was also Plantagenet, my brother's son, and with guidance he could have been a good king. Edward placed him in my care. I failed him. Failed them all. Elizabeth should have been wed years since, before she could fancy herself in love with me. I am not sure, even now, that she has made the right choice in choosing to marry Scotland…And Anne... Who was my first and only true love, she has been dead so short a time. Am I betraying her, my memory of her, by putting another in her place so soon? Give me your counsel, Father."

Dominic hesitated. "Richard, your Grace, let me speak now to the man. You did as the people wished, lords and commons both, when they begged you to take the throne. You did not wish to be king. You are clean of that. Queen Anne is surely with God. Be sure she would not condemn you. As for the young Princess… You will do what you must do, for the good of the Realm, and if it is God's will, get sons for England.

Now, *ego te absolvo*, my son." Dominic made the sign of the cross over his bent head.

*****

"You're remembering your wedding to Anne, Dickon." Francis, ever prescient, cast an expert eye over his friend's wedding finery, the purple cloth of gold and white damask furred with ermine.

"This is going to be an altogether grander affair, Francis. Anne married the Duke. Isabella is marrying the king..."

"Richard, third of that name, by the Grace of God King of England, Ireland, and France, marrying the Infanta Isabella, of Aragon and Castile, princess of Asturias, daughter of the Most Christian Kings." Francis performed a last-minute adjustment to the great livery collar of suns and roses. "I wish you happy, Dickon. Truly." His voice shook a little with an overwhelming emotion.

Impulsively, Richard embraced him. "You are the best of friends, my Francis! I could not wish for a truer companion." He stood straight. "Well," he murmured to himself, "let us get this done." And took a deep breath.

The Abbey was packed full with all the nobility of England, and the air was thick with incense, the voices of the choristers soaring unearthly sweet, as he stood waiting for his bride, Francis at his shoulder.

The Spanish Ambassador escorted her to the altar. Don Roderigo de Puebla was smiling, murmuring to his charge, and Richard saw her smile at something he said, relieving for a moment her solemnity.

She was all in white cloth of gold and figured velvet and white satin damask. The veiling over her loosened hair was a pale silvery cloud about her shoulders. Her train, carried by four ladies – two of Spain, Dona Lucia and Dona Maria, and two of the English court, Lady Anna Lovell and Jane Vaux - was fully ten yards long, of crimson satin edged with fur. Behind her paced Elizabeth, as the eldest daughter of York, her face without expression.

And it was done, the vows spoken, the rings exchanged, and Nuptial Mass celebrated. King and Queen processed together out of the Cathedral into the bright spring sunshine, and together acknowledged the cheers of the people.

She was Isabella, Queen Consort of England. She presided over the celebratory banquet, under her Cloth of Estate, and he made sure that she ate, seeing her a little pale and sensing that the rigors of the day had overtaxed her. As well they might. He was feeling it himself, and he had made sure to eat as soon as he might, though of course he had gone fasting to the altar to receive the Host. Francis had brought wine and manchet bread and half a baked chicken as he was divested of the heavy and elaborate wedding finery, and watched him while he ate it. He hoped the Infanta's ladies had had the foresight to do something similar for their mistress.

The wedding feast was elaborate, and king and queen sat together under their Cloths of Estate, with his White Boar Crowned and her Scallop Shell and Pearl. The music of the king's players was a background to the feast, while tumblers and clowns entertained the guests. Dish after dish of extravagant foodstuff was presented to the two monarchs on bended knee. He was pleased to see that once started, she had a good appetite, tasting each dish politely, even if she took only a mouthful. He guessed that her secluded upbringing in the convent had not offered much in the way of dainties. Like Anne, she was abstemious, and did not overindulge in anything, however, even the fantasy of marchpane, fashioned after the arms of England, the Lion and the Unicorn. She applauded it, and deigned to taste a morsel of it, laughing.

Inevitably, the time came for the bedding, and the rituals that accompanied it. His chamber grooms took his banqueting robes from his shoulders, dressed him in his nightgown and helped him into a rich green damask velvet chamber robe, furred with squirrel. And Francis and a select few of his friends escorted him to the bridal bower. He had issued strict instructions that there was to be none of the usual bawderies, and Francis had seen that everything was done in a seemly fashion. The bed was blessed, the attendants departed, and he was left alone with his new bride.

She lay stiffly among the piled pillows, and could not bring herself to look at her husband, gazing instead up at the pleated crimson silk of the tester above. An Infanta of Spain does not show fear. She was the daughter of great Isabella, who had led armies into battle, unflinching. She was the child of kings, raised to wed and bear kings in her turn. It was her destiny. But now, alone with this man, this stranger, she was afraid.

He must have sensed it. She felt him shift in the bed beside her. "What is it, sweetheart? Look at me?"

In the light of the single candle, his face was shadowed, gaunt. She made herself look at him, this man she hardly knew, who was now her king, her lord, her husband. She had thought when they first met that he was more handsome than the portrait that had been sent. Lady Lovell, when she had mentioned this, told her that it had been painted shortly after the death of his beloved Queen Anne. Now he had lost that distracted look. And when he smiled... She liked his smile.

"I hope Your Grace finds me pleasing," she whispered, and prepared herself mentally for what was to come.

"I think it would be well if we got to know each other better, lass." He left the bed and crossed to light more candles. The wash of light was both comforting and alarming. She sat up, clutching the covers to her breast.

"My lord…"

"Richard. Remember? I would have you know the true self of the man you have to husband." He pulled the fine silk of his nightgown over his head and let it drop to the floor.

Her eyes widened. She had never in her life seen a man entirely naked. His skin was white where the sun had not touched it, but evenly tanned elsewhere. He was lean in build, but muscles moved smoothly under his skin. He turned his back. There was a twist to his spine that raised one shoulder, and she wondered if it hurt him. She hoped it did not. Slowly, she let the covers drop to her waist. She could not, in honour, do less than her lord. The ribbon ties of her night gown came lose with a tug, and the gossamer-fine silken fabric whispered apart, baring her.

Her hair, brushed to a shine and perfumed with rosewater, fell about her shoulders, but wisps escaped to curl about her face. Slowly, she drew the covers aside so that she lay exposed to him. "I hope Your Grace – Richard – I hope you are not – I hope I do not disappoint…"

He smiled, and came to sit beside her on the bed. "My sweet, I would need to be blind not to find you fair. But it has been a long and tiring day for us both. Can we sleep together? I would like to hold you. The rest – the rest can wait."

She woke slowly, to a sunlit morning, a maidservant pulling back the bed curtains. The room was bright with sun. One of her ladies – Lady Lovell? – was quietly instructing the chambermaids to stir up the fire, to bring warm water for washing, to bring manchet bread and small ale to break the queen's fast.

Queen. She was Queen. And Richard the King was her husband.

She could not help giving a little wriggle of pleasure. He had been so – so sure, yet so gentle.

"Your Grace slept well, I trust?" Lady Lovell curtseyed and came to the bedside. "Dona Lucia waits without."

"Oh. Yes. Admit her, please." She realised that she was still naked, but Lady Lovell helped her into a loose gown of carnation satin damask, held the little velvet slippers for her feet. As she stood, she could not avoid seeing the stain on the pristine sheets.

Well. That was what Dona Lucia would see, and report to her parents, that she had come to the king's bed an untouched virgin bride, and that the marriage had been consummated.

They did not need to know anything else. She was Queen Consort of England, and she thought she might be in love with her husband.

Who was—where?

"His Grace the king heard Mass, and now meets with the lords of his Council, madam. Also, with Don Pedro, to discuss your dowry. Will it please your Grace to choose your gown?" Lady Lovell smiled at her and Dona Maria, as Mistress of the Wardrobe, awaited her orders.

She deliberated. Raised quietly, as she had been, she had not had many choices in her wardrobe. At her mother's court, there had been her ladies to make the decisions, as if she was a doll, a poppet to be dressed and made fine. During her years in the convent she had worn the dress of a postulant, plain unadorned linen. Now ---

"I think – the tawny? My lord my husband much favours the colour, I think."

"He does, madam. But on you, I think any colour would find favour." There was a shift in silk, embroidered all over with leaves and vines. The overgown was in rich velvet, deep russet, reversed in gold satin with pullings in white silk down the sleeves, and girdled with braided gold studded with amber and topaz. She studied her reflection in the polished metal of the mirror Lady Lovell held for her, and was pleased. "As queen, you may wear your hair loose, madam. Or perhaps a coif or caul of gold net?"

They combed and scented her hair, brushing it into a sleek cape over her shoulders before pinning it up and confining it in the little gem-sewn cap and the attached net snood.

"Oh, yes, madam. That does very well."

"I will go to my husband now," she said decisively – so pleasant, to make decisions and to be instantly obeyed, "Lady Lovell, attend me, if you will."

The company in the council chamber scrambled to their feet as she was announced. She gathered from their expressions of surprise that she was not expected. Richard alone greeted her with a smile and gestured her to a vacant seat as his side. There were some surprised looks, and a few frowns, which the king ignored. "My lords, by this marriage we cement the alliance with Spain. Our countries have much to learn from each other, and much to gain. We are fortunate in that our new queen will truly be an ornament to our Court, and an helpmeet for me." He gestured to a page to bring wine, and to fill each cup. "My Lords – let us salute Isabella of England, our new queen."

The company raised their cups and echoed the king's salute. She dipped her head in acknowledgement. Some of the lords on the Council she knew – Viscount Lovell, of course, at the king's right hand – and the Lord Norfolk, and John of Lincoln, who smiled. Cardinal Archbishop Thomas Bourchier had a dour churchman's face, but nodded to her – he had officiated at the wedding. Dr. Russell, who was Bishop of Lincoln. Sir William Catesby, Lord Chancellor. John of Gloucester and Richard of Shrewsbury – the latter seeming very young. Lord Dacre. His lady was her newly-appointed Mistress of Robes... She liked the lady – a forthright Yorkshire woman. She must put names to faces. These men were the backbone of her husband's administration. It was important that she knew them, and they knew her.

"We were making plans for your coronation, my burde," he said. "Our tradition has kings and queens crowned in Westminster, and we must give the Londoners their show. You shall be crowned Queen Consort there, before we make Progress. Our people must see their queen. We thought just after Midsummer. I will take you to York, to my favourite city, and show you the North. Now, Sir Robert, pray continue."

"Let's hope she's not a meddler like the Woodville," she heard someone mutter. "A woman on the Council can only cause trouble..."

"Ah, she's a young woman, she'll learn. She hasn't got a tribe of brothers to interfere. Or sisters to be married off. Besides, it's obvious the king dotes on her already. I've not seen him smile so much in an age."

"That'll be at the size of her dowry, I'll wager!"

Three weeks later, on the Feast of St. John, she and the king were feted through the streets of the capital, entertained with pageants and tableaus. The crowds threw flowers, and the white rose was everywhere along with the scented orange flowers of her homeland, dizzying with their perfume. Roses and orange flowers had been braided into a coronal doing duty until she was crowned in truth. As was customary, she spent the night in the queen's rooms in the Tower, to be woken before dawn to begin the long process of being made ready. She heard Mass first. Then there was the robing, in white cloth of silver, a great mantle of purple velvet furred with ermine overall. She thought the weight would crush her. But she was the daughter of the Christian Kings, and she would bear herself like the queen she was. They had told her that Richard would not take part in the ceremony, but would be watching from a screened closet. She resolved to make him proud. And hugged to herself a small, barely acknowledged secret. She would not tell him until she was certain…

She was anointed with the sacred oil on brow and breast, and the palms of her hands, had two archbishops lead her by the hand to the ancient throne of kings. They gave her the Rod and Orb to hold, and Bourchier raised the crown of the Queen Consort from Its velvet cushion. It was a thing of delicacy, a fantasy of finely-worked gold, studded with gemstones and pearls, and as the Cardinal Archbishop placed it gently on her head, and she heard the peers' acclaim. "My lords, I present to you Isabella, your undoubted Queen!"

"*Vivat!*" came from a thousand voices. *"Vivat Regina!"* And she knew that her mother had been right, that this – this, was her destiny. "*Help me to be a good queen, and a good wife, Lord God,"* she prayed in her heart. *"Let me serve You and these my people rightly. And, Lord God, in Jesu's name, send me a son!"*

As each of the lords came to kneel and offer homage, the choir sang an anthem. It could have been the voices of angels, soaring up to the vaulted roof. It was all very stately and solemn. But Francis Lovell, who she knew was her husband's most beloved friend, looked up at her as he knelt at her feet to recite the oath of homage, and *winked!*

It was most improper. She wanted to giggle.

And “God save the Queen!” Francis cried, as he got to his feet, and was echoed by everyone.

*****

It was customary, she understood, that part of the festivities that accompanied the Royal event was to be a week-long tournament. The announcement brought knights and their retainers from every corner of the realm, and from Germany and France and Italy as well. The tourney had always been a great leveller. The late king had enjoyed the contests, and his favourites had vied for his notice, the Woodvilles prominent among them. The premier jouster, Sir Antony, was not among them, having been executed years before. But Thomas Lord Dorset, his nephew, was determined to show himself the equal of any.

The tiltyard at Smithfield was as it had been then; it had not seen any change over the years, save maybe more room for spectators. The market stalls and food vendors were making the most of the celebration. But at the tiltyard proper, the contestants' pavilions bloomed like so many exotic flowers. The Royal Lodge required the ladies of the Court to be carried there by litter, so as not to soil their finery with the dust or mud.

It had taken Isabella some time to decide on her dress, choosing at last a gown in ivory silk over rose, but refusing the fashionable steeple headdresses offered. They felt heavy and cumbersome. Her scallop shell emblem in silver and gold was embroidered around the hems of her gown and the hanging sleeves. As queen, she could wear her hair unbound, but had had her tire-woman braid it with ribbons, with a little cap of ivory satin sewn all over with rubies and pearls. From comments she heard whispered, she thought this new fashion was an innovation that might be taken up by others. Certainly Katherine, the king's natural daughter, loved it, and had devised a kind of crespinette, formed of silver braiding that confined but did not hide her hair. There was a little veil that went with it, weighted with seed pearls and peridots, and Katherine wore leaf green, girdled in gold, where she sat in her place of honour on cushions at the queen's feet. Above their heads the Royal Standard fluttered, and already the contesting knights were drawing lots for their place in the competition. Their great destriers stood impatiently, held by squires, and the whole field was a blaze of colours. Richard was in his preferred indigo, on a tall throne that matched the queen's, and pointed out some of the contenders, their shields proudly borne by their attendants: the knights themselves gleaming in their ceremonial armour. Richard identified some of them to her, the intricacies of English heraldry being foreign to her.

Norfolk, as Earl Marshall, gave the command to open the competition. The contestants lined up in procession around the tiltyard, acknowledging the applause, squires carrying the lances and the armorial bearings of each knight aloft. Several of the Spanish contingent jostled for precedence before their Infanta, begging a favour from their countrywoman, and she laughed delightedly, saying she could not possibly choose one over another. Until an armoured knight came forward, making his grey horse curvet. "Francis," said the king, acknowledging his friend with a smile.

Lovell bent his head before his queen, extending his lance in salute to his king. "A favour, my queen, from your Royal hand?" She looked at the king, who nodded, smiling, and she stepped forward to give him a silken kerchief in shades of ivory and rose. He tucked it into the gorget at his throat, grinning.

"For the honour of Spain," she said seriously.

"And the Honour of England, my lady!" he responded, "For truly now both are one!"

And "Laisez Aller!" Norfolk boomed, and the first of the jousters took the field. The thunder of hooves, the shouts and cheers of the crowd, worked like wine in the blood, the clash of lances, the cries of adulation or despair as knight after knight fell. Sir Roland of Provence took a stunning blow from his opponent that unhorsed him, though he was able to limp to the shelter of his pavilion. The victor was a Spaniard, Don Diego of Seville. Isabelle applauded him loudly. He in his turn had his lance shattered by a young courtier from Italy, one Cesare Borgia, who showed a remarkable talent for one so young.

"He'll be one to watch, madam," Richard opined, thoughtfully. The youngster had all the exuberance of youth, and a skill that more than matched it. His horse was a magnificent black beast, barded in cloth of gold, and he made it caracole before the Royal pavilion, his raised visor showing a vivid dark face, bright with delighted laughter. His next opponent was a Burgundian, who barely kept his seat as the lances clashed.

There was a lull as the order of precedence was arranged, and Isabella and her ladies took the opportunity to partake of a drink flavoured with lavender syrup, cold and refreshing. Richard and the attendant lords chose cider, and some surreptitious wagers were being made. Odds were against the young Borgia. "Showy," was the general verdict. "Won't last the course."

A big bay horse, barded in azure and silver, pranced impatiently in place, his rider Thomas Lord Dorset. A man in his prime, well-versed in athletic pursuits – a hard man to beat.

The Borgia boy's first lance struck Dorset on the helm, and he was borne backwards out of the saddle to somersault onto the dusty earth. There was a gasp of surprise from the onlookers, particularly when it was seen that Dorset's helm was so badly deformed by the blow that his squires were unable to remove it.

"Oh, dear. Call the blacksmith, someone..." Richard murmured. "Roland," this to a hovering page, "Go and see if my lord is badly injured?" And, raising his voice; "Well-ridden, my lord Cesare, well-ridden indeed!"

Francis was to ride next, a little disappointed as he had secretly wanted to challenge Dorset, and that gentleman was in no state to accept a challenge of any kind. Hobbes said no permanent damage had been done, but his face was badly bruised, his lips split and nose bloody, and his ribs ached. So Francis ran his three courses with faultless technique, and was likely to win the Champion's award. Dorset did not care. What rankled with him was the loss of his best tourney horse, now claimed by the Italian. "A fair beast," that young man was saying, "though a little light for the purpose. And I have stallions enough at home, so I have no need for another to stand at stud. Perhaps my lord would choose to buy him back? I am sure we can agree a fair price."

And Dorset had perforce to agree.

Cesare Borgia won the tourney prize – a feather fashioned in silver gilt and enamel – but it was Francis who was judged overall winner. It was the queen herself who stepped from the dais to give him the golden rose and announce him Champion. "Queen's Champion," Richard said, pleased to see his friend honoured. "Just like the old stories."

"My Lancelot," she agreed softly, giving him her hand to kiss.

It was moot which of the jousters was more popular at the feasts that followed the tourney – Francis, still flaunting the queen's favour, or the darkly-handsome Cesare, for his sheer exuberance. He was exotically dressed in parti-coloured hose of crimson and gold, and a stunning fur-trimmed short doublet, in gold brocade, hanging sleeves lined with scarlet. He danced every dance, and Isabella's ladies declared themselves quite in love with him. Even Lady Dacre, who said he put her in mind of her eldest, Geoffrey. "I should not have a favourite," she admitted, "but dear Geoff was so like to my late father, God rest him." She blushed like a girl when Cesare bowed over her hand and begged her for a dance.

It was soon clear that the Borgia had an agenda aside from the tournament.

"I have a little sister, Lucrezia" he told Isabella as he escorted her in the gardens. "Ah, *che bella*, your Grace! She is very young yet, but my father hopes for a great marriage for her. One of your great English lords might make her a fine husband, when she is grown."

"There you must petition my husband the king, Lord Cesare. But what of you? Are you promised to any of your Italian beauties?"

"Oh, I am for the church, lady. So my father wishes. He is ambitious for our family." He paused and went to one knee. "Speak for me before the Council, madam? Your husband values your advice, I know."

*****

From the beginning, Richard had Isabella made privy to all of the Council's deliberations. It was not a role she had expected, but she found that she came to relish it. Her husband and his trusted lords actually listened to her now when she ventured an opinion. She did question it, at first, uncertain of her welcome. This was England, after all, not Spain. True to her word, she spoke up for the young Borgia, but Richard said such arrangements were premature. Cesare would have to go home dissatisfied. In the meantime, the Italian was enjoying making the acquaintance of the lords of the Court. And especially their ladies.

Isabella and the king were making ready for bed, and with their attendants dismissed, Isabella asked, a little hesitantly, why he had agreed to a point she had made that day. Oh, everyone had listened very politely, and Richard had simply said it should be written into the Council record and implemented. He gestured for her to come and join him by the fire now, drew her onto his knee.

"A mind, my queen, is a terrible thing to waste. And God in His goodness has sought fit to gift you with a brain as sharp or sharper than some of those who sit in council! Your Royal mother rules Castile and Aragon jointly with your father, does she not? They sit in Council together. Just so, I will have you share in the rule of England. And in a fashion, you are by way of being an ambassador for your homeland."

"You do me great honour, my husband..."

"It is a great responsibility, dear heart. There are those who share my burdens, to a degree, but few I can trust absolutely."

"My Lord Lovell ..." she said hesitantly.

"Yes, Francis has my absolute confidence. He has a mind like a rapier. I should listen to him more! He always has my best interests at heart. I owe him more than I can say, and not in coin alone." He drew her closer, and she rested her head on his shoulder, locks of her unbound hair falling over his breast. He drew a lock to his lips and kissed it. "My brother used to say we were like Roland and Oliver, inseparable! I am glad you like him. I would have you be friends."

"I used to think," she murmured drowsily, "When I was very small, that one day my knight would come riding on a white horse, like in the stories..."

"Well, I have the white horse, anyway." She felt, rather than heard, his chuckle.

"And I have my handsome prince, into the bargain. My king, rather. I do love you, Richard..."

And I never thought to know love again, when Anne died.

*****

York was a city gone mad with joy. Their Princess, their own Elizabeth, was wedding the Scots Prince, and there surely had not been such an occasion in living memory. The late summer weather, always capricious, gave pause for some concern, however, dawning grey and overcast.

"But they say it will break," Cecily said, helpfully selecting the prettiest white roses for the bridal coronal. "And the sun will shine for you, dearest sister, as it did for me and Dom Manuel." She was a Duchess of Portugal now, but had made the journey home, with her sister Cathy, for the wedding. Cathy was to marry a Portuguese grandee, had been swept off her feet at the Christmas Court when Joanna had arrived, and was delighted by it, as the king had offered a generous dowry.

"And are you happy with him, Cis?" Elizabeth let her tire-maids brush her hair to a sheet of live honey-gold.

"Oh, yes. He's good to me. Gentle. Considerate. Anything I want, I can have."

"Well, you are *enceinte,* after all."

The wedding gown was sea-blue damask, sewn over with pearls and brilliants – it sparked, catching the light, at every movement. The hanging sleeves were reversed in darker blue, and trimmed in ermine. Cecily regarded her with pleasure.

"Yes, and everyone knows that breeding women entertain strange fancies. Strawberries in March..."

"Cis, you didn't!" Elizabeth turned wide eyes on her sister.

"No, because that would be impossible. But he did find peaches.... There. White roses for a White Rose." Gently, she crowned her sister with the woven flowers. "There. You look like a Queen of the May."

The sun did struggle through the clouds to greet the bride on her way to the Minster. There her brother Dorset waited to lead her to where Rothesay stood. Her hand in his was cold, and she gripped his arm to still her trembling. The Minster was full to overflowing with the nobility of the land. She kept her head high, made her pace match his as he brought her at last to the altar where the archbishop waited. Where Alexander– her 'Xander – stood smiling at her, resplendent in dark blue and silver. She gave him a rather tremulous smile in return, as her brother relinquished her hand and Alexander took it in his. Cecily helped her put back her veil. And in turning, she caught sight of the king and his Spanish queen sitting on twin thrones a little to the left. The king's eyes were on her, sombre, unsmiling. She could not read his expression, but she thought – wished? -- that there was regret there, and maybe an unfulfilled passion...

"Do you, Elizabeth, take this man to be your lawful wedded husband? To love him, to honour him, and obey him; in plenty and in want, in sickness and in health, and forsaking all others, to keep you only unto him as long as you both shall live?"

Her assent was a mere whisper. *Oh, Dickon, Dickon...I would have willingly become your mistress...*

Alexander repeated his vows in a strong voice. The rings were exchanged, and the prelate pronounced them wed.

"Whom God hath joined together, let no man put asunder."

And Rothesay was turning her so that they could make obeisance to the Royal couple, and she dared not meet the king's eyes as he and Isabella came to give the pair their blessing.

"Be happy, Bess," Richard murmured, kissing her brow. "I think you have a good man here. And if he is not good to you, by God we will make red war on Scotland. You hear me, Rothesay? We have given into your keeping this peerless pearl. See that you cherish her as she deserves."

And Alexander, bowing hand on heart: "She is my chiefest jewel, Sire."

Every bell in the city was pealing out in rejoicing; there were flowers strewn underfoot, and flower petals like scented rain; voices calling blessings on the pair.

It came as somewhat of a surprise when Richard announced that he was making her Duchess of Berwick, she and her heirs, by way of a bride-gift.

*****

Isabella was beginning to find that the endless rounds of Court life were becoming more and more exhausting. There were Council meetings to attend, ambassadors to entertain, so many duties that fell to her, as Queen Consort, to perform. She did not want to disappoint the king, but now she found she wanted to rest more, to follow Spanish custom and take siestas, and when Dona Lucia said one morning that she was becoming a slug-a-bed, Isabella snapped at her and then burst into tears. The duenna took her charge into her arms, rocking her. "Hush, child. Hush…" The familiar voice, the enveloping arms, soothed her, and she hiccupped a little. "Tell me, dearling, when did you last bleed?"

Isabella had to think. With one thing and another, she had not kept a count. "I think – there was a little show six weeks ago?"

The duenna, who had after all been with her since infancy, asked some more questions, consulted with the woman who dealt with the queen's linen, and finally gave a small satisfied smile. "We had our doubts, your mother and I, seeing that his first marriage had produced but one son, and that one sickly. And you are still young. But it would seem that you may be with child, *muneca*. You and His Grace the king agree well, I think."

Isabella sat up straight. "Do you think so? When can I tell him? It is too soon?"

"Another month, perhaps. But you should not be riding. We will use the litter your mother sent."

Which perhaps gave Richard an inkling of the possibilities. He would say nothing, of course, until he could make a formal announcement, but Francis knew his friend very well. "You are looking indecently cheerful, Dickon," he said as they walked together towards the Council Chamber.

"I have cause, Francis. The midwives and the lady duenna believe that the queen may be pregnant."

"That is excellent news!" Francis said, delighted. "The Privy Council can hardly object to anything you suggest now. The move to the North?"

"They're coming around to that idea. I told them I wanted the queen out of London. There is too much risk of plague. Which reminds me, I must put forward ordinances to keep the streets cleaner. When it rains we are ankle deep in filth. Yes, we can put down straw, but it just gets trampled into the general mire. And even the river stinks."

Francis looked thoughtful. "What did the ancients do, I wonder?"

"Besides the roads? Well, London was a somewhat smaller place in Roman days! I'll see what I can find out – and light a fire under the City burgesses to *do* something instead of just talking endlessly about the problem! In Rome itself they had a network of drains and sewers."

Francis frowned. "The *Cloaca Maxima.* I remember my tutor telling me about it. Is it not in ruins?"

"I'm not sure. But that might be a solution for our cities."

"Good luck with that," Francis snorted. "I can just see the Council's faces when you suggest it."

Richard gave him an urchin's grin. "You can back me up."

"Well, we'll be out of the city in the worst of the heat. At least, late summer is a good time to go on Progress."

"Indeed. Dona Lucia tells me she is ordering the Royal litter to be made ready, although the queen would prefer to ride."

"It will be a taxing journey, Dickon. The lady duenna knows what she is about, I am sure."

She did. The litter was roomy, well-cushioned, hung about with crimson velvet, and harnessed between two splendid bay horses. It had every comfort save stability, as the procession wove ponderously over roads that were sometimes no better than rutted farm tracks, dusty when dry and muddy when it rained. It seemed to rain a lot.

"It is why England is so green," Richard told her as they dined one evening at an inn in Northampton. "Is the chicken not to your taste, hinny? I will have them bring you something else..."

"No, Richard, your Grace. I thank you. But I am not hungry, truly."

But the queen grew paler and paler as the journey went on, though she was faultlessly courteous at every town where they stopped, and the people seemed delighted by her when she was presented by her husband the king. "So sweet," they enthused, "so pretty, so unassuming!" So unlike the Woodville, they meant, but did not say.

It was at Lincoln that she was sick. Richard was distraught, seeing her green-pale and shivering and unable to speak to him save in a small hoarse whisper that it was nothing, nothing at all, and she would be well soon. It was Dona Lucia who refused his order for physicians and would not let her be bled, trying to ban him from her side, for had he not done quite enough? She fussed around the queen, who uncharacteristically let her without protest.

"I will send for Master Hussey," Richard said firmly at last. "He has my trust, Dona. And speaks your language."

The Moorish doctor came without delay – saluted the queen gravely, and questioned her gently, turning to Dona Lucia to ask for details. Richard understood barely one word in ten, but was reassured when the doctor turned to him.

"It is a passing indisposition, your Grace." He smiled. "One that will resolve itself, *insh'allah,* before the year is out. In the meantime—" he beckoned to his page. "Madonna, a tisane of ginger will help to settle the stomach...My servant will see to it."

The boy, so self-effacing as to be almost invisible, made that graceful gesture of compliance. Except --- as Richard realised, this was no boy. He shot a look of enquiry at the Moor, who bent his head and moved from the bedside, allowing Dona Lucia to bustle forward to take his place by her charge.

"My servant, Soraya, your Grace," the doctor said, "As you might say, my apprentice. She is skilled in herbals, and I have trained her myself in chirurgery." She had brought the cup, and Isabella was being supported by the duenna to sip at the fragrant liquid, but it was the girl Soraya who held Richard's attention. She had doffed the velvet cap, and a thick glossy plait of black hair, released from confinement, hung past her shoulder-blades. Skin of a deep olive tan, a face that could have been male or female, with clean-cut features, and dark eyes. "She was a slave, a child I discovered in the marketplace, of Egyptian birth. It is an act of merit to free such a one, in the name of Allah, and I have never regretted it. I had her garbed as a boy for her safety as she travels with me. I deemed it wiser. If you will accept her into your Household, she can dress more befitting her sex..."

"She will be welcome," Richard said, smiling, and acknowledged the bob of the head she made in lieu of a curtsey. Clad as she was in tunic and hose, she could have been a boy indeed. "Do you speak English, child?"

"English, Spanish, French and Arabic, your Grace," she murmured.

Isabella had set the cup aside, and was frowning into the dregs. "You are a Moor, girl? Like your master?" she said sharply.

"I do not know, lady." She looked puzzled at the question.

"My mother is driving the Moors from my country." Isabella regarded the doctor narrowly.

"Indeed, your Grace." The Doctor inclined his head gravely.

“I like it not that we should entertain a heathen at our court, Richard –” She would have said more, but the king drew the doctor and his assistant from the room.

“You will forgive the queen, sirrah. She is very young.”

“There is nothing to forgive, Sire.” Hussey shrugged the apology off. “Perhaps I can suggest that Soraya remains apart from the queen’s company? If it displeases her? Though she would be useful in my absence.”

“I will speak to the queen myself. I will not ask that the girl be punished for what is no fault of hers. You yourself are a follower of the Prophet?”

The Doctor bowed his head. “I am, your Grace. But Soraya --- I have not insisted that she follow my beliefs.”

“So. Would she speak with my chaplain, do you think? It would please the queen, I know.”

“Soraya will do as you command, Sire.” He turned to the girl. “As the king requires, my child. There are many learned and holy men here in England. The Holy Office holds no sway here.”

“Nor will it, while I am king, sir. Soraya, I will ask Father Dominic to speak with you. You need not be afraid.”

Isabella was feeling more comfortable, the nausea having abated, and accepted Richard’s kiss on her brow.

“I am sorry, Richard,” she said quickly. “I should not have been so discourteous to the good doctor. Moor though he is, I think he is a good man.”

“Indeed. And I will ask Father Dominic to speak to the girl. The Doctor tells me that she is no Mohammedan. Or of any religion. It is our Christian duty, is it not, to bring a soul to the Truth."

Isabella signed herself. "Oh, yes. To bring a soul entire to acknowledge Christ our Saviour – that can only be good."

*****

Soft-footed, the Doctor's assistant entered the dimness of the little church. It smelled of incense, of frankincense and myrrh. There was a hooded man kneeling at the altar, and he rose to greet her.

"Peace be upon you, daughter," he said, and smiled. "Don't be afraid. The king has asked me to speak with you. Come, sit."

He drew her to the bench at his side. "Your name is Soraya, yes? I am Dominic." His voice was gentle. She nodded. "Tell me, do you hold to your master's beliefs?" She looked into the kind blue eyes, and shook her head. "So, tell me, if you can, what god you pray to?"

"No god," she said in a whisper. "I know of no god who listens to such as I, or cares."

"God cares for all of us, daughter, for He is a God of Love."

She shook her head violently. "No! No, sir, for I have seen much cruelty and evil in the hearts of men."

"Tell me," Dominic said gently. It was as if the words released a floodgate of memories. She told of her earliest years. Of being slave to one man after another, of some who were kindly and many who were not. She had seen the injuries her Master had treated. She carried the marks of the whip herself, together with the brand on her shoulder. She had seen other children violated and abused as she had been until the kindly Doctor had taken her from that nightmare life.

"I cannot worship a god who allows such things, Ser Dominic." She was shaking now, and he laid a hand over hers.

"We cannot know the ways of God, my child, or why He allows such suffering. Will you come and talk to me again?"

It was Doctor Hussey who attended the Queen the next day, and mentioned that the girl Soraya was taking instruction from the King's own chaplain. It could not be other than good, he said. And Isabella agreed. "She has pretty manners, Master Hussey. It would please me if she would accept some gowns from the wardrobe. Lady Dacre, my Mistress of Robes, will see to it." She settled herself against her cushions. "If she is to be about our Court, she should be dressed appropriately."

It was not long before Soraya had become an accepted part of the Household. Isabella quickly warmed to her for her youth and her knowledge of the Spanish tongue. She could soon be found more and more in the Queen's company.

"I shall speak to the King, and you shall be one of my boon companions!" Isabella decided, after Soraya had entertained her with Spanish songs. She had a gift for the lute. And when the queen was melancholy and missing her homeland, Soraya was there to comfort her.

"As you wish, Bel." Richard was pleased to see her looking so much better, though he was still inclined to treat her like spun Venetian glass. "She's a handsome wench. If she makes you happy, then good. Father Dominic speaks well of her. Master Hussey agrees? Then of course, Bel. You know I can deny you nothing!"

Soraya fitted into the queen's household without incident, taking much of the burden from Dona Lucia. Lady Dacre had replaced Dona Maria, who had returned to Spain, and had quite taken to the queen, her own brood grown and living their own lives, and the royal wish was her command. As Mistress of the Robes, she put her mind to finding suitable clothing for the Moorish girl, and soon dresses were found in the queen's wardrobe and fashioned to fit her slender frame in colours and styles the queen chose. "It is like having a real poppet to dress!" Lady Lovell laughed, watching them as the garments were taken apart and remade, and the queen's rooms were filled with chatter and laughter. So it was not long before the girl was one of Isabella's chosen companions. They were much of an age, and delighted in their new-found friendship. Particularly as the queen's pregnancy progressed, and she was confined more and more to the hated litter for travel. Padded with cushions, with furs of sable and marten and fox, it was palatial indeed, and commodious enough for a companion or two. Usually it was Soraya. They found ways to amuse themselves, from Soraya's skills in the cosmetic arts and talent for music, and Isabella's love of books. Fluent in spoken languages though she was, Soraya's abilities with the written word were scanty at best.

"Though my master has taught me a little," she confessed. "In the Arab script, I can make shift to read."

"Then we will teach you!" Lady Katherine Plantagenet chimed in, delighted by the prospect of anything different. Though baseborn, she was daughter of the king, and she had been one of the first English women chosen by Isabella to join her ladies. A slight girl with a merry disposition, she and Isabella agreed well. The queen nicknamed her Kati, and in return Lady Katherine began to call her Bel. Soon it became common usage among her intimates, so much so that even the king began to use it. And soon, Soraya made three in their amusements every evening – Soraya strumming on the lute, Isabella singing Spanish songs, while Katherine twirled in dances of her own making. A pretty child, graceful and playful as a kitten, the name suited her. Her father the king, they knew, was already looking at potential matches.

They dressed Soraya's long raven locks with pearls and peridots, found the peacock colours that suited her so well, and Lady Kati sighed in envy at such looks. "I have my sire's colouring," she said, sadly. "I am not a flaxen-haired blue-eyed beauty, nor of such red-gold as your Grace, Bel."

"But I cannot wear white, after all." Soraya pointed out comfortingly. "I look as if I were drowning in buttermilk. I am swart as any blackamoor."

"*'I am black but beautiful, o ye daughters of Jerusalem, as the tents of Kedar, as the curtains of Solomon',*" Isabella quoted softly, and kissed her. "You are both my dear friends, and you make this tedious journeying bearable. Sing to us, Kati. The new one Sir Francis made, about the lady with the green sleeves."

"Tch." Lady Dacre, bustling past with another three of Isabella's made-over gowns, looked askance. "Sir Francis should know better than to make songs about loose women."

"Oh," Kati said, looking bemused. "I thought it was a love-song. And it is a pretty tune."

"Is it truly about loose women, Lady Dacre?" Isabella asked innocently. "I thought the lady refused the singer's suit?"

"Green is the colour of hope," Kati suggested. "He hopes she will return his affections. '*Come once again and love me.*'" Soraya took up the tune on her lute, and the three of them sang the refrain. Which was when Richard entered, and joined in, his pleasant tenor in counterpoint. Isabella, delighted, begged him to sit and sing with them – it happened too rarely that he had the leisure. Kati and Soraya made room for him on the cushions next to the queen, and he reclined there at ease. "I have news for you, daughter," he addressed Kati. "How stands your disposition to be wed?"

Kati blinked at him. "As my lord father pleases..." she said hesitantly. Isabella pushed herself upright.

"Oh, tell us, husband! Who has asked for my Kati's hand? Do we know him? Is he worthy?"

Richard laughed. "He is indeed. Would I consider anyone less? He is William Herbert, Earl of Huntingdon. A good man, loyal to our House, of Welsh nobility. You shall meet him, daughter and, if you like him, you and he can become betrothed."

Kati blushed. "As you wish, my lord father..."

"A wedding to prepare for!" Isabella was delighted. "You shall have the best of everything!"

Isabella's earlier indisposition soon passed without incident. She found instead a ravenous appetite, which Dona Lucia warned she should not indulge. Her husband thought the northern summer suited her well – she bloomed, he said fondly, like a rose. As soon as it was deemed safe, they rode out together, he in deep green velvet, and she matching him, with lighter green kirtle embroidered all over with the white rose of York, and a jaunty little cap adorned with pheasant feathers. She loved those rides, when pressure of business gave him leisure to escape the duties of kingship. They would sometimes be joined by Lady Katherine or others of the favoured ladies, riding to Asgarth Falls and other picturesque spots, and picnicked there on the smooth green sward, and musicians played to them, the muted roar of the water in counterpoint, while Isabella and Katherine talked about the wedding to come. "Can you bear to wait, Kati dearest, until I am delivered?" Isabella asked wistfully.

"You are full young for marriage as yet, my daughter." Richard pointed out fondly when he joined them. "Lady Stanley was wed at twelve and gave birth at thirteen, and never again after. I would not have you wed so young, lovedy. I am selfish, and want to keep you with me as long as I might."

"I am in no hurry," Kati confessed, dimpling. "Though I like the Earl well. I shall be sad to leave Court, and you, Bel."

"Then we will make it a condition of the marriage that you spend as much time with us as you may. And we can visit you in your new home when we are on Progress!"

*****

Although Richard's Court was not so ostentatious as Edward's had been, still he knew how to put on a show for any visiting diplomat. And Lorenzo de Medici was de facto ruler of the Florentine Republic, and was representing the great banking family. He and his retinue were appropriately and royally received at Court.

He was dressed in the height of Florentine fashion, in crimson damask, reversed in cloth of gold, and his chaperon hat bore a great enamelled badge that matched the plaques on the wide belt that encircled his ample middle. He swept the hat off with a flourish as he bowed before the throne. "Your Grace," he announced, straightening. "I bring greetings from the Florentine Republic, and from the House of Medici."

"You are welcome to Court, Ser Lorenzo. My queen and I---" He was interrupted by a series of whimpering yelps as a page tried to control the puppy he held on a leash.

"Your pardon, your Grace. This creature is by way of a gift, if her Grace will accept it?"

It was small brindled Italian greyhound, and Isabella fell instantly in love. She stepped down from the dais to crouch beside the dog, gathering it up into her arms and laughing as it desperately tried to lick her face. Hector, the largest of the King's hounds, got to his feet and came to investigate the pup.

Which showed no fear at all as the great hound thrust his nose in to investigate the newcomer.

It was Francis who stepped forward to take Hector in charge. "A fearless beast," he commented, one hand on the big hound's studded collar.

"Then I shall call him Leon," Isabella decided. "For his bravery. And he shall have a velvet cushion to sleep on beside my bed."

"You have made a conquest, my lord Lorenzo," Richard said wryly, wondering if the little dog might spend its nights elsewhere than in the royal bedchamber. One of the pages might be deputed to take it in charge, velvet cushion and all.

Lorenzo was an accomplished negotiator, and knew it. The gift of the dog had been something of a gamble, but his informants had told him that the young queen might be susceptible to such a gift. Being aware of his own somewhat unprepossessing appearance, he relied on his considerable charm.

"Your Grace does me too much honour," and he bowed deeply again. He gestured to one of his entourage, who brought forward an ornamental casket, which, when opened, revealed a standing-cup in enamelled gold. A stylised crowned boar ramped around the cup proper, wreathed in white roses, along with the king's achievement of arms, and Isabella's badge and the arms of Spain.

"A noble gift, Ser Lorenzo," Richard took the piece in hand, admiring it.

"Designed by a young sculptor of my acquaintance," the Medici murmured. "One Leonardo da Vinci. I am a patron of the arts, in some small way."

The banquet arranged to greet the Florentine was the finest the Royal kitchens could provide. Dish after dish was presented, a rich pottage followed by venison and wild boar, swans and peacocks roasted and re-dressed in their feathers. Sweet tarts and pastries, fruits both fresh and candied, and as a centrepiece a fantastical castle made of marchpane. Throughout, the king's musicians played, and the diners were entertained by jongleurs and tumblers led by the king's Fool, Roland, in motley of scarlet and black. Privately Francis considered that the man was getting too old, and resolved to have him pensioned off as soon as a witty replacement could be found. Richard disliked the so-called 'naturals', finding them pitiful rather than amusing.

Ser Lorenzo was loud in praise of the food, of the music, and politely applauded Roland's antics, though it was doubtful he understood the half of the jokes, delivered as they were in a broad Yorkshire accent.

The high point of the evening, however, was the masque.

Walter Halliday, Master of the Revels, while nominally under the jurisdiction of Francis as Lord Chamberlain, had a deservedly high opinion of himself, and Francis allowed him to use his talents to the full. He had contrived a new masque for the Italian's visit – it was to be the Visit of the Queen of Sheba to Solomon's court.

"Oh lord, I don't have to dress as Solomon, do I?" Richard queried when Francis broached the idea, sauntering into Richard's private study and perching a hip against the desk.

"Don't you want to, Dickon? It can be arranged. The wisest king in Christendom…" He rolled his eyes to heaven dramatically, sniggering.

"There are times, Francis, when I could happily dunk you in a horse-trough." Richard muttered. He was struggling with a difficult report from the treasury. The Medici had made it plain that a loan was perfectly possible. They just had to agree collateral. And get Parliament to agree in their turn. He did not appreciate distraction. Especially when Francis was in one of his antic moods.

"Ah, you'd have to catch me, first, Dickon. And it would hardly be a very kingly thing to do, now would it." Francis managed to avoid the ledger Richard threw at him. And made his exit. He had an appointment with Master Halliday.

The queen's solar was a rainbow of coloured fabrics, silks, satins, velvets, all tumbled together as the ladies tried and exclaimed, and generally enjoyed themselves. It was a bit like walking into an aviary, all exotic colours and twittering. He had to chuckle.

"What amuses you so, Lord Francis?" Kati wanted to know. The queen cocked an eyebrow at him.

"Why, the thought of my lord the king in splendour as King Solomon, my lady."

Kati gasped. The queen regarded him in amazement. "As King Solomon, Francis?" she queried.

"Ah, alas, for my best arguments could not persuade him. Now, let me see what Master Halliday has found for all of you..."

*****

Sheba and her eight ladies processed in stately splendour to the elaborate draped dais that would house her 'court'. All were masked in gold and crimson, their gowns a fantasy of figured velvet and cloths of silver and gold, designed out of Halliday's fertile imagination. The queen herself wore a fantastical headdress dripping with pearls and gems, her hair dressed with ribbons of sheet-gold, a great collar of sapphires and emeralds encircling her slender throat. Her pregnancy was just beginning to show, but cleverly disguised by the voluminous silken drapery. She was not masked herself, but her attendants, the York princesses among them, all wore delicate filigree masks in silver and crimson and gold. The gentlemen of the court were likewise disguised, and Francis leaned on the back of the king's chair, commenting in Richard's ear on the choices made.

There was Shrewsbury as an owl, and Warwick had adopted his parrot's plumage. And Cesare Borgia, who had prolonged his visit, was a prancing satyr. The Medici had an eagle's beak, which unfortunately did him no favours, the gentleman being somewhat portly. "Not so much an eagle, Dickon, but more an egg-bound rooster," Francis muttered.

"Roosters, my Francis, do not get egg-bound. But I take your point."

"And the young Borgia? A satyr, forsooth. All that's missing are the hairy legs."

Richard cocked an eyebrow at his friend, who, in lavish Lincoln green, was being Robin Hood. "Is not green the very colour of envy, Francis?"

"He's a stripling. Scarce out of baby skirts. Nothing to envy there."

"Is there not? He's got half the ladies making cow-eyes at him."

"And he's angling after your daughter. When's he going home, Dickon?"

Richard laughed out loud. "He came for the queen's tourney. No reason for you to take against him. He'll have no joy of my Katherine, I tell you that."

"They say guests and fish stink after three days," Francis said sourly. "His three days are long past. He makes me feel old."

"There I can agree with you, my Francis. Were we ever that young?" He shared a moment with his friend, remembering their youthful years. Battles, uncertainty, exile, danger. But he shook the memories off. "Well, we greybeards must make the most of what we have left, so let us stir our ancient bones and join the dancing!"

Richard joined the dancers and took Isabella's hand. As the measure finished, he commanded them to unmask, and the ladies curtseyed deeply to the polite patter of applause. The Italian was loud in his praise. "*Brava*, ladies! Honour a poor guest with another dance?"

Couples formed up again for a pavane, and Thomas Dorset sidled to Soraya's side. "My beautiful lady – will you partner me?"

He was dressed in his best, and fairly dazzled the eye with blue damask faced with white fur, long legs in parti-colour hose of blue and white. His mask had been that of a wolf. Soraya looked towards her mistress for permission, but Isabella was laughing with Francis, and did not see. Francis had his wife and Lady Vaux in hand 'unable' to decide who should partner him. "The Judgment of Paris," he declared. "Surrounded by beauty!"

"Well, Sheba's queen can give her hand to no man but her king," Richard decided. "Come, Bel!"

The musicians struck up a lively measure, and Dorset drew Soraya a little apart. "I would have you dance with me, my Dark Beauty," he purred.

"Your pardon, my lord. I do not know these dances..." she demurred, pulling away from him.

"I am sure there are other measures you know well," he said. "Privy measures, *bella donna…*"

Soraya gazed at him, at the sapphire blue of his eyes and the flaxen locks that fell to his shoulders. He was tall and well-proportioned and tended to extravagance in dress – he wore a blue to match his eyes, trimmed with silver, and there were pearls pendant all around the brim of his hat. He looked good, and knew it, and used his looks to full advantage. It had gained him a reputation for unprincipled behaviour, and he had had no difficulty in finding partners. Elizabeth Lambert, better known as 'Jane' Shore, after Edward's demise, had found comfort with Hastings, but Dorset had been one of the last of her lovers before she wed Thomas Lynom and gained a measure of respectability. He had been quite taken aback to find she wanted nothing more to do with him after that. He was somewhat at a loose end, therefore, and Soraya's singular exoticism piqued his interest. She was also a favourite of the queen, which he thought might be to his advantage.

"You are forward, sir."

He smiled. It was a good smile, and usually effective. "Forgive me, then, if I am overcome with such beauty. I venture I know why the king seeks to keep you close."

"His Grace the king is all kindness—" she began.

"Of course, sweet lady. A true *preux chevalier*—" He would have said more, but for the approach of the formidable Lady Dacre. "For shame," she scolded, interpreting Dorset's languid sidelong looks, and steering Soraya away. "Come, Mistress, to your duty. Attend the queen."

Dorset laughed, made a leg, and kissed his hand to Soraya, who bemusedly smiled back. He sought her out again as the evening drew to a close. "Do you dance attendance on her Grace tonight, lovely one? Will she excuse you this once?"

He had an arm around her waist, drawing her close. He smelled pleasantly of some herb she could not immediately identify. "Shall we go into the gardens? The air in here is too warm..."

Soraya could not remember when she had lost her virginity, and she had been careful not to scandalise the queen with any loose behaviour, but in the scented darkness she rediscovered a sensuality she had long forgotten, if she had ever known it. His hands roved up from her ankles, stroked and teased, until she was more than ready for him to go further. Her skirts proved no barrier, and the grass beneath her was soft, and he was kissing her, murmuring endearments...

In the morning, heavy-eyed, she made her way to the still-room for the herbs she needed. If this affair was to continue – and her lover was insistent that he wanted it to continue – then she must avoid any chance that she might get with child.

It soon became common knowledge that Lord Dorset had a new amour in Soraya. It hadn't taken him long. Paying her compliments, choosing her company above all others, finding little gifts to offer her, he continued to flirt with her shamelessly.

The queen had made sure she was always suitably dressed, in gowns that complemented her colouring. Her innate grace made her a popular partner in the fashionable dances, for she was quick to learn them, and it was not long before it was obvious that she had succumbed to the blandishments of the tall handsome courtier. And he had seduced her into his bed.

It was Lady Katherine who first guessed at their liaison. Seeing Soraya slumberous eyed and with a small secret smile on her lips, she felt it imperative to tell the queen. Who felt that she must warn the girl that he was not entirely trustworthy.

“He is wed, Soraya.” The girl was brushing the queen’s hair preparatory to braiding it for the night.

“His wife is not at Court?” she queried.

“She is not. My dear, understand that he cannot offer you an honourable marriage. If you wish to be wed, then there are men here at court, even high lords… Let me speak to the king. As one of my ladies, your hand is in his gift. He will not see you wed unsuitably.”

Soraya smiled. “I do not want Lord Thomas as husband, Madam! He contents me well enough as he is.”

Isabella concealed her disapproval. Soraya, she was sure, was well able to take care of herself, and hopefully would not scandalise the Court. “Be careful, then, my dear friend…”

She did not immediately confide in the King. It was as they lay together in the great State bed, she uncomfortable with the weight of the child in her womb, and unhappily aware that she needed to use the privy, that he knew she was wakeful.

“What is it, Bel?” he queried sleepily. “Do you need anything?”

“No, Richard, I thank you.” She slipped from the bed and padded awkwardly to the curtained alcove. She was chilled when she returned. She snuggled into Richard’s warmth, her back against his chest, his arms wrapping her round. She relaxed with a sigh, and the child within, taking advantage of the freedom offered by his mother’s empty bladder, performed several lazy somersaults.

Richard laughed softly. “He will be a tumbler, this little prince of ours, my hinny! Jesu, but your feet are freezing!”

"I am not used to the cold stone floors..." she confessed contritely.

"I will have rugs put down. Finest sheepskin from our good Wensleydale sheep, if it will content you, lovedy." He kissed the back of her neck, under the silken curls, and she purred her pleasure.

"Oh, I am so lucky, Richard, husband," she murmured. "You are so good to me..."

"No less than you deserve, sweetheart. You have made me very happy." She smiled, safe in his arms.

"I wish everyone could be as happy, Richard."

"You think they are not? Their queen but a month from bearing – how can they not rejoice?"

She shifted a little, trying to ease her position "Richard," she said. "I am afraid for Soraya."

The change of subject took him by surprise.

"Why? What has she to fear? Has anyone offered her insult?"

"Insult, no. But my Lord Dorset---"

Richard swore under his breath. "That bloody tomcat!" He refrained from saying what he would like to do to the aforesaid lord, but it involved surgical alteration. "What has he done?"

"He has taken her for his mistress. It is wrong, Richard, he is already wed, and he is toying with her!"

"Be easy, Bel. I will find her a position away from temptation – "

"No, Richard! No, she is my friend, she is dear to me! I need her to be with me when I am confined, I am so afraid ---"

"Hush, Bel. Hush. Do not weep. She shall stay with you, of course she may." Her nightshift was damp with tears. He cradled her, tenderly.

But I shall have something to say to Tomcat Thomas, he resolved silently.

*****

Thomas Lord Dorset was increasingly concerned. Although he still had some considerable status at court, he also had a lifestyle that outstripped his income. It had never mattered before. His mother had always been open-handed with him. Now he had increasing debts, and he needed funds, and although his second wife was a considerable heiress, she kept a tight hand on the purse-strings. He'd had to borrow heavily to buy back his horse from the damned Borgia, who, God be thanked, had finally gone back to Italy.

He and his wife kept separate households, now, as she did not like Court, and rarely saw each other unless there was a matter that involved the children. She was a prolific breeder, he had to say that for her. But the children cost money. She did not indulge them, but they wanted for little. Her husband, however, was another matter, and now he had a mistress in the Moorish wench, coin just did not stretch as far as it might. Not that the girl was grasping, demanding gauds to deck herself – she was delighted by the smallest of treats. The king had given her a palfrey, a roan mare, so that she might accompany the queen when she rode out. Dorset had won some pretty coral harness ornaments in a game of primero, and gave them to her. It had cost him nothing, to please her, and by so doing pleased himself.

He knew he must tread warily. Being a Woodville meant that he was not among the trusted inner circle, though he had been a Privy Councillor under Edward. Richard, he knew, did not like him, and the feeling was mutual. Needs must, however… He screwed up his courage and went looking for the King. He found him in the queen's chamber, engaged in a game of chess, and Richard was winning. He looked comfortable and relaxed, and nodded a cool greeting to Dorset.

"What is it, Thomas?" he enquired, quirking an eyebrow. Yes, he must speak to the man about his liaison with the Moorish girl. But later. The queen must not be upset.

"Your Grace," he said, bowing, and "My Queen."

"You are welcome, my lord," Isabella said smiling. "Will you take wine? Soraya, if you will…"

It was the Saracen maid who poured for him with silent grace before returning to her seat. Carefully he avoided her eyes.

"I thank your Grace." He did not drink, though his mouth was dry. "I need a favour, my Lord King."

"I'm not paying off your creditors again, Thomas." The king said shortly. "Once was enough, and that was only at your mother's entreaty."

"No, sire. I need *occupation.* England is at peace, my lands are ably administered by my wife's steward, and I feel – useless." He tried a shrug. "If your Grace might consider…"

"Really?" Richard steepled his fingers, leaning back in his chair. "We will think on it…"

The result was not what he expected.

"The Royal *library*?" Jesu, a task that might be done by any puling clerk! A Knight of the Garter, one-time Privy Councillor, advisor to the late king, son of the queen, and…

"You have the acquaintance of William Caxton. You can advise on what manuscripts; what books should be acquired. There would be a modest honorarium involved…" Kendal the King's Secretary did not meet his eyes. He did not say that Dorset was lucky that the king had not packed him off to some obscure post in Ireland.

Richard summoned Dorset to his Privy Chamber, by which Dorset knew he was not going to enjoy the interview.

The king let him remain standing, which was another hint. "I understand that you have debauched one of the queen's ladies, sirrah."

"Debauched?" Well, there was no way he was going to let that stand! "I have done no such thing, sire!"

"You deny, then, that you have entered into a relationship with the Moorish maid Soraya?" The curse of the fair-skinned meant that Dorset blushed scarlet.

"I do not deny it. It is a mutual attraction."

"I will remind you, if you need reminding, that you are a married man. And as such, you can offer her no honourable estate."

"Nor does she expect it, Sire."

"Understand me well, then. I will not have any breath of scandal disturbing the Queen's Grace. I know well the kind of behaviour that was tolerated at my brother's court, and I will not have it here. You will be discreet, my lord Dorset. Or you may find yourself on a fast ship to Ireland. Do you understand me?"

Speechless, Dorset nodded. The king steepled his fingers. "Very well." A gesture of dismissal, "Don't let me detain you..."

Master Caxton professed himself delighted by the visit of the 'King's commissioner' as Dorset now styled himself. It sounded better than mere librarian.

"Honoured, my lord, honoured! How may I serve?" The little man bustled around him, beaming.

"The King's Grace is minded to expand his collection, Master Caxton. I have been tasked with acquiring works of worth." He cast his eyes around the shelves, stacked as they were by sheaves of manuscript as well as bound books. Some titles he already recognised – a dissertation on the game of chess, which he knew was in Richard's possession; Tristan and Isolde; and Aesop's Fables. There was even a copy of Xenophon's *Anabasis*, and Wycliffe's translation of the Bible: The king had that already, the first in the country. And a very fine edition of Chaucer's Canterbury Tales. Excellent. He could hardly do better.

"Then allow me to show you this..." It was a beautifully bound volume, the red morocco leather stamped in gold. Reverently, the printer laid it on his desk. "Le Morte d'Arthur. Tom Malory's own transcription."

Dorset opened the book, and his eyebrows rose. It was a treasure. Clearly printed, with illustrations in jewel colours, the story of Arthur and the knights of the Round Table leaped from the page.

"The king would think me remiss if I did not purchase this," he said. "Beautiful work, Master Caxton."

The queen agreed with his verdict, when the volume was presented to her, carefully and exquisitely wrapped in silk.

"Kati, Soraya, come see!" Lady Katherine exclaimed with pleasure, and the Moorish girl's eyes lit. Isabella, heavy with pregnancy, was finding the curtailing of her activities irksome. "Oh, Richard, thank you! Lord Dorset, you have done well!"

Dorset bowed himself out, and Richard beamed at his wife, taking her hand and kissing it. "I know you are bored with naught but policy and needlework to occupy you. Perhaps you will enjoy reading with your ladies. And I have another gift – but you cannot ride until you are delivered, my sweetheart."

*****

Some weeks before her due-date, Isabella took to her chamber for her confinement, as was customary. She and her ladies heard Mass, took the Sacrament, and the whole Court prayed for the safe delivery of the queen.

The room, prepared under the instructions of Dona Lucia and Lady Dacre, was sumptuous, with every conceivable luxury – the walls were lined with tapestries, the windows tight-shut, a good fire burning in the hearth, and various devotional items on the little private altar. Richard had sent to Rievaulx Abbey for the girdle of St. Ailred, and it reposed there in a golden box.

There was nothing to do then but wait. She read from the tales of Arthur and his knights. She played desultory games of cards with her senior ladies, which they generally won, as her mind was elsewhere. She attempted needlework. The beautiful Spanish blackwork was beyond her competence when she could not concentrate on setting more than a stitch at a time. She longed for fresh air. She wondered what was happening outside. There could be no men within, no pages to bring news or gossip. Even her confessor, Fra Inigo, was allowed only to the anteroom, but held a Mass for her there daily, and administered the Sacrament.

Then, halfway through a game of merels, she felt the first pangs. The chief midwife, rather appropriately named Dame Elizabeth for the cousin of the Virgin, and a saint who protected women in childbed, was summoned, and curtsied deeply to the young queen, who was looking pale with nerves, but answered the soft-voiced questioning steadily. The great state bed was ready, with its coverlet in white satin embroidered with roses, but there was a small pallet bed besides, and a birthing chair. She did not want to look at that. Her ladies meant well, she knew, but some of their stories of childbirth were terrifying. Dona Lucia helped strip her court robes and eased her into a linen shift and chamber gown. She felt horribly alone, although the room was full of her ladies. She could have done with less of them. A lot less.

However, Soraya was with her and that was a comfort. Custom required that no one who had not experienced childbirth should be in attendance, so Kati was perforce waiting outside. But when Lady Dacre remonstrated with Soraya, Isabella insisted she stay. The pains had been mild to begin with, but had become a cramping ache, worsening all the time.

"You should walk, *mi reina*." Soraya murmured. "I will walk with you. Come, give me your arm…"

"Oh, but I hurt, Soraya..." To her horror, it came out as a whimper. The Moorish girl urged her to take another step, and another, pausing when the pain surged like a tide, and then walking again. It seemed like hours before there was any surcease. At last Isabella gasped that she could walk no more, and Dame Elizabeth helped her to the birthing chair. Soraya gently unbound her hair. It fell down her back like a sweat-sodden cape, sticking to her bare neck and shoulders. She was running with sweat, desperately thirsty, and gratefully accepted the cup of honey-water Soraya offered, but her belly could not hold it, and she vomited it up with the next spasm.

She could hear herself groaning, a guttural sound, like a hurt animal, and Soraya was behind her, supporting her, as the pains became stronger. She felt as if she was being torn apart. The midwife palpated her swollen belly. "Push, madam." Dame Elizabeth commanded. "And -- wait a little, and breathe... and push again..." The midwife gave a small grunt of joy. "One more push, lady. Your child is ready to be born---"

A rush of liquid, a feeling of something sliding from between her legs. Relief from the cramping pain. "Once more, madam..." The afterbirth was delivered, and the midwife turned to her exhausted patient, beaming.

"There he is, the bonny lad! You have borne a boy, lady. A fine healthy prince for England!"

Isabella pushed herself up on one elbow. "Show me! Show me my son!" Soraya took the infant from the midwife's hands, wrapped him in the linen cloth, slimy with his mother's blood and the white vernix of the newborn, and gave him into Isabella's reaching hands. "Oh, *hijo mi...mi joya...* Soraya, tell the king..."

But it was Dame Elizabeth who had that honour, smiling broadly as she curtseyed to the man waiting impatiently in the antechamber. "Your Grace has a fine son, God be praised."

"And the queen?" Richard demanded anxiously.

"My lady is well, your Grace—"

He waited for no more. Isabella had been moved to the great bed, and was now propped on pillows, her hair combed, in a chamber robe of green satin lined with fur, sewn with pearls, and a smile of ineffable joy lighting her face. "Richard, husband – we have a son!"

He could not speak for some moments, but took her hands and kissed them. "Thank you, dear heart…" Then, "Let me see him."

It was a sturdy child, skin velvety as the petals of a rose, with wisps of red-gold hair. Remembering the pale fragility of Edward, his first-born, Richard felt enormous relief. He handled him now with the ease of one used to young creatures. A starfish hand waved out of the lacy coverings, and the little fingers wrapped around his own forefinger in a determined grip. *My little Prince. Thanks be to God, England has an heir again.* He remembered holding his frail little Edward in just the same way, so unlike his natural children. Of course, he had never seen them newborn. But there was a strength he sensed in the child in his arms, one with a strong grip on life.

"What name shall we give him, Bel?"

"Oh, dear my lord, what else but Richard, of course!"

"Indeed. Richard Plantagenet, fourth of that name." The child gurgled, as if in agreement, and Richard laughed. "He is a fine boy, and God grant he will be a fine king after me."

"And God grant that be many years hence," Isabella said, signing herself devoutly.

They chose young Richard of Shrewsbury for one of the godfathers – his last court appointment before he left for Chepstow to learn statecraft there, along with young Edward of Warwick, who was his closest friend. Until the new prince was grown, the king had decided, Shrewsbury would have the governorship of Wales – and then act as guardian when the prince went to Ludlow and his own Household was established there. Norfolk's son Surrey was the other godfather, and well-aware of the honour. At the Christening, they knelt together and pledged their allegiance. Isabella wanted Soraya for godmother, but Soraya begged to be excused, as she had never been baptised into the Christian faith, nor did she want it. "But many Moors are *converso*," Isabella pointed out.

"Give me leave, my queen, to remain as I am."

"Of course, if you wish it…" But she was more than a little disappointed.

It was Kati, instead, who stood sponsor for the babe with Surrey and Shrewsbury, and Cardinal Bourchier who performed the rite. Heralds cried the prince's titles *'the Right High and Mighty Prince Richard Plantagenet, Earl of Chester, Duke of Cornwall, Prince of Wales'."* It was against custom for the new mother to attend, but the new prince was carried back to her as she sat in state, and it seemed that the world had sent gifts. The king had sent word to her parents, and proclamations had been sent out to all the courts of Europe, announcing the birth of Prince Richard. And he himself presented her with a collar of emeralds and diamonds.

"Thank you, my sweeting," he murmured. "Thank you for my son."

"May he be the first of many," Norfolk pronounced, "A quiverful of boys for the Royal Nursery!"

And Isabella, having just endured one childbirth, managed to keep a smiling countenance. It was to Soraya that she voiced her true feelings. "If my lord of Norfolk had ever borne a babe, then he might not be so quick as to wish another in my belly! The king my husband at least does not trouble me – nor will he until I am churched. It is tradition, you understand," she explained, "for a newly-delivered woman to undergo a ceremony to cleanse her of the defilement of childbirth, to give thanks for a safe delivery, and accept a blessing from Holy Mother Church."

Soraya cocked an eyebrow. "I cannot think that childbirth is a defilement..."

"Well, a thanksgiving, then, that God in his goodness has vouchsafed to send me a healthy male child." She stretched luxuriously. "And now I can enjoy the Twelve Days of our Christmas Court! I shall dress all in white velvet, with trim of ermine and crystals. Soraya, you shall wear the scarlet silk. Oh, and Kati, cloth of silver for you!"

*****

The weather was foul, and Shrewsbury was mired to the eyebrows by the time he reached Sir John Nesfield's estates. Sir John gave orders for a bath and clean clothes, and it was evening before the young man presented himself to his mother. She was sitting close to the hearth, wrapped in furs. She had always felt the cold, he knew. He remembered how she would sit with her skirts drawn up, like any housewife, to feel the warmth on her legs.

"Oh, Dickon, my joy!" She rose and embraced him, and he smelled the musky scents of her furs. "It has been so long since you came to me!"

"I had been much engaged with business at court, mother." He eased himself from her clutches and found a seat across from her. "I go to Chepstow within the month. But I was given the honour of becoming godfather to the new Prince. A fine boy."

She grimaced. "Indeed. Well, you are best away from that court."

"The king did wonder why you refused to come to the Christening, Mother. You know the girls would have enjoyed your company. Do you not miss them?"

“Miss them?” Her face twisted. “They are traitors, my son! Have they forgotten that it should have been your brother who took the throne? It should have been your brother’s court!”

“Mother…” he sighed. This was an all too familiar complaint. “The king has been good to all of us. I am content with what I have, and will have.”

“You should have had more, so much more!” She dropped her face into her hands and wept. He crossed quickly to kneel at her feet and took her hands.

“Do not weep, Mother, I beg you!”

But she was not weeping. Her eyes were dry. She clutched at him instead. “My Dickon, dearest boy. Would I could turn the clock back and make all right again, with my little Edward in his rightful place … ”

“That was not to be, Mother. You know that.”

“Yes…yes. I know. But ah, if things were different…”

*****

“There are more petitioners?” Richard asked. His back was aching, and he wanted to summon Doctor Hussey for one of his remedies.

“Just one, Sire.” Kendal consulted his notes. “John Cabot. A seaman out of Bristol.”

“Can it wait?” Francis said impatiently. “The king needs—”

“—to hear one more. Peace, Francis.”

Admitted, the man made obeisance, doffing his cap and remaining on one knee. He was plainly dressed, lean and deeply tanned, and his eyes were bright.

"Your Grace. I thank you for agreeing to see me. My lord Lorenzo informed me that I have an enterprise that might interest you." Interestingly the accent was more Italian than English.

"Indeed? Say on, Master Cabot."

The man opened the leather satchel at his side, and drew out rolls of parchment. "By your leave, your Grace." He glanced around, spying the table beside the window. "If you will permit?"

At Richard's nod, a page removed the wine flagon and cups, and the man unrolled a number of what appeared to be maps. "There is, I believe, a whole new world lying unexplored to the far west. It was thought, by many eminent scholars, that there was a route to the riches of the Orient by sailing west. But I think otherwise. I have studied the Viking Sagas, and they tell of a land to the west, one they called Vinland the Good. They are not mere traveller's tales."

"So, no fast route to the riches of the Indies and far Cathay?"

"No, your Grace. But riches unknown, undreamed of. I have sailed there," he went on, "I want to return. I come to you, to the great princes of Europe, like Ser Lorenzo, for money to finance another expedition."

Richard wondered if there might ever come a petitioner who did not ask for money. But this was different. And intriguing. He crossed to the table, Francis at his side, and they began studying the intricacies of Cabot's maps.

At last, the king held up a hand, cutting the enthusiastic details short. “Yes, Master Cabot. But it is clear there is considerable risk involved.”

Cabot made a rather Italianate shrug. “Always there are risks. But Marco Polo travelled the Silk Road, and all the world knows what we have learned from his adventures.”

“You say true.” Richard conceded the point. “So, sit and tell me more. I promise you nothing. I will take your proposal to my Council. If they deem it merits more investigation, then you will hear from me. And tell me – Is Cabot your real name?”

Again that Italianate shrug, and a grin.

“I was born in Genoa, your Grace, and baptised Giovanni Caboto. But I have come to love England. And I believe that English ships are most fit for my enterprise to the west. I am building one, to my own design. But it will cost more in gold than I have.”

“So, the Medici.”

“Indeed, your Grace. Ser Lorenzo is interested in a financial gamble. But he said that you also might consider it.”

The Italian explorer had been gone an hour or more, but Richard sat still regarding the maps laid on the table. Francis closed the door, and his friend looked up. “Well, Francis. Tell me what you think.”

“I think he’s a dreamer, Dickon, for true. But it’s a magnificent dream.”

“Yes… Do you remember, when we were boys at Middleham, how we’d have adventures, and pretend to voyage to Cathay and the Indies, and rescue doe-eyed maidens from terrible dragons?”

"I remember." They had recruited Anne or her sister Bella to play the 'maidens', and others of the pages and squires to act as crew, or brigands, or pirates... Warwick's aged destrier, long retired, made a good dragon, his stable the beast's lair, and his straw bedding became his golden treasure. Francis traced the topmost chart with one finger. "*Terra Incognita*, Dickon."

"Indeed. *Here be dragons*... And he is in need of a patron. I must say I am tempted." He leaned back in his chair, stretched, winced as his back twinged. "As God sees me, my friend, if I were not a king, I think I'd go adventuring with him! But as I cannot – where is he building his ship?"

"Bristol, I think."

"Yes. The poverty there is troubling. I'll reactivate their shipyards. That should help, and encourage Master Cabot."

*****

It had come as some surprise to Francis and to Anna his wife that she discovered herself to be pregnant. In fact, she was unsure of the fact for several months. Concerned about her own health, she had consulted with Dame Elizabeth, the senior of the midwives.

"My courses have never been regular, and twice since I was wed to my lord my husband I had hoped, but it came to nothing. But now I have not bled for three months. And my breasts are tender. For the last week I have been unable to attend the queen in the mornings, my belly will not accept food."

The midwife nodded. "Those are indeed signs that you are carrying, my lady. I would advise against riding, and I will brew you a potion that will help assuage the sickness. You should tell my lord as soon as you may."

Francis alternated between delight at the news and concern for Anna's health. It seemed the simplest thing to do was to remove from Court to the peace of Minster Lovell.

"Unless you would rather go north and stay with your mother?" he suggested tentatively.

Anna made a little grimace and shook her head. "She has not forgiven me yet for the last time I slipped a babe. She will have me wrapped in swaddling for the whole time, forbidden to stir from my bed, or eat what I like, or ride, and you, my lord husband, would not be allowed near me! No, if the queen permits, I will go to my own place, and be mistress there."

"Be sure the queen with give you leave. I will ask the king for permission to accompany you."

Permission was granted. Isabella was happy, for Lady Lovell was a favourite of hers, and the thought that their children would share the royal nursery delighted her. "You must let us know if there is anything you crave, dear Anna! If Francis cannot instantly obtain it, I am sure we will find a way! The royal litter is at your disposal, also."

Minster Lovell was a peaceful place, well-founded, with every modern convenience. In the gardens there, with the river chuckling by, Anna was content to walk a little or to sit in the blossoming bowers, and dream of the child that stirred under her girdle. She felt well, and surely this time would bring a happy outcome, and give Francis his longed-for heir.

The months passed. Francis came to spend time with her, when the king's business allowed. He was, as always, courteous and careful of her. As she grew larger, and more uncomfortable, she kept more to her bed, but insisted on taking daily exercise in the garden, his supporting arm around her. They would talk a little, desultory, about the coming child, and he would give her news of Court. Until, one morning, before cockcrow, one of her ladies roused him from his bed. His wife had begun her labour, and it was not going well.

September 1488

It had been raining solidly for a week, and late summer's gentle benison had turned into savage autumn with the onset of wind and chill. It made Richard's bones ache. But the harvest, thankfully, was in, and safely stowed. There was an abundance of fruit – thanks to the warm spring; it had been a particularly good year for apples. Will Stanton, Richard's page, brought a dish of the fruit and set it down at the king's side.

"Thank you, Will," he said absently, then smiled at the boy. "Here, take one for yourself." The boy bobbed an acknowledgement, obeying. Richard selected one in his turn, and bit into the juicy flesh. He thought he must be careful not to get juice on the letters he had been writing, to tell Isabella's parents that she was pregnant again, and seeming healthy. He smiled to himself.

"Will there be anything else, sire?"

He did not get the chance to answer, for there was a disturbance at the door, and Francis staggered in. He was soaked to the skin, shivering as if with ague. "Dry clothing for my lord Lovell, Will, and hot wine." Richard ordered quickly, and himself pulled a chair up to the hearth. Francis was stripped of the sodden cloak, the furred jerkin, while Will Stanton eased off the high boots, the fine Spanish leather muddied and shapeless. Another page stirred up the fire, and a welcome heat filled the room. Richard splashed wine into his own cup.

"Drink it, Francis," he commanded. Obedient, his friend gulped at the wine, coughed, drew a ragged breath.

"She's dead, Dickon." It was a croak. "My Anna. She's dead."

Richard dragged the heavy crimson coverlet with the wolfskin lining from the daybed, draped it over his friend's shoulders. "Tell me." he said quietly. "What happened?"

Francis took another gulp of wine. "You gave her leave to go home to Minster Lovell, to bear the child there."

"We agreed it best, Bel and I. Yes."

"She was well. Blooming with happiness. Then the pains came. A month early, the midwife said. She was a day and a night in labour. They would not let me see her, but I could hear...God help me! I could hear, and they would not let me go to her, Dickon! And at the last, the boy was born – God knoweth how – but he had torn her and the blood did not stop...The babe. A puny, sickly thing. The midwife baptised him... Nicholas. They showed me. He was blue-white, shrivelled...Oh, Jesu, Dickon, I should never have got her with child!" He was weeping, the hard-choking sobs of a man unused to showing his emotion. Richard signed to Will.

"Go to the queen, lad," he said quietly, "And ask if she will come, in charity..." The boy nodded, leaving the two men alone. "Francis," Richard said gently. "Be easy, my friend. Anna wanted the child, I have no doubt, and it is a hard fate that took her and the babe. Be easy, man, and never doubt they are with God."

"Would God they both were, Dickon. She -- Oh, Jesu, why take her and leave him!"

"The child lives?"

"They had a wet-nurse waiting, and put him to suck." He drew a harsh breath. "I used to envy you, Dickon. What you had with your Anne – that was rare. We were wed too young,

Anna and I, and there was no great passion between us. We were more like brother and sister. Oh, we rubbed along well enough, and she did her duty by me, but I saw what you had and I wanted that. Before God, I would have given my heart's blood to have her look at me just one time the way Anne looked at you."

There was nothing Richard could say to that. He sat in silence, his arm around his friend's shoulders, the silken flutter of the flames and Francis' harsh breathing the only sounds in the room. He had calmed a little by the time Isabella arrived, going immediately to embrace him.

"There can be no argument," Isabella said firmly to Richard, when Francis was settled in his own bed, with surreptitious doses of sedative in wine to help him sleep. "When the babe is strong enough to travel, we will take him into the Royal Nursery at Middleham; he can be companion to our prince. And we will stand his godparents at his Christening. It is the least we can do."

"A good thought, Bel." Richard looked into the ruby depths of his winecup, thoughtful. "I wish I could do more... He was a good friend to me, the best, when my Anne died, and my little Edward. I was near crazed with grief. He stood by me, my rock against the storm. I think I might have truly gone mad without him." She was silent for a moment. Then he said "Will you help him, Bel? I cannot be with him, I have too much business here and in the North. He will need a friend."

"Anything I can do, husband, I will. For your sake as well as his. Will you give him some employment? Other than he already has?"

"God knoweth he has enough just running the Household, but...yes, Bel, there is something. The last letter your mother sent – did she not mention an Italian seaman?"

"A Cristobal Colon. Yes. He has been asking for money around the courts of Europe to finance his explorations."

"And a John Cabot – another Italian -- came to our court, and brought maps of lands to the west. I had them copied but thought no more about it. I will ask Francis to research the possibilities, I think." The maps so lovingly embellished with sea-monsters, with careful script. *Here be Dragons. Terra Incognita.* "We will finance an expedition. I'll find the money somehow. I've reactivated the shipyards in Bristol, where he was building his ship. Who knows, there may be advantages in this. Trade, and alliances." He gave a short laugh. "Though who we may make alliances with, I have no idea. But it will give Francis occupation, and perhaps ease his pain."

The Middleham nursery was staffed by Bet, the wet-nurse, two rockers, and three nursery maids. They took Nicholas to their hearts.

"Poor motherless wean..." The prince, they told Francis, was thriving, could already crawl about and needed constant watching. His innocent mischiefs had earned him the name of 'Imp'. It was the youngest of the nursemaids, though, Nina, who took Nicholas into her especial care.

Even in his grief, Francis liked her on sight. She was a small girl, the top of her head barely chin-high to him, and a little plump, and neat as a pin in her blue linen gown with the white apron over all.

"He's doing well, the wee lad, for all his sorry start. Would you like to see him, sir?" She lifted the child from his cradle, unwound the swaddling. He was small, still, but a healthy colour, and clearly appreciated the freedom for his limbs. He crowed, reaching out, and Francis picked him up. "He's feeding well, sir, Bet says. Guzzling like a drunkard." And she blushed. Francis laughed. It felt odd, to laugh again. The nursery was a pleasant place to be, and he found himself wanting to spend time there. It seemed that here was a hope for the future, where before there had been none.

*****

3 Shadows on the Sun

Spring 1489

The abbey at Bermondsey was a rich one, endowed by kings and queens over many years, but the sisters did not indulge themselves or their guests. Richard was received with all due courtesy by the Abbess, a bony woman who looked as if she might be stern, but her voice was gentle.

"Yes. The Lady Margaret came to us four years ago in deep distress, sire, having lost at one stroke both her husband and her son. For a time we feared that she might do herself harm, but her deep faith, fortunately, prevented that. However, some weeks ago, we noticed that she was no longer having care for herself. To be blunt, your Grace, we began to fear she had lost her reason."

"Indeed? May I see her? Speak with her? If you think it would not distress her further?"

"Sister Joseph the Infirmarer will take you, sire." A bell summoned that worthy, who bent her head to him.

"This way, your Grace." Silent-footed, she led him through the cloister and past the sisters' cells, out through the gardens to a cluster of buildings at the very heart of the foundation. "It is here we house those who are in greatest need, sire. God's sick. Those who will not recover health or strength..." Two solid doors, both locked, allowed access. There were small rooms either side of a short corridor, and the sister led him to the furthest, took a key, and unlocked the door. "Meggie," she said gently. "Here is a gentleman to visit you."

She was crouched on a pallet-bed under the single high window. And she bore no resemblance whatsoever to the spare and elegant woman who had served as one of Anne's ladies, the one who – signal honour! – had carried the queen's train at the Coronation. Her hair was an uncombed rats' nest, her dress a robe of the same unbleached linen as the sisters' habits. She was clutching a bundle of – what? Rags? – and crooning to it. Sister Joseph took a step forward, and the woman's eyes came up. He could see nothing of sanity there.

"Meggie," Sister Joseph said again. "Will you not greet this fine lord? He has come to see if you are well-served here. We call her Meggie," she said in a quiet aside to Richard, "because she would not answer to any other name when she became like this."

"My knees are raw," the woman said suddenly, her voice high-pitched, like a child. "I pray so much, my knees are raw. God sent his angel to tell me that I would bear a son. 'Blessed is the fruit of thy womb,' he said. 'And you shall call him Emmanuel…' Do you see him, my blessed babe? He will be a king, you know. God told me so. He will be king of England…"

And she fell to rocking the bundle again, singing to it in that same high reedy voice.

"Lady Margaret," Richard said, keeping his voice steady, though her condition had shocked him to the core. "Lady Margaret, it is I, Richard. Do you know me?"

The vacant eyes lifted again. But there was a spark deep within, he was certain. "Know you…? No. I know no Richard. "

January 1490

The courier pulled his lathered horse to a halt, dismounting and opening his bag before taking the reins of the fresh post-horse the stable lad held waiting. "A letter from Antwerp, for Dame Grey." Sir John Nesfield raised an eyebrow. She did not correspond with many people that he knew of. He took it to his study, broke the seal. Nothing of import. Gossip. No need to hold it back. He took it into her solar. “Madam,” He gave a short bow as he handed it over. “The courier brought a letter for you.”

“For me?” There were few enough people to correspond with her—young Dickon of Shrewsbury, sometimes, and her daughters Cecily and Elizabeth, very rarely. The king had invited her to attend Elizabeth’s wedding, but she had ignored it. She had not been allowed to travel to see Cecily wed.

Sir John proffered the letter, one eyebrow raised in mild enquiry, but she merely thanked him and waited for him to leave. Why should he be privy to all her business? The letter was a little the worse for wear, having travelled from Antwerp in the courier’s pouch. It had been opened, she guessed, and read, but the seal though broken across was not one she recognised. Looking closely at it, however, she saw a figure done very small in one corner. A dragon.

She caught her breath and sat to read. The hand was one she knew. “*Cher madame, ma cousine* – I greet you well. I am fortunate to have found shelter here, with a merchant in silks, one I had met before when my husband was yet alive. We are in partnership now together, and we agree well and may wed. I pray that you may find the same happiness, for widowhood is a grievous burden…” It went on, innocent and gossipy, talking of nothing and at some length. The final words, though, she read with a growing excitement. “…I would I could send you some of the fruits we have here. The lemons, especially, are very good, and I remember how you used them to lighten your hair…”

She had never used anything to lighten the silver-gilt of her crowning glory.

Dismissing the hovering maid, she crossed to where a solitary candle fought against the gathering gloom of evening, held the letter to the light, not close enough to scorch, but close enough to read the words emerging from between the lines, faint brown but readable still. It was signed ‘Ned’.

She read the brief message twice, clutched it to her breast, kissed it, then dropped it into the flames of the hearth, seeing it crisp and crumble. Then crossed to her prie-dieu, and knelt.

Her heart was too full for formal prayer.

Sir Edward Woodville had taken the opportunity offered by the late king's death to abscond with a good quantity of the Royal treasury as well as more than ten thousand pounds in gold and one of the best ships in the fleet. To know that Ned was alive and well would have been enough, but the letter spoke of a plan to unseat Richard and put her boy on the throne in his place. She was instructed to contact Margaret Beaufort, who in turn would be in touch with Jasper Tudor. The three of them, with whatever allies they could discover, would raise their affinities and march to kill Richard and all who supported him.

She lost no time in sending a message to her son Thomas. Who asked permission of the king to visit her and came three days later, bearing some of her favourite sweetmeats as an excuse. She received him in her solar, and beamed at him as he bent the knee in salute before rising to kiss her cheek.

"Dear Tom!" She embraced him, her tall and handsome son, and exclaimed her pleasure at the candied cherries he proffered. "Dearest boy, I am happy that you do not forget your old mother. How are things at Court?"

"Old?" he scoffed. "You outshine the moon, Mother, as you ever did."

"But no longer the Sunne in Splendour." Her mouth twisted. "Be sure, if Edward were not dead, I would kill him myself," she hissed. "All our troubles stemmed from his lechery." Then she shrugged. "Well, what's past is past, I suppose. Come, Tom, the sun is shining – let us walk in the garden."

And while they wandered aimlessly along the gravelled paths of the pretty little knot garden, the scents of lavender and roses sweet on the air, she told him of Ned's letter, and all that it implied.

He stopped dead, staring at her. Elizabeth plucked some stems of lavender to make it seem why they had halted. One never knew who might be watching. For sure, someone always was. Thomas regained his composure quickly enough, and they continued to stroll. "Madam my mother," he said hoarsely, "I must ask – are you in favour of this?"

"Would I have told you if I was not? Think, Tom. Your brother on the throne. Think what it could mean for us. For you."

*****

Margaret Beaufort ran her beads through her fingers, the aves and the paternosters, without thought. They comforted her a little, in these endless days of her imprisonment, although it was a gentler confinement than she might have expected. Feigning madness had been a good plan to begin with, though difficult to sustain. It had saved her from more strait imprisonment, and allowed her to be alone. The priests who served the convent had been of small comfort, until one Robert Baxter joined their number. Margaret was not slow to recognise her old ally, Reginald Bray. The good sisters were pleased to see her improving, and put it down to the visits of her ghostly advisor. He had been her envoy to the outside world. And now he would be the agent of her vengeance.

It had been unexpected when Dame Grey had visited, bringing a basket of preserved fruits and small cakes. And news from outside the convent walls, even more welcome...

The good sisters allowed her to join them for the Divine Office almost every day now. There was comfort in that, also, the singing of the psalms, the hymns, the readings... It was past Compline now, and the convent was settling into sleep until Prime.

She slept ill, these days. So much haunted her dreams. Sometimes she saw her dear son, saw him crowned and enthroned, surrounded by angels. She would weep, then, on waking. In the bad times, the nightmare rode her and she knew him dead, slain on the bloody field of Redemore.

She heard the scrape of the key on the lock, and huddled further into the tumbled bedding, her eyes on the doorway. The heavy door creaked open – a figure stood there, silhouetted against the flaring torchlight. Tall, broad, not one of her nun-jailers. And a voice – dear god, a voice from the past! "Lady Margaret?"

Was he real, or a phantom, a fetch, sent by the Devil to torment her? Was her mind so disordered, the feigned madness becoming real, that she was imagining him?

"My God!" she gasped. "Sweet Jesu, Jasper? I thought you dead..."

"No, Margaret. Though I wished it for many months. Your agent Bray has been in touch with me. Come, sister. I have come to take you home."

She sobbed, and took the hand he offered her to help her to her feet. "Home? Has the king relented, then? Jasper, I am close-confined here..."

"The king knows nothing of this. And gold opens many locks. Here---"

He swept a heavy cloak about her shoulders, pulled the hood up to hide her face. "Come, sister," he said again gently, and led her out of the cell. The corridor was dim-lit, and the only sounds were the sweet voices of the nuns as they sang Prime.

Jasper was silent as a cat, and moved like one, his feet sure. Then he paused, pushed a door open, and – oh, the sweetness of the spring air, as intoxicating as wine! She muffled her sobs in the folds of the cloak. If this was a dream, then she longed not to wake.

There were horses waiting beyond the walls.

"Can you ride, sister? Or will you go pillion behind my man?" Jasper's strong arms lifted her to the pillion pad, and a lilting welsh voice muttered a greeting.

"Hold tight, m'lady."

Once beyond the Abbey grounds, they picked up the pace. Margaret, clutching the broad leather belt of the man before her, was grateful for Jasper's cloak. The streets were never quiet, but if anyone saw and noted the passing of the two horses and their riders, they did not mark it.

They did not pause until they were well clear of the city, and in the grey dawn light took shelter at a nondescript manor where clearly Jasper was known. Stiff from riding, she was lifted down by Jasper, and saw, with horror, that he was missing his right eye. A patch covered it, a terrible line of scar tissue from temple to jaw.

"How...?" she faltered, and reached to touch his face. The one eye left was still the blazing blue she remembered. She had always loved his eyes.

"A York arrow. It doesn't matter. Come, sister, eat a little."

"Where are we going?" Pembroke would be closed to them, of course, but Jasper had the unswerving loyalty of his Welsh adherents.

"Chepstow. Here, there's bread and honey. You must eat, you are too thin."

She had never been otherwise. "We have a long road ahead of us."

"Why Chepstow?" The bread was coarse, but the honey sweet on the tongue. There was fresh milk, also. Everything tasted so good, sauced by freedom.

"That's where Richard of Shrewsbury, is now. Are you done? Sleep a little, if you can. I have sent my man to find you some clothing other than those convent cast-offs."

A kindly goodwife gave Margaret a kirtle and gown of brown homespun, a woollen shawl and headwrap. They smelled quite strongly of their previous occupant, but Jasper smiled at her grimace of disgust. He was better clad in leathers, an archer's jack and trews. If it was not for the quality of the horses, they might have been commoners. So Jasper traded his big black and his man's bay for two less recognisable mounts, sturdy but nondescript beasts.

It took three full days before they reached the river, and Jasper had a boat ready, and there were the walls of Chepstow castle looming large, blood washed by the setting sun.

A cowled figure came to meet them as they approached the great gate.

"God's greeting," he said coolly. "You are pilgrims *en route* to St. Melangell's shrine."

"We are," Jasper confirmed., swinging down from his horse. "My sister and I beg the indulgence of the Lord of this castle, in charity. I doubt my sister can go much further without rest."

"Enter, then, in God's name."

They were conducted into the Great Hall, where bread and meat and ale were set before them, and servants divested them of their travel-stained outer garb.

"If we may," Jasper said, "we would thank the young Lord for his kindness?"

The castle steward went to enquire, conducted them up the stairs into the solar, a fine painted room hung with rich tapestries. Margaret stiffened, with a hiss. "That one, beside the window, is mine, Jasper. Mine!"

It was of the legendary unicorn, who lays his head in the maiden's lap. The hunters waited, with nets and spears.

"And it may be yours again, sister." Jasper murmured. Then, doffing his cap, he bent the knee to the tall, fair stripling before them. "My lord Richard," he said, as the cowled monk did likewise, and Margaret swept a deep curtsey. "I am Jasper Tudor, and this is the Lady Margaret Beaufort."

"And I," the monk pushed back his cowl, "am Edward Woodville, and your uncle."

"But—but you were declared dead…" the boy stammered. He had gone white as milk under his tan, looking from one face to another, the cowled monk, the other two in homespun like a pair of peasants.

"It was politic for some to think so, your Grace. No, do not call your guards, we mean you no harm."

"I bring word from the lady your mother, your Grace," Margaret, said softly, taking his hands. "By right, the throne of England is yours. And we will help you to claim it."

The boy disengaged himself from her grasp and backed up until a chair stopped him, and he sat down hard. "This...this is a lot to take in," he said at last. "You will stay here tonight, and we will talk more. I shall need to know all your plans. Do you have the money to finance such an enterprise? And what troops can you call on?"

They sat late over the wine, telling of their plans. Shrewsbury gave orders for chambers to be appropriately prepared, and for Lady Margaret, some better clothing. "My sorrow, my lady, that I can provide no better for you. Where do you go from here?"

"My affinity will be gathering at Pembroke," Jasper said. "I can be sure of support there. As for money – well, your uncle Edward managed to take a certain amount before the Usurper took power. I hope it left him bankrupt and begging to the bankers of Europe!"

That made Lady Margaret laugh harshly. "I wish I could have seen his face when he found the well was dry!"

With fresh horses, and a pack-pony loaded with supplies for their journey, they left the next morning. Richard went straightaway to his writing desk, taking a sheet of paper, quill and ink, but words did not come to him. The ink dried on the quill.

Jasper had given him a list of people to contact, to join his affinity. Were there so many disaffected among the lords and nobility?

"Who are you writing to?" Edward of Warwick wandered into the room, his pet parrot riding his shoulder. He had taught it a variety of unsuitable phrases, much to the despair of his tutors.

"I have business," Shrewsbury said, thoughtfully.

"Oh. I am glad they're gone, aren't you? He scared me, with that scar." He shuddered. "And her – what a hag! She was just like the witches my nurse told me would come to get me if I was bad. She didn't like Pedro. I'd like my sister Meg to visit, I'll write to her myself. I want to tell her about Pedro. He can count up to ten, did you know? And I'd love to hear from cousin Bess. She hasn't written in an age. We should go and visit her."

"Scotland is too far. Let me finish this, Ned, and then we'll go and see your new falcon in the mews. If Pedro isn't jealous!"

*****

"Gone?" Richard stared in shock and amazement at the Abbess of Bermondsey. The woman wrung her hands. "How *gone*? She was to be kept close confined!"

"She was, indeed, your Grace," the woman stammered, "But it seemed to us that she was a little improved as time went on. She was moved to another cell, and given access to our garden – under supervision, of course – so that she might sit sometimes and enjoy the sun. It seemed to help her. Her appetite improved, and she ceased to dandle that ragged poppet, and helped with the herb garden and stillroom, and could even join the sisters in their devotions…"

"God give me strength!" Richard cursed. He had to contain his fury in front of the Abbess. "My lady Abbess, Margaret Beaufort was not sent to you to become a professed nun, she was a prisoner! Jesu! I should have sent her to the Tower!"

"I must tell you, your Grace, that it was not you alone who visited her, but also Dame Grey, the queen that was." She wrung her hands again. "She brought some small comforts, sweetmeats and the like. I was not privy to their conversation. None of us were. They knelt together in the chapel, we thought they prayed. Her confessor has gone, too. Father Robert was her preferred counsellor, rather than our own chaplain."

Richard resolved to find out more about 'Father Robert', who for certain was not what he seemed.

*****

The journey had been long, though the great north road was in decent repair, and the holy houses where Dame Grey sought a night's rest and refreshment were welcoming. Rothesay castle on its high rock looked dour and grim, and the lowering clouds masked any hint of sun. She huddled into the marten fur of her cloak against the chill. *Summer in Scotland*, she thought with a shudder.

"I am Elizabeth, the Queen Dowager," she announced herself, as her chamberlain assisted her out of the litter. "Announce me to my daughter the duchess."

Elizabeth laid down her embroidery as her mother swept into the room. Her curtsey was that of daughter to mother, irrespective of rank. "Madam my mother," she said as she rose. "This is unexpected. Your courier arrived but a few hours ago. Are you well?"

"I have endured days in a litter that jarred my very bones, but yes, for your asking, I am well enough." She shrugged out of her furs, which puddled on the floor until a maidservant retrieved them. "And you – are you breeding yet?"

Elizabeth coloured. "Not yet, Madam."

"They say the Spaniard is *enceinte*. Again."

"So I hear. We pray God sends her and the king another fine son."

"So." The dowager queen's voice was sharp as a blade, and as cold. "He wed this Spanish Infanta, and now he has got her with child again." And like a striking snake, her palm smacked into her daughter's cheek. "Dear God, girl, did I raise a wittol? Did you learn nothing? I made sure to put you in his path, I came out of Sanctuary, had you there before his eyes all the while the queen was deathly sick. You could have had him eating out of your hand! You could have been queen! Now a simpering Spaniard sits on the throne that should have been yours!"

Elizabeth flinched from her mother's fury, her hand going to her bruised face. "You wanted me to marry the Tudor... You and Lady Margaret."

"Yes, and we saw to it that he made that promise public! If your damned uncle had not slain him on Redemore field, then he would likely have been king and you his queen! *Queen,* do you understand! Whoever ended up on the throne, you were to be queen!"

"We are uncle and niece, Mother!" She would have gone on, but an impatient gesture from her mother stopped her.

"Grease enough palms, God knows the Curia is greedy, and a dispensation would have removed any obstacle." She shrugged that objection aside. "Both the Spaniard and the Portuguese wench are close kin. We got a dispensation for the Duke and for Cecily, we could have got one for you. Margaret was ready to get one so that you could wed her son." She turned away, and the train of her gown swished through the rushes like the tail of an angry cat. "*You could have had the king, daughter!* Or did you mislike him so much? Let me tell you, liking has little to do with it, and he would not have said you nay. I saw the lust in his eyes when he looked at you."

"I didn't mislike him!" Elizabeth protested. "I loved him!" And flushed scarlet as the words were out. She had never spoken them aloud.

The dowager turned on her, livid with fury. "Then why did you not tell him so?"

She snatched her daughter's arm in a steely grip, dragging her to the mirror in its gilded frame. "Look at yourself! Fresh, ripe, even more beautiful than I was when I snared your father. One glance from you, one word, and he'd have had you in his bed. He'd have to wed you then, he'd have had to, or made you his whore."

Elizabeth's fists were bunched in the rose velvet of her skirts. The flush was gone, she was white and shaking. "And I'd have been his whore willingly!" she shot back.

"The Tudor thought you already were! If Richard had got you with child… think then, another bastard for the House of York. As if there aren't already enough! No one else would have had you, you may be sure, you'd have been shut away with your shame in some convent or holy house, like the Beaufort. You could have been a queen. But you were too nice, or too stupid, and you lost your chance."

Elizabeth pulled from her mother's grasp, straightened to her full height, taller than her mother by three fingers. She had inherited her father's regal stature, and like him she knew how to use that to her advantage.

"I am wed now, Madam, to one of the premier lords of Scotland, a Duchess in my own right, thanks to the king. Seeing what queenship made of you, I am content with what I have."

"Do not name that usurper king! God grant he'll not be so for long!"

"What are you saying?" Elizabeth said, appalled.

"I've said too much."

"You have not said enough," Elizabeth bit out. "Tell me all."

"Where is your husband?" The Dowager looked around her as if he might be hiding behind an arras.

"Hunting," Elizabeth said. "It is his passion. Mother! Have you run mad like that bitch the Beaufort?"

"She is not mad. I sought leave to visit her, as an act of Christian charity, or so I let it be known. Immured in Bermondsey, the feigned madness was by way of a defence."

"What is that to me?" Elizabeth snapped, impatiently. "I have no love for that woman. She can rot, for all I care."

"Will you listen, girl! She is not mad. She has friends, still. Archbishop Morton is returning from France. And Jasper Tudor did not die on Bosworth Field." Her voice dropped. "He is raising his affinity. He rescued her from Bermondsey, and took her to Chepstow, along with your Uncle Edward."

The young woman's face was a mask, white as chalk save for the imprint of her mother's blow. "What is that to me?" she whispered.

"Think, girl! Your brother will take the crown that is his by right. And if he dies without issue, then the heirs of your body--"

"No more, Madam, for the love of God. I think you have run mad in truth, or maybe bewitched! This is treason!" She turned to the little table under the window, where her writing things were kept. "I will write to the King. He may be inclined to spare you------"

"You will not!" the Dowager hissed, and seized her wrist, twisting it so that her daughter gasped. "One word of what I have told you, and your brother goes to the block!"

"He knows?"

"What do you think?"

"He would not--- he is loyal---"

"With so glittering a prize?"

*****

September 1490

Letters from the Duchess Margaret were frequent, but one in particular led Richard to call an emergency meeting of the Council. "My lords," Richard addressed them "My sister writes to me that Burgundy and Brittany are under threat from France. This is surprising, since it is common knowledge that France is in chaos at present. A child king, an unpopular regent. I believe it is time we considered our options. I cannot in truth ignore my sister's call for aid. We are, by ancient right, King of France."

"Your Grace, the country is sick of war." That was the Archbishop.

"I know it, who better! But soldiers need employment. Inactivity breeds insurrection, my lords. Whereas our armies relish the chance for action."

"You're thinking invasion," Lincoln said, an anticipatory smile on his face. And Norfolk was on his feet.

"Yes, your Grace! There's not a man here who will say you nay!" The old warrior glared around at his fellow Councillors, daring them to object.

"My Royal brother," Richard said, "Made a contract of peace in the Treaty of Picguigny. And the French bought him off with gold. The seven years of that treaty are up, and the fifty thousand crowns spent, and this time we will have the support from Brittany and Burgundy we were denied before; I have my sister's word on it. Louis broke his promises as often as he made them; witness his renunciation of my niece's betrothal to the Dauphin."

A grumble went around the table. That had been a sore point for years. "Parliament will grant us six thousand pounds for this enterprise," Richard went on. "Our aim will be to re-establish our English rights in France, the rights that Henry the Fifth won at Agincourt. We can take Boulogne, Guyenne and Paris and all of Northern France."

There was a shout of approbation. "Yes, and the rest!" Norfolk bellowed. "And by God we'll have you crowned in Rheims, my king!"

Richard smiled wryly. "One thing at a time, my lord. While we are away, my queen will act as Regent and Captain-General here. She will have Visount Lovell to aid and advise her at need."

Two faces turned to him, two pairs of eyes. Isabella's face had lost colour, and there was a shimmer of tears in her eyes. Francis was simply staring at his king as if he could not believe what he had heard. Then the queen moved, thrusting back her chair abruptly and sweeping from the room.

When the council meeting had been concluded, Richard excused himself from the discussions arising and followed her. He found her not in her solar as he might have expected, but in his Privy Chamber. Every line of her body radiated tension. He dismissed his attendants with a gesture. This was going to be difficult, he realised. There had been disagreements before, of course there had, but nothing that could not be swiftly resolved. He bent his head to her in salute. "My lady Queen," he said shortly.

"My lord Husband." She gave a bob of a curtsey, clearly too annoyed to offer more. "My lord," she burst out, "why did you not inform me of your plans before announcing it in open council?"

"Because, madam, it does not look well to have you call into question any decisions I make! You have a seat on my Council. We listen to your opinions, young as you are. That should content you. I do you great honour in appointing you Regent, you realise?"

"An honour I do not want!" She stamped her foot in annoyance. "You are going to war, my lord, and it is my wish to ride with you! Do not you tell me there is no precedent! Duchess Eleanor of Aquitaine, when she was Queen of France, went on Crusade with her husband! My mother herself donned armour and rode to defeat the Moors! Can I do less than they? I am young, yes, but I can fight!"

He should have known she would cite her mother's exploits.

"Your mother, valiant as she is, would not have you endanger yourself. Not at this time, with the child in your belly," he pointed out. There were two spots of hectic colour on her cheeks, and tears of anger in her eyes. She was quite clearly furious, and the delay in confronting him had not mellowed her. Rather the opposite. He was aware of his own rising temper and reined it in. "Your mother miscarried a son not four years after your birth. It was another three before she conceived your brother Juan." She opened her mouth to raise another objection and remembered instead seeing her mother grieving over that dead infant. She had been but four years old at the time, and had not been able to understand why her mother no longer wanted to embrace her, instead sending her away to live with the holy sisters. Reflexively her hands went to the small hard bulge of her belly, hidden beneath the satin of her kirtle. "Bel," he moderated his tone, "I cannot allow you to risk yourself and your child. Our child. As Regent, you must hold the realm for me, for our children yet to come. Who else can I trust?"

*****

"Dammit, Dickon, this is unreasonable!" As soon as they were alone, Francis turned on his friend. "You're going without me!"

"Francis," Richard said calmly. "Don't take this amiss, I beg you. Bel is bad enough, swallowing her tears whenever she looks at me. She's afraid for me, I can understand that. I have appointed her Regent, but she will need help. You are the best person to offer that help, and to keep her safe. I swear, if she were not carrying a child, she'd have donned armour like her mother and ridden into battle at my side!"

"Very like," Francis agreed wryly. "But so is my place at your side, Dickon. Not nursemaiding your child-queen."

Richard looked at him. "Francis," he said quietly. "Francis, you have my absolute confidence. I need you to do this. I could ask it as your friend, but as your king, I must command it of you. Who else can I trust?" Francis was mute. When Richard put it like that, what could he say? "And know this. There are rumours, stirrings in the west. Catesby has his best man on this, but as yet there is nothing sure. It's like a heath-fire, smouldering underground but likely to burst into flame at any time. It may not come to anything, but if it should then I need you to deal with it in my absence. I would not have the queen worried by this, Francis. She is Regent, but you are Viceroy until I return."

Francis joined with the queen to say farewell to the king as the Royal Army mustered at Southampton. It was a bright blustery day, and the flags and pennants snapped and fluttered in the freshening breeze. Richard was not in full armour – a brigantine and breastplate were enough for the voyage. The harbour was a cacophony of noise – shouted orders, the stamp of many feet, the unhappy whinnies of horses as they were loaded into slings and lowered into the holds of the horse-transports. And Richard and Norfolk seemed to be everywhere, the Duke using his battlefield bellow to good effect. Richard's eyes were bright with anticipation as he paced the deck of his flagship, the Rose Victrix. He did not seem to feel the chill of the wind, but Isabella did, huddling into her hooded sable-lined cloak. She was composed and queenly, as she should be, sending her king off to war. Francis stood at her shoulder, steadfast and unsmiling. More than almost anything he longed to be joining his friend in this enterprise.

Above his head the sails filled, bellied, and the ship seemed to quiver, like a horse that is ready to run, or a hound that scents the prey.

Richard crossed to where they stood, took Isabella's hand and kissed it, and drew her into an embrace, but the hard steel of his breastplate was between them. "Farewell, my heart," he said, smiling into her eyes. "Be brave, and guard my country well."

And to Francis – "I leave all in your charge, my friend."

Francis went to one knee, bowing his head. "To the best of my ability, my king." And as he rose, a whispered – "Give those garlic-eating Frogs one from me, eh, Dickon?"

Richard laughed, and for a moment looked like a boy again. "To the best of my ability, Francis!"

The trumpets sounded, the court disembarked, and the Rose slipped her moorings and made her way seawards, the fleet following, for all the world like a gaggle of goslings following the mother goose. It was a brave sight, and Francis and the queen watched them sail down channel until the sea-mist took them.

"Francis, will you join me?" Once inside the walls of Southampton Castle, Isabella shed her cloak and allowed Soraya to tidy her windblown hair. Her eyes were quite dry now. Tears were not appropriate when sending men into battle. She would save those for her private moments, when she was alone with only her beads to console her. "I will go to Mass to pray for the king and all our valiant men."

"With a good will, madam." And she laid a hand on his arm for him to escort her into the chapel.

*****

The Court was at Winchester, a favourite palace of the king's, close enough to the port city of Southampton that couriers could reach it in a day, and while it was not large, it was comfortable. Isabella liked it, as it appealed to her romantic nature, housing as it did the fabled Round Table. She was finding it hard, though, to be alone. Even among her ladies, she was alone. She almost resented the child within her – which thought she knew was wicked, and confessed it to her chaplain. But if she had not been with child, perhaps he might have taken her with him.

She knew that Francis felt the same, and that he longed to be at Richard's side. Their shared anxiety brought them more into each other's company, and she found comfort in that closeness.

"Madam, will it please you to walk a little?" Francis suggested, knowing that she was growing more and more impatient with the constraints her advancing pregnancy were placing on her.

"Well, I am not allowed to ride. But it is true, I am finding the confines of the queen's suite stifling."

He could understand that. She must feel like a caged bird, vainly beating her wings against the imprisonment.

"I have heard from the king," he offered, as he escorted her out into the pretty walled garden, redolent with the scents of late summer. "The Channel crossing was smooth, and he wasn't sick once Or so he says."

She halted, looking at him. "Does he get seasick, then? He has never said..."

"Madam, he would hardly confess such a weakness. He did tell me once of the time he and his brother had to flee the country, and the weather was so adverse he thought it might be easier to die than endure another hour of their voyage."

"Oh, my poor love!" Her laughter made him smile.

"Your husband is a proud man, your Grace. It is the face he shows the world. It has always been so, since our shared boyhood."

"You know so much of him, Francis. Things I can never know. Tell me of the days when you first met?"

As they walked slowly down the gravelled paths, he regaled her with stories of Richard's boyhood – the time they escaped their tutor to go rabbiting on the moors, and got a whipping for it, and when Richard broke his collarbone trying to ride one of Warwick's warhorses, to win a wager, and how he desperately tried to pretend there was nothing wrong. Her eyes never left his face. He plucked a late rose for her. He liked to hear her laugh, knowing he was lightening her burden.

The long September evenings grew shorter, and soon there was a definite chill in the air. He made sure she was warmly clad against the brisk winds, wrapping her in fox-fur and velvet. Richard had left her, his Queen, in his charge, and it was not a duty he took lightly.

They made time each evening to talk together, to read from the books he had had sent to Winchester.

"What shall it be this evening, Francis? The Chaucer?"

"A knightly tale, I think. Of noble deeds and high courage."

"You read my mind! *Sir Gawaine and the Green Knight.*" She settled herself in the high-backed chair, her feet on a footstool. He brought the candles nearer, and she smiled at him as she opened the book. Soraya knelt to take off the little kid slippers, and began a gentle massage of her queen's feet. Kati unpinned her hair, and brushed it out before spreading her skirts and seating herself on the cushions beside the chair.

It was all very peaceful and domestic. Francis leaned back in his chair and closed his eyes, letting her voice flow over him, the softly-accented Spanish cadences like music…

"Francis? Fie, my lord, you were asleep!"

Jolted out of a formless dream, Francis blinked awake, then laughed. "My apologies, my queen!"

"Tch!" she scolded. "You do not fall asleep in Council!"

"There are no voices as dulcet as yours, your Grace, in the Council."

“And that is probably true,” she agreed with a smile. “Ah, but you are weary, my friend, and I have kept you from your rest. Go, seek your bed. I shall see you in the morning.”

“Your Grace.” He bowed deeply, “God send you sweet sleep.”

*****

Francis handed the latest communication to the waiting courier, wondering again how things were really going across the Channel. His thoughts were interrupted by a tug on his sleeve.

“My Lord, my Lord Francisco!" It was the Moorish girl, the physician’s assistant, her face sallow-pale, and the veil over her hair disordered. “My Lord, it is *mi reina*, it is the queen, she needs help!”

Francis turned. “The queen? What’s wrong?” She had been merry that morning, laughing at something Soraya had said, and announcing her intent to visit her new Arabian mare, a gift from the king. “Where is she?”

The girl swung on her heel, making for the stable-block, running, so that Francis was forced to lengthen his stride. He was able, then, to hear the whimpers from the shadowed and fragrant interior. Fragrant, but with an overtone of something else.

Blood.

Isabella was crumpled in the hay, almost under the hooves of the little dappled mare she had christened Estella – Star – and the mare was shifting uneasily at the unfamiliar smell. Soraya flung herself to her knees beside her mistress. “My Lord, please to help her!”

Francis took in the situation at a glance. Taking the mare by her headcollar, murmuring reassurance, he led her to an adjacent stall, tethered her there and went back to crouch by Isabella. “My Lady,” he said quietly, “what ails you?”

She looked pallid in the dim light. “The babe, Francis. It is too soon...”

By four or five months, he calculated. Even as he knelt there, a fresh surge of blood gushed from beneath her skirts into the straw. “Soraya,” he ordered quietly, “Have the queen’s rooms made ready. And have her women send for the midwives.” There was no way she could walk, or even stand. He bent and gathered her into his arms, lifting her carefully. The shambles stink, the butcher’s bloody reek, was stronger as he stood, and he felt the wetness soaking into his shirt.

“Be easy, Lady,” he said, the reassuring tone he had used to the mare. “All will be well.” By the time he reached the stairs to the queen’s rooms, there was a gaggle of her women about him, hindering him as he climbed. “Are the midwives here?” he demanded, and carried his burden through to her bed, easing her down onto the white satin coverlet sewn with roses. It would be white no longer very shortly, he guessed. The women bustled around, edging him back, but the queen reached out a hand, and her fingers tightened on his.

“Francis...” she whispered. “Please. Don’t leave me...”

It was unheard of. It was completely unfitting, even scandalous, for a man to be witness to the women’s mysteries of childbirth and parturition. He ignored the shocked mutterings, and knelt at the bedside.

“While you need me, dear Lady,” he promised, “I am here.”

It was an ugly time, and he kept his eyes on her pale face, taking no heed as the women stripped her of the bloodsoaked skirts and shift, and packed linens in an attempt to stem the flow of blood. They washed the stains from her thighs, slipped a clean shift over her head, and Soraya brought a posset cup and raised her mistress' head to let her drink. It must have held a sedative, for her grip loosened, and she sighed and let go of his hand.

"She will sleep now," the midwife said.

It was a stern dismissal. Francis climbed to his feet, stiff from kneeling so long. He desperately wanted to shed his stained clothing, and to wash. And he must send word to the king in France. He felt a surge of pity for the suffering girl – she was hardly more than that, after all – and remembered Anna's dreadful death. Isabella had been so kind to him after that...

It was late the next day when he sat down to compose the letter that he knew would break his king's heart, when the Moorish girl came to him. "My lord, the queen –"

"I know, Soraya. I am writing to tell the king---"

"You must tell him, then, that the queen is well, and the child she carries thrives within her womb!" Her eyes glowed with delight. It came to him that she was a remarkably pretty girl. "The midwives are certain, my lord!"

He would need to talk to them, he thought. He would not, could not, dash Richard's hope, and Bel's.

The senior midwife was certain. "The Queen's Grace was carrying twins, my lord. She miscarried one, but the other lives. With care, I believe she will bring it to term."

Care. He seized on the word. "Whatever she needs, she must have. I will give the order." And here, at least, was something he could do.

*****

It had become his habit, as Chamberlain as well as councillor, to confer with Richard over business at day's end, perhaps to relax with him over chess, to share a cup of wine. He had not found it necessary to change this habit in the king's absence. Isabella had a brain in that pretty head, as Richard knew, and he was not inclined to waste it.

They had built up something of a rapport, he thought, from spending time with her and the king together. He had been careful not to overstep the mark, but there was a growing friendship that Richard had encouraged. How not? His queen and his dearest friend – Richard had no compunction about leaving her in his charge.

Now, he began to realise, things had changed.

"The queen is sleeping," Soraya told him, opening the door when he tapped on it.

"No matter. I will come back –" he began, but there came a stir from within and that slightly accented voice said:

"Francis?"

"My queen."

"Admit him, Soraya."

He stepped inside, into the warm rose-scented bower that was the queen's solar. The sun was gilding the tapestries, and gleaming on the sleep-tousled hair. She gave him a drowsy smile, patted the coverlet on her day bed, with its embroidered roses. "I had forgot the hour, my lord. Come, sit. Will you take refreshment? Soraya, fetch us some of the fresh orange-juice. Richard likes to cut it with wine, but I love it as it is. It is the taste of home to me."

It was tart, and sweet, and delicious. He took the cup from Soraya with a murmur of thanks, unable to take his eyes from Isabella. Rumpled from her siesta, she looked younger than her years. A young woman, scarce more than a girl, and lovely, with bright eyes and flushed cheeks…

But it had not been the young girl who had come at Richard's call, who had held him and let him weep out his grief over Anna's death. Who had helped the king strip him and put him to bed that night, who had held the cup with the potion that brought blessed sleep. Whose face had been the last thing he saw before his eyes closed, and the first thing he had seen when he woke, who had sat vigil together with his friend all that night.

That had been a woman, a woman grown.

And as sudden and as startling as a levin-bolt, he knew he loved her. Heart and body and soul.

And not as his Queen.

Isabella stared in surprise at the spill of juice on the white of the satin, and at the precipitous exit of the Viscount.

"Did a wasp sting him?" she wondered aloud, as Lady Dacre tutted and removed the overturned cup, and the stained cover, replacing it with a different one in embroidered scarlet.

"Most like the smoked eels at supper misliked him," she said. "Takes some men that way, madam. My dear husband cannot stomach shellfish, though he has an inordinate love of them. Aye, and regrets it after! But that is men for you. Can I get you anything else, my lady?"

"No, I thank you. Soraya, have you your lute to hand? Sing some songs of my homeland…"

And as the plangent notes drifted about the room, she drifted smiling back to sleep.

Isabella was instructed to keep to her bed, and not to stir save to use the close-stool. To this end, she was accompanied at all times by one or more of her ladies, as well as one of the midwives.

After a week of this confinement, however, she felt strong enough to make objection to this stricture. "I am well now, Soraya. Madam midwife, do you tell them that I am recovered!"

"Your Grace, surely you would not endanger the child!" The midwife looked askance.

"I will do nothing that would do so, be sure. But send for Lord Lovell, if you will. I must consult with him. I am still Regent, even tied to this bed! Perhaps he will cheer me with good news. Soraya, Kati, make me fit to be seen!"

Francis, appealed to, would not hear of her going against the midwives' advice.

"Alas, you must bear this, my queen." He gave her a tight smile. She looked small as a child on the wide daybed, reclining against the heaped pillows. Her hair was bound up and covered by a little gold-sewn cap, and a shawl of Indian silk in peacock colours was around her shoulders. "But is there anything else I can do for you? The king will rejoice to know you are well. And if you are strong enough, there is business to conduct." He asked for and gained her permission to send for John Kendal.

The king's secretary Kendall, a little uncomfortable to be in so feminine a setting, looked around for a stool and something to do the duty of a desk.

"I may not be able to ride out or even stir from this bed, but I can make shift to set my seal and sign-manual on State papers! My lord my husband has left the realm in my care, and I will not disappoint him. Soraya, set the pillows so that I can sit. I should head the Council, but since no one will let me stir, you must do that duty for me, Francis. Now, is there word from France?"

"The reports are all positive, madam." He passed over the letters that had arrived over the past few days. "Our men are in good heart, and our losses are few."

"Now God be thanked," she said at last. "Is there anything else?"

Francis helped Kendall to gather up the papers, all business now.

"Not at this time, Madam. Are you fatigued?"

"A little." Kendall bowed over her hand, and left, but when Francis would have followed, she called him back. "Stay, Francis. Would it be possible for someone to fetch me one of the books that were in the king's gift?"

"I will send for one directly," he promised. "The Chaucer, madam?"

"No, the tales of King Arthur, I think. And Francis, if you can spare me the space of an hour, perhaps we might read together? And I have oranges." She gave him a dimpling smile. "My mother sent them! Share them with me?"

"Alas, Madam, I must decline. Enjoy your fruit."

It was too much of a temptation. He sent young Owen for the book, and then leaned for a moment against the closed door. It was becoming harder and harder to see the queen as queen, and he knew his thoughts were wicked and wrong.

She was wife to another man. She was Queen of England. And not for him. Never for him.

Isabella hated to have her windows closed, save in the worst weather, and was in a running battle with Lady Dacre, who was convinced that all kinds of evil airs could enter. This night, however, Soraya had waited until that lady had bidden her queen a good night, and then had reopened the shuttered windows to the freshness and scented coolness. Isabella gave a sigh of pleasure, and Soraya, whose duty it was that night, joined her in the great bed, and was soon asleep. Isabella was not so inclined. She missed her husband, and not only for bedsport, which was forbidden anyway until she was delivered. She rested a hand on the small bulge of her belly. Another son? Or a girl? Richard had said he cared not which it was, so long as she and the babe were healthy. She breathed a prayer for him. She would make pilgrimage, she decided, to Walsingham, for his safety, as soon as she was delivered. Maybe he would be back by then. She longed to have him with her again, to see that slow smile, and feel herself beloved... Her thoughts drifted to Lord Lovell, then, and she found herself wondering if she might somehow have offended him. He was always courteous, always ready at her slightest command. She remembered how he had saved her life, carrying her from the stable and then staying at her side during the bloody horror of the miscarriage.

How delighted and relieved he had been to be told that her child survived. Yes. But she sensed that something was indeed amiss. He was never less than gallant, but there had been a change. Was he still grieving for poor Lady Anna? She and Richard together had tried to keep him busy, in the hope that he would not brood over the tragedy. Maybe they had succeeded too well. And now he was assisting her in the Regency. She was doing her best, she knew that, but it was wonderful to have him at her side, helping with that enormous responsibility. He would rather be with his king, she thought, in France. She could understand that. She had not wanted to part with Richard, wanting to go with him. He had been adamant in his refusal, and that had hurt. It had been the first real argument they had had, and it had changed something between them. It occurred to her then that he had responded to her in a different way, as his Queen Consort, an equal, a woman grown, not as the child who he had wed, needing to be protected. That was worth thinking on. And maybe Francis had felt the same resentment at being left behind? That could explain why he had changed towards her. They did not read together now, or make music. She missed her Lancelot.

But most of all, she missed Richard.

"Blessed Mother," she whispered, "Keep the king my husband safe."

*****

It was raining in Calais when Richard's flagship the Rose tied up at the dock, and Richard was glad when he could get within walls.

"My lord Father," the young Captain of Calais bent the knee before his king. "I bid you welcome to Calais."

"Johnnie!" Richard raised the youngster to his feet, "It is good to see you," and embraced him. Like his father, John of Gloucester was not tall, but he carried himself with Plantagenet pride, and no one could have doubted whose son he was.

"And you, Father. Sir James Tyrell and I have arranged quarters for you here in the Castle, and also for my lord of Norfolk and his son."

"Jocky will be grateful for that, I can tell you. He loves wet weather as much as a cat. Now, before we go in to dinner, I require the services of your secretary."

"I can do that duty for you, sire." John said quickly.

"I am sure, but you have more important matters, my son. I will need to see and speak with my commanders, as well as those from Burgundy and Brittany, and inspect my troops. You should make yourself known to them. You are their Captain. Now, send for your secretary?"

"William of Montgomery, sire." He was a well-set-up youth, with a tangle of black hair, and the build of a blacksmith. Which he admitted was his trade, and why he was one of John's men, because every army needs men with smithcraft. He was awed almost speechless to be brought before the king. "Educated by the good fathers at the abbey, sire – your Grace. I can read, and cipher, and write a fair hand. As well as smithing. And fighting."

"Well said. We'll need all those skills ere long. This letter to my Council – and three fair copies. My couriers will be waiting. "*To our right trusty and well-beloved lords of the Council,*" Richard dictated now, *"We are ten thousand strong, well-armed and provisioned, thanks to a generous grant from Parliament, and have crossed the Channel without incident. We are quartered now at Calais while we finalise our plans...."*

He had most of it in his head already. He had learned from his brother, and from his brother's captains. Now he argued and discussed strategies over the dinner table, with the senior commanders from Burgundy and Brittany, and though he would not have admitted it, enjoyed himself.

The maps John provided were clear and up-to-date, and his knowledge of the country was going to be a bonus. He had an efficient spy network, as well.

"...I can tell you, sire, that the taxes imposed on the people are ruinous, and there is much discontent."

"Well, we can do something about that. No, thank you, Rob," this to the page about to refill his winecup, "I'm cutting down on strong liquors. I need a clear head. Ale will do. What of the French army?"

"In a parlous state. Desertions are rife. Not to mention the recurrent sickness. They call it *Sudor Anglicus* – the Brittany Sweat would be a better name for it."

"Aye, and Tudor's mercenaries brought it to England... Johnnie, I'll have you for my aide-de-camp, so I'm knighting you. We can do the pretty when we have the leisure, but that's for later..."

John slid from his chair and knelt to kiss his father's hand. His eyes were shining. "Your Grace does me too much honour," he murmured. Richard smiled.

"Be warned, my son, I shall work you hard."

They marched out to meet the much-depleted French army, and Boulogne fell with barely a struggle. Paris was a harder nut to crack.

On the first day, as the Army set up camp beneath the walls, Lancaster Herald rode to the closed and fortified gates. "People of Paris! King Richard, king by ancient right of these lands, now demands your surrender. Resist, and suffer our wrath. Open your gates, and we will spare your citizens."

There was no acknowledgement.

Richard gave them five days to consider. As with the other towns, he gave the command that there should be no looting, no pillage or abuse of the citizens if they surrendered.

Norfolk, however, was on fire to deploy his artillery – it had not been required for the other towns. And there was also another weapon close to his warlike heart. "The five days are up, Dickon," he said, thrusting into the king's tent in the half-light of dawn. "I say we bring up Long Meg and her daughters." Richard put down his knife and pushed the dish of eggs to one side.

"As you suggest, Jocky. Give the order."

The wagons transporting the trebuchets – Long Meg and her daughters, the soldiers called it, in insulting reference to the deposed Margaret of Anjou – were trundled forward and the parts of the assault engines assembled. Norfolk regarded them fondly.

"There's my girls. Load 'em up, lads."

The freight of hemp-wrapped rocks daubed with pitch were unshipped, hauled into place, and in the instant before launch, set alight. Trailing fire like a comet, the missile soared into the dawn sky and impacted the walls above the gates, splattering burning material like fiery rain.

Grinning like a fiend, Norfolk stood gauntleted hands on hips and roared his appreciation. "Give 'em another one, boys!" he bellowed, "That'll soften their flinty Frog hearts!"

Three more missiles flew from Long Meg's grasp, setting alight the brushwood piled in front of the gates in a crackling sheet of flame, before Norfolk called a halt.

"Do you think they got the point, Jocky?" Richard said, with a quirky smile.

"If they didn't we'll give 'em a reminder with some cannon-shot."

"My Lord," a sergeant panted up. "My Lord King, sire, we caught a whiff of wine on the wind."

"Aye, well, I'd be stinking drunk too if I'd been on the receiving end of Meg's billet-doux!" Norfolk laughed.

"They're dousing the flames with wine, my lord."

"Are they, by God! Then they're short of water! There's been no rain for a week, and it was a dry winter. They're short of water, Dickon."

John was acting as esquire, helping his father arm and seeing to his other needs. "My spies confirm that," he said quietly. "If they're using their supplies of wine, as my Lord of Norfolk suggests, then they're seriously short of water. They'll maybe last another day or so."

"And we'll be ready for their surrender, by God!" There was bread and cheese, and apples. Norfolk helped himself to all three, grinning as Richard got to his feet. He chortled. "Five crowns they'll surrender today!"

"I'll not take that wager, Jocky. But I think we have time to arm. Johnny, if you will..."

So it was that when the portcullis creaked up and the blistered gates groaned open, the supplicant city-fathers were greeted by cheering and jeering soldiery. Norfolk, still munching on an apple, stepped aside and gestured to where Richard stood, a slight figure in gleaming armour, the helm crowned with bright gold. As one, they went to their knees, and doffed their caps. The dawn was clear and cold, with a pale sun just taking the edge off the frosted grass. The party who exited wore the look of defeat as they crossed to kneel before the slight figure of the king. They bore the symbolic keys of the city. "Paris is yours, dread king. We throw ourselves on your gracious mercy."

"It is granted," Richard said.

The army marched on Rouen, and the weather worsened, Constant rain turned roads to quagmire, the wagons became bogged down axle-deep in mud, and no one, lord or commoner, was dry.

Richard, being Richard, did not spare himself but shared the discomforts of his men, and it cost him. His attendants did what they could, but there was nought they could do about the king's habit of going among his men in encouragement.

"You're doing yourself no favours, man," Norfolk, opined, finding his king divesting himself of sodden cloak and boots while his pages brought hot wine. "And what would the queen say?"

"She's not here," Richard said shortly, taking a drink of the wine and coughing. "Thank God." And coughed again. "It's just a chill, Jocky." He shivered, grateful for the heavy fur-lined bedcover John had placed over his shoulders. *Just a chill,* he told himself, remembering what he had been told of his brother's last illness. A chill caught on a fishing trip. And less than a week later, bedridden and dying. *And I didn't know. I didn't even know you were sick. She didn't want me to know, the bitch. And you died without me at your side.* He shuddered, and another spasm of coughing shook him.

"Right," Norfolk said, levering himself to his feet. "I'm sending for a leech. Here, Rob," to the hovering page, "whatever your name is, tell the surgeon the king requires his services. Quick about it, now."

Thus summoned, Master Perry ignored the king's increasing irritation and took his pulse, listened to his chest, and announced there was a rheum, an element of fever and an ague afflicting the king.

"Could have told you that," Richard snapped. His head ached, and his back. He accepted, with bad grace, the draught he was given.

It didn't seem to help. He allowed himself to be dosed again, after Mass, and set about the orders of the day, coughing throughout. He hated being ill. He hated this damned rain. He hated France. He wanted this godforsaken enterprise to be over. He wanted... Oh, he wanted to go home!

It was Surrey who stormed in, pushing the pages out of the way. "My lord King, you forbade looting and abuse. There has been an incident among the troops, expressly against your given command."

"What?" Richard croaked. His throat was clogged and sore. "What now?"

There were four of them, standing drenched and miserable before his tent, wrists bound and noosed with hempen ropes.

"They are Harry Wycombe, George Farrier, Will of Montgomery, and Sam Turner, sire. Accused of theft, rapine and murder."

"Evidence?"

"Caught in the act, sire."

Will of Montgomery. Johnnie's secretary, the smith.

"Hang them," he said hoarsely. A rage was bubbling within him with his rising fever, the fateful Plantagenet temper. "Hang them. Now."

"Father..." Johnnie said, clearly desperate to mitigate the sentence on his friend, however deserved it might be. He took a step forward, but his father ignored him.

"No arguments. Get it done." He turned on his heel. "My orders were clear."

"Your Grace, should they not be shrived...?" His chaplain asked, deferential.

At least Hastings had been shrived before I had him headed.

"Make it quick, then."

"Father?" John was standing near the accused men. Of course, Richard realised, he and the smith were friends. It did not matter. Justice must be done. "Father, can I ask mercy?"

"You may not." He cut his son off. "They are to die. My lord of Surrey, do your office." And coughing, he went back into his tent. He had a disturbed night, seeing his son's face as his friends were executed. *It was necessary,* he reminded himself, *Justice must be done, and seen to be done. Or I am leading a rabble in arms, not England's disciplined militia...I'll beg pardon of Johnnie when I may. But not yet.*

The word quickly got about that the king's orders were not to be flouted, that the king's own son had been denied his pleas for clemency, and it was a chastened force that marched on Rouen, while Richard recovered his health.

Rouen, birthplace of his brother, the Rose of Rouen. The Sunne in Splendour. *I cannot match you, Edward, but with God's help I do the best I can...* The city, having heard of the fate of Paris, welcomed the brother of the Rose with open arms.

"*Vive le Roi*!" was the shout as he rode through the city gates. "*Vive le Roi d'Angleterre!*"

And then, Rheims, where the French king had been crowned by Joan the Maid in the reign of the fourth Henry.

"A perfidious people, the French," Norfolk opined. He sat with Surrey his son in the tent they shared outside the city walls and availed themselves of the local wine. "They had an inspirational leader—mad though she was – or God-touched, who knows – but they sold her to the enemy!"

"His Holiness the Pope declared her a martyr," his son said idly.

"Much good that did her!" Norfolk grunted sourly. "A perfidious people..."

"Da," said his son tentatively, "what does the king intend? Will he accept the crown?"

"He will not, for all our counselling, while there is a legitimate heir. He may agree to take over the regency. He may establish a protectorate. He hasn't told me. And with Lovell back in England holding the queen's hand, I doubt he's told anyone else what's in his mind. Oh, he'll establish a military presence here, no doubt, with one of us to head it and hold it." He grinned widely. "Fancy that, do you, son? Viceroy in France?"

"Can't say I'd mind, at that!"

"No, you wouldn't, I'll wager! And a pretty French doxy to warm your bed, to boot!"

*****

Miles Bluett reined in his hardy little Welsh pony at the side of Llyn Coch, at the foot of Snowdon, in Cwm Idwal. There was a thin mist over the water, a mist that coated the sides of the valley that sheltered the little gathering of men under the banner of the Red Dragon.

There stood Jasper Tudor, last scion of the Tudor line. Owen, his sire, had been headed in Hereford marketplace. Edmund, his brother, was dead of the plague. But not before getting a son on Margaret Beaufort's unwilling body. And what a son – a puling squint-eyed pipsqueak of a boy that she had managed to squeeze out of her skinny loins. But by that time Edmund was dead, and Jasper had done a brother's duty in caring for the widow and her boy. Jasper, Miles acknowledged, was a man among men. Look at him under the banner, hair grey-grizzled ruffled by the ever-present wind, straight as a lance. *Hen un Llygad*, they called him. Old One-Eye. Welsh to his fingertips. He could have ruled Wales, Miles thought wistfully, for he was a man to follow. Henry, his nephew, had been raised abroad, scarce spoke a word of Welsh, and it had been Jasper who had protected him in exile, who had rallied an army to fight for him at Bosworth. An army of gutter-scrapings and mercenaries. And turncoats. But they had come against the might and courage of a king who rivalled Caesar...

Jasper was speaking, his deep voice announcing that soon they would have a bloody revenge on Richard the Usurper. Miles took notice of all that was said, joining in the bellow of *'Cymru am Byth'* roared as Jasper drew his sword and brandished it high.

'*Cymru am Byth!*' Wales forever.

There was a diminutive figure small as a child at Jasper's side, bundled in layers of wool and fur. Margaret Beaufort, sharp-eyed, sharp-featured, sharp-tongued, the woman who had been the driving force behind her son's abortive invasion. She was speaking, her voice thin in the damp air. Miles could almost feel her enmity. He shivered under his leather cloak.

"We have the support of Richard of Shrewsbury, the true heir to his father's throne, and we will put him in his rightful place! King of England and of Wales!"

There's interesting, Miles thought. *Does Master Catesby know that? Duw Mawr, that'll be worth gold!*

*****

January 1491

Rothesay was feeling cock-a-hoop – it had been a good days' hunting, they had taken two stags and a great boar, with the sow charging to avenge her mate, leaving a litter of sucklings. He much enjoyed a roast suckling pig. He had lost two good dogs to the savage tusks, though. He would regale his wife with the bloody details, but tone them down a little so as not to upset her. She was past the difficult first months of pregnancy, but even so…

Now, changed out of his hunting leathers and with a cup of wine to hand, he strode into her solar. "How now, Bessie?" he beamed at her, feeling very content. It did not last. She held out a letter, her face a mask.

It bore the Dowager's seal, he saw, but he hardly needed to read the contents. His wife's face told him he was not going to like it.

"Well, Bessie? What does she want from you now?" He had no great love for his wife's mother, regarding her as a meddling beldame who should by rights be confined in a convent somewhere. Or locked away where she could do no harm.

"Read it, 'Xander," Elizabeth said, with barely controlled fury. "She and the Beaufort are determined to unseat the king, and put my brother on the throne, and she wants me to join with her---" She did not see the blow coming and it stung her cheek. Alexander, eyes blazing, stood over her.

"You little fool!" he bellowed. "Do you want to end on the block like your grandsire and your uncle?"

Elizabeth did not flinch. Facing him down, she was not conciliatory. "Do you think me such a fool, then, husband?" she snapped. "My lord the king has only ever been kindness itself to me! Do you think I would betray him on the whim of that witch the Beaufort and my stupid mother? I was a pawn in their game when they plotted to wed me to the Tudor. I swore

I would rather have gone into a nunnery before they forced me to the altar!" She paused, gathering her dignity. "I could not marry the man to whom my heart was given, 'Xander. I have never been less than honest with you."

He drew her to her feet. Yes, she had been honest. He knew of her old unrequited passion for the king. She had cried out that name, "Dickon!" on their wedding night, as he took her. It had been only the one time that she had let her real feelings show. In all other ways she had been all the wife and helpmeet that he could desire. And he had come to love her, in his own way, his bonny Bess. His only sorrow was that although she had conceived twice, she had not carried full term. But there was time enough for that, and maybe this time she would bear him a son. Or a daughter. He did not care which. It was still a wonder to him that he had won this lovely creature. "Indeed, Bessie. Forgive me. I should not have doubted you. But this---" he held the letter as if it were a snake. "We cannot ignore it. Write to your mother, prevaricate, tell her you need to talk me round, whatever. And I will write to the king, to warn him."

*****

The king's messenger from France, by Francis' order, delivered his news directly to the queen before the Council was informed, so she heard the news of the taking of Paris before they did, and sent for her chaplain, Fra Inigo, to offer masses of thanksgiving to God.

She and Francis were reading the latest dispatch when she caught her breath, grimacing, her hand going to her belly.

"My queen?" The dispatches scattered as he stood up.

"Call the midwives, Francis," she gasped. "Then, I beg you, absent yourself until I send word."

The child was early by a month, the lying-in chamber unprepared, but Isabella remained calm as the bustle of preparation went on around her. Soraya was there at her side to support her, and before long she was walking steadily into the room, her glance telling her that all was ready for the coming of the babe.

The pain was different, this time. It felt as if her bones were grinding together, and there was no surcease, just a constant monstrous gnawing. She could hear herself sobbing, wailing, demanding that they do something, anything, to assuage this anguish. There was a short period of respite, as Dame Elizabeth consulted with her assistants – but Isabella did not hear them. She was back in the fountain courts of home in Granada, drifting in the rose-scented sunlit air, and it came to her that she must be dying. *Lo siento*, she thought. *I'm sorry, Richard. So sorry…* She could not fight the pain when it returned. She had not the strength. Her mother's voice was in her ears, stern. *This battle is one you must win, my daughter, as I won against the Moors. Fight!*

I cannot, mi madre. It is too hard…

Are you not a daughter of Spain, child?

I am dying, mi madre! I can fight no more! Oh, Richard, I would you were with me, so I could say goodbye…

And it seemed that he was there, supporting her, loving her, although rationally she knew he was in France and not in this birth-chamber, reeking of blood.

Fight for me, my Bel!

She made one last convulsive effort, crying out his name, and then, suddenly, the pain was less and she heard the faint kitten-wail of the child before a welcome darkness took her.

When she woke, the chamber was blessedly quiet, and there was the homely scent of lavender on the air.

"The child?" she queried weakly.

"A girl, madam. A princess for England!" Dame Elizabeth said triumphantly.

"Send for Sir Francis," she demanded. "Tell him to notify the king!"

He must have been waiting outside, because he was there immediately. "Are you well, madam?" he asked softly.

"Dear Francis," she extended her hand for him to kiss. "Tell my husband the king that he has a daughter. Will you stand as her godfather? She is to be called Philippa. The king and I decided that she would be Edmund, if a boy, but I am happy to have a girl."

"A Princess for England," Francis agreed. "The midwives let me see her. She will be as beautiful as her mother." He must warn Richard that the babe was not strong, being early. He had not told Isabella, herself too weak from the birth.

"Be easy, madam, until the bleeding stops," she was instructed, and she obeyed. She felt weak and drained of strength – that would be the blood-loss – and longed over all to sleep. She dozed, in fact, for some time, and woke to find Francis at her bedside again. Somehow, it did not matter that her hair was in a snarl, or her clothes disordered, or that the room still had an underlying scent of blood. This was Francis, and her dearly beloved friend. She held out her hand, and he took it in his

To His Grace the King. Your daughter is born, Dickon, and the midwives tell me that she came before time, and is not strong. She is, of course, having the best of care, and I am told that she has taken to her wet-nurse better than was

hoped. The queen asked me to stand godfather, which I willingly do, though I have advised no ceremonial Christening. She was, in fact, baptised by the midwife as soon as she was born, as they thought her not long to live. She has proved them wrong. She is all Plantagenet!

I have not informed the queen of the child's condition, as she herself was much weakened by the birth. I am happy to say that she mends daily, and obeys the midwives, resting as they instruct. She still insists on reading all the dispatches, and doing Council business from her bed.

The queen begs me tell you that your daughter is named Philippa.

She sends, as always, her love and duty.

The queen was resting on her day-bed, with Kati beside her, when Lady Dacre entered, looking flustered. "There is a messenger from your mother, your Grace, with a parcel. I have never seen the like – black, he is, as an ape, and so outlandish!"

Isabella sat up, intrigued. "Admit him, then, my Lady..."

The person who entered was clearly one of her mother's blackamoor servants, outlandishly dressed in a rainbow of colours – gold loose trousers tucked into scarlet ankle boots, a flowing purple shirt, and over all an open bronze robe thick with bullion. He was also a dwarf, scarce the height of a ten-year old child, though a preposterous turban in vivid green brocade gave him extra inches. Isabella liked him on sight. He had an impish grin and bright dark eyes. He performed a deep obeisance before her, and beckoned to the page to bring forward a large parcel wrapped in white silk and bound in scarlet cords.

"*Con permiso, Infanta...*" He cut the cords, unwrapped the silk with a flourish, and revealed the most stunningly beautiful fabric either young woman had ever seen.

It was silk, but silk of a quality and weight that defied description, woven all over with a design of phoenixes and dragons, on a background of the purest turquoise.

Isabella extended a hand to touch – "Feel, Kati, this is not embroidery but woven into the very fabric! Oh, it is beyond beautiful! This is from my mother, *senor*?"

"She sends it as a gift, *mi Infanta*, to celebrate the birth of your daughter, the princess Philippa. It has come, I am to tell you, many month's journey from far Cathay, along the Silk Road, to Venice, and thence to Granada."

"Your name, *senor*?" Isabella enquired. He bowed.

"Domingo, *Serenissima.* And I am at your service. Your mother sends me to be as playfellow and guardian to your Royal children."

"They will be enchanted, I know. You have our thanks, sir. I shall tell my mother." He performed a deep bow and backed from the room.

"Oh, Bel, you must have a gown of this!" Kati said excitedly. "To greet the king on his return!"

Isabella considered. "Yes. With an underkirtle of white silk, or cloth of silver, I think. And, Kati, I think there will be enough to fashion a wedding-gown for you as well."

Kati was speechless for a moment. "Oh, Bel! You are too generous...! It is too fine for me..."

"Nonsense. You are the king's beloved daughter, and my favourite among my ladies. We will commission our Master Court painter to paint a portrait of you wearing it, so that your sons and daughters to come will see how fair you are!"

*****

Father Dominic, chaplain and confessor to the king, was about to dowse the candles and divest himself of his sacerdotal trappings when he saw a cloaked and hooded figure enter the chapel, genuflect, and slide into the penitent's seat. It was too dim to see anything of the man's face, but he took his place, none the less, and kissed the stole he wore. "Yes, my son?" he asked softly. "Do you wish to confess?"

"I must, Father. Bless me and let me unburden my heart."

"It is my duty and privilege, my son. Now, tell me. How long is it since your last Confession?"

The ritual words seemed to reassure the penitent. He began to speak – awkwardly, desperately. It was no catalogue of venial sins. Rather it was one terrible mortal sin that made Father Dominic's blood run cold, and stirred him to pity. The penitent loved a woman forbidden to him.

"...I cannot help how I feel, Father. I love her more than life itself. She is the very breath of life to me, but she is his. And God help me I come near to hating him, my best friend, that he has what I cannot."

"Does she reciprocate? Is she your partner in sin?"

"She does not know how I feel. I dare not tell her."

Father Dominic ruminated for a moment. "Then this I can tell you, my son. If you wish absolution, then you must truly repent. Avoid the occasions of sin."

"That will not be easy, Father. She – bears a great responsibility. And I have been tasked with helping her with that burden. Until the king – " He stuttered to a halt. Then: "Until the king comes home."

Father Dominic knew him then, though his face was still shadowed by the hood. “My Lord Francis,” he said softly. “I do not know what I can tell you. I cannot grant you absolution unless you are truly contrite. I do believe that you have no wish to hurt the king…”

“I would cut my heart out before I did him harm!”

“Just so.”

“She called me her Launcelot,” he said softly. “I am torn two ways. My love for my friend, and my love for his wife. Dickon and I are as twin souls, but she is his queen, and forbidden to me by all the laws of God and men. She troubles my sleep. When I am not with her, I am in hell.”

*****

March 1491

The whole of England rejoiced at the return of the king; all his objectives had been achieved, although he forbore from accepting the French crown, becoming Governor General instead as part of a triumvirate with his sister Margaret and the Duke of Brittany, and installing young Surrey as Duke of Normandy. While there was a legitimate heir, though a minor as yet, Richard would lay no claim to the French throne. And he would have the raising of the boy, with a Council of his choosing to guide him. There had been approaches of submission from the Aquitaine, from the south of the country, but these he considered were for another campaign. If indeed it could be called that. France had welcomed his rule rather than that of the self-serving Regent.

He rode in triumph through London, was greeted at the Guildhall by the Mayor and aldermen and other worthies in their red and gold, and where Isabella joined him, her face alight with pleasure and thanksgiving. They held festival together in the Great Hall of Westminster, in Royal state, gowned and crowned as King and Queen Consort. "That gown," Richard said to her, under cover of the music and chatter. "It becomes you well, dearest."

"My mother's gift," she said, smiling. "I am having another gown made up for Kati, as a wedding gift. Let it be soon, Richard?"

"Well, young William did bravely in France. It will be fit reward. And I was surprised by how well Lord Dorset did," he added. "Mistress Soraya must be good for him."

*****

Soraya woke from a dreadful dream where she was struggling in the coils of a great snake as it oozed from its hot and swampy home. It was almost dawn, the windows grey with morning, light cobwebby between the bed curtains. She was alone, she realised, but the bedding was tangled around her limbs. The pillows and sheets were sodden as if a river had overflowed.

"Tom?" she queried softly. "*Querido?*" She heard a hoarse cough, and kneeling up, parted the bed curtains. He was huddled in the chair by the dead ashes of the hearth, naked but running with sweat, hair glued in elf-locks to his neck and shoulders. The face he turned to her was pallid, eyes slitted, red-rimmed.

"I'm sick," he croaked. "Cold..." He was shivering violently, in spasms. "Head hurts…"

She crossed to kneel at his side, and felt the fever-heat from him as if he was burning inside. She dragged the fur-lined coverlet from the bed and wrapped it around his shoulders against the rigors shaking him, only to have him throw it off. She stood up. "I will go to my master," she told him, and pulling a shift over her head, fled the room.

The Moorish physician came almost immediately. “This is *Sudor Anglicus*, I believe,” he pronounced, having examined the moaning Dorset. “The English Sweat, it is called. A new disease, possibly brought from France with Tudor’s mercenary army.”

“Can you help him, master?” Soraya was stripping the bedding.

“To be honest with you, child, I do not know. There are no nostrums, no cures that I have heard of.” He stood up. “If we treat each symptom as it appears, perhaps. It seems to be highly infectious, from what little we know. You have been exposed – you should isolate yourself, leave him to the care of others.”

“Who will care for him, master, if not I?” she asked simply.

Who indeed, he thought, looking with sympathy at the girl. Thomas Dorset had few friends at court, and none at all who would be willing to risk their health for him. “You have courage, child. As you will. Keep him well-covered, in spite of the sweating and fever, and give him plenty to drink – broths, ale, whatever. Good clean water, if you can get it. Listen to his chest for fluid on the lungs, for that would surely kill him. I will go now to warn the king – it is imperative that he and the queen remove themselves immediately to a more healthful location.”

Richard did not hesitate. “We will take the Court to Richmond. The children are safe in Middleham.”

“But, Soraya---” Isabelle began, to have the physician shake his head.

“She has chosen to stay with the lord Dorset. She knows what to do. I advise you to distance yourself and your people as much as possible. If any fall sick, isolate them.”

Lady Dacre nodded. "I will so instruct the Household, your Grace." She bustled off. Isabelle, looking concerned, gathered her ladies and followed in her wake.

Richard took Francis aside. "Have there been other cases, do you know?"

"None that I know of. He probably caught it from one of his Southwark doxies."

"Or in France. Make enquiry. If it's not in the city already, then there's hope."

But the plague was already in the city. It struck without warning, rich or poor, young or old, and death stalked the streets like a reeking shadow.

Nor was the Court untouched. Katherine Plantagenet, the king's natural daughter, Bel's Kati, newly betrothed to one of the Herbert sons, was visiting her soon-to-be family at their London house. She sickened while she was with them, as did the maidservants assigned to her, and two of the grooms. Death took her swiftly and mercifully. She was well in the morning, but dead by sundown.

News reached the palace the next day. It was Francis who took control, as Lord Chamberlain, ordering the Court into mourning black. Together with Sir William Catesby, he consulted with Master Hussey, and ordered the draconian measure of having the city gates shut, none to go in or out until the pestilence had run its course.

The king was out riding with Isabella in Richmond Park, taking their hawks. Francis waited in the stable yard. He heard Isabella singing as she rode, and Richard joining in. And he had to be the one to tell him of his daughter's death. It was not going to be easy.

Richard swung down from his horse, lifted Isabella down from her saddle, laughing. The austringer took the birds back to the mews, and that was when Richard noticed what Francis was wearing.

"Why the gloomy garb, my friend?" he asked with a smile. "What, has someone died?"

For a moment Francis could not speak. Then; "Dickon," he said hoarsely. "It's Kati. Your daughter."

"What?" Richard was staring at him as if he had brought word of his own death, his colour that of unbleached linen. Isabella, at his side, listened unbelievingly.

"It cannot be..." she stammered, "She was due to return to Court tomorrow! How can she be dead?"

"It was a swift sickness." Francis said. "There was no time to send word."

Privately he thought that was as well. They had not had to watch Kati suffer, or see her death-pangs. But that did not assuage Richard's pain, or that of the queen. They closeted themselves in their Privy Chambers, seeing no one.

"I keep remembering what she was like as a babe," he whispered to Isabella. "I can recall her mother writing to tell me she had been born, and sending a lock of her hair... it was some months before I was able to see her. A pretty babe, she was... And when I took her into my Household after her mother died, she was so brave... Anne loved her, too. She was our light in darkness after Edward –" He broke off with a sob. Isabella clung to him, wetting his shoulder with her tears.

"We must arrange a Requiem Mass for her..."

"Francis will see to that. Oh, Bel, I wanted so much to bring her to the altar, and maybe in time see her gift me with grandsons..."

They wanted no company. It was Francis who saw to everything. When they did emerge, it was to go first to the chapel where Kati lay coffined, her body lapped in lead and waxed cere-cloth within the coffin.

They attended a Requiem Mass, and the Cardinal spoke the obsequies, and praised Lady Katherine for her many virtues, and that she had died a virgin. "Be sure she is in Heaven, among the blessed that die in the Lord," he intoned, censing the coffin on the bier. Isabella, veiled in black silk gauze, rose from her knees to lay a posy of rosemary and lavender, while Richard laid a wreath of white roses. Both were red-eyed with long weeping and clad in the unrelieved dark blue and black of court mourning. "Dearest Kati," Bel murmured. "I thought to have dressed you for your wedding..." Kati's lovely gown, unworn, clothed her now in lieu of a shroud. Lady Dacre said she should be shrouded in white silk, as became a virgin, but Isabella overruled her.

She clung to Richard that night, as they lay together in the great State bed. A single candle burned on the night-table, illuminating the shadowed face of her husband, and the gleaming tear-tracks that reflected her own. "I thank God for you, my dearling," he said in a choked whisper. "You are my strength, my very present help in time of trouble. I loved my Anne, and cherished her, but she was not strong, and after Edward..."

"Tell me about her," Isabella murmured, curling into his embrace. "I think I would have liked her..."

"I am sure of it. She was so gentle... You know I was her second husband? She'd first been wed as a matter of policy to Edouard of Lancaster, but he never touched her after the first night. And then he was killed, and my brother George took her in ward and tried to take her inheritance away from her. He hid her away. In a cookshop in London, would you believe? But I found her, and wed her, and we were happy at Middleham.

Then I was made king, and it was a burden she was not able to bear. God forgive me, I set a crown on her head, and she wilted under the weight of it."

"And Edward, your son?" she prompted softly.

"A dear lad. But he died, and she wept that she could not give me more sons…"

After a little while, his embrace loosened, and she knew he slept. *She could not give you more sons*, she thought. *But I can, Richard. I can.*

It was on that night, she was certain, that he got her with child again.

Dorset was slow to recover, and there were frequent relapses. He was unable to stand for more than a few minutes at a time. Soraya was an attentive nurse, not shying away from the often-unpleasant chores of the sickroom, encouraging him to leave his bed for the chair or the close-stool, coaxing him to eat. He found her unflagging patience astonishing, and relied on her more and more, used her as a sounding board for his thoughts. She listened to his ravings, thinking them the outpourings of a mind disordered by the fever. Surely they were not the thoughts of a sane man?

"It will not be easy, to unseat him," he said, clutching sweatily at her hands as she assisted him back to his bed. "Soraya, my love, think what it will mean for us. I will put my wife aside, put you in her place. You shall have anything you desire."

"I want nothing, *querido*, if I have your love." She stroked the sweat-sodden elf-locks back from his brow, soothing him. "Who is it you wish to unseat?"

"The Usurper Richard, of course! He has no right to the throne, I can tell you."

She stared at him, at the fever-gaunt face, the burning eyes in shadowed sockets. The fever was back, she thought.

"You cannot act against the king, Tom!" she said, trying to reach what sanity was left to him. "It would be madness!"

"But it must be done. It must be. He is a canker on the heart of England. But if we can remove those who support him… That snake Lovell, to begin with. We will defame and destroy him. Drop poison in the ears of any who will hear us. Let it spread like oil on water, like the very plague." He nodded to himself. "Oh, yes, the rumours have been started already, I've seen to that, Morton and I."

Soraya did not know who Morton was but, in an effort to soothe him, murmured: "But what of the queen, Tom? She is my friend and I would not hurt her for the world."

"Nor would we. To depose her would mean war with Spain, and that would be disaster. No, she shall be persuaded to marry young Shrewsbury. They are of an age. Trade one Richard for another!" He gave a harsh laugh that triggered a coughing spasm. Soraya proffered a cup of blackcurrant and elderflower cordial, and he gulped at it with a grimace of distaste.

"Get me paper and pen, woman. I must write to my mother. She must know my mind…" It was a scrawled letter, barely readable, and Soraya did not attempt it. She took it from his shaking hands, as he commanded. "By courier, to Dame Grey. Use Peter the ostler. He's trustworthy. The man will know the direction, and to keep it secret. He can't read any better than you. Take a gold angel from my purse to pay him. God's Nails, but I am weak as a kitten."

"You must rest, *querido*." She guided him gently back onto the pillows.

"She is a witch, my mother," he mumbled. "She and her dam, Jacquetta. Both witches. And bitches, too. Oh, yes. Enchanted poor Ned… He was king, and they snared him in a web of witchcraft. Poor Ned… You don't know what I am talking about, do you?" She shook her head. The fever-heat coming off him was scorching. "Tell you something, darling girl. Poor Ned… And his brother George as well, not an ounce of brain between 'em. It was little Dickon the Runt who was the smart one. Damn him… Now the Runt rules England…" Tears of weakness oozed from his eyes. She wiped them away, gentling him with her touch. "You'll help me, won't you, my love? You'll help? My mother doesn't like you, but that don't matter. I'll set you up like a queen…"

"Yes, Tom. I'll help you."

"Promise?" It was a childish whimper. "Promise me?"

"I promise…"

*****

November 1491

The Privy Council were assembled in York, and were loud in praise of the queen's regency rule.

"Her Grace clearly showed a wisdom beyond her years," Norfolk said, smiling. "She is a worthy daughter of great Isabella."

"I had no doubt of her ability, my lord." Richard nodded. "She and my sister Margaret are two of a kind. They don't need us men to rule their lands. Meg is of the opinion that she can outfox any ruler in Christendom and I can well believe it!"

There was a buzz of amusement from the Council. Only John Kendal did not smile. "Your Grace, there are matters arisen which I thought must wait on your attention. I did not wish to disturb the queen in her delicate condition."

He took folded papers from the portfolio before him, rose, and gave them into Richard's hands. The seals were of Richard of Shrewsbury, and Alexander, Duke of Rothesay.

To his Grace, Richard, Third of that name, from his loyal nephew, Richard of Shrewsbury. Uncle, I greet you well. Alas, I have ill news. Jasper Tudor and Margaret Beaufort have visited me, along with my Uncle Edward Woodville. I thought them both dead, and her confined. I do not know details of where they were until this time. Your Grace, it pains me exceedingly to reveal to you that they are fomenting rebellion against you. They told me they are raising their affinity, their aim being to dethrone you and set me in your place."

Your Grace, they spoke arrant treason. I dissembled, pretending to hear their plots, and let them think I agreed to this most heinous plan.

My lord, I beg you to believe that I will offer them no aid, in any form. I am, I remain, your most loyal and loving subject and the letter was signed *Loyaulté me lie, Richard of Shrewsbury.*

In silence Richard read first one letter, then the other. The genial expression on his face was gone, hardened into stone.

"Christ above!" And he brought both fists down hard on the table before him. "Sweet suffering Jesu!" In what was clearly an effort to control himself, he threw the documents down. His face, Francis saw, was chalky under the tan, the lines of stress livid. "This is what mercy buys me! I try for justice, and this -- *this* is how I am rewarded!"

"Your Grace...?" Bewilderment was on every face

“Read, my lords!”

Francis was the first to peruse the two sheets of parchment. He looked at his king, read the red fury there, and felt it in himself. “Treason,” he stated flatly. “I thought it was ended, after Bosworth. But…”

“No. Treason indeed, and by the Blood of Christ, we will have an end to it!” He swept the table clean of papers. “My lords, call out your affinities. We will muster at Chester, in seven days’ time.”

Once they were gone, he thrust himself from his chair and paced the room. “Jasper Tudor – why did I not make sure of him? Dorset, and Edward Woodville and that snake Morton…” He spun around and slammed his fist into the wall. Francis saw the shock of the blow jar his friend’s shoulders. And again. “*Damn them all! And those double-damned bitches Beaufort and Woodville…*”

Francis moved then, to put his hands on Richard’s shoulders. “We’ll sort the bastards out, Dickon. This time, for good.”

Richard drew a deep shaken breath and some of the tension went out of him. “Thank God for you, Francis.” He turned and grasped Francis’s wrists. “My dearest friend, faithful and just to me.”

“*Loyaulté me lie,* Dickon.” Francis whispered. “Always.”

The king rested his head for a moment on his friend’s shoulder, drawing strength from him. Then straightened. “We have work ahead of us. I must send to the queen. She must go to Middleham, and hold it against Tudor and his rebels.”

“Tudor won’t get that far,” Francis reassured him.

“Let’s hope not.”

*****

Word came from Rothesay that he was marching south to the muster point, bringing with him a force of five hundred battle-hardened Borderers. He also brought copies of the letters Elizabeth had received from her mother, revealing the plans already set in place by the conspirators. She had been clever enough to agree to nothing, to make vague promises of assistance and saying that her husband would most certainly support them.

"She has a head on those pretty shoulders," he told Richard proudly, and when the Council of the North, the War Council, convened in Chester, he was in attendance. "That witch her mother thought her daughter as treacherous as she is. She doesn't know my Bess!"

"This is valuable information," Richard scanned the letters. "'Price above rubies', my niece. How is her health?"

"Oh, bonny as ever, sire." He smiled.

"Would she come to Middleham and stay with the queen, do you think?" Richard suggested. "Bel is seven months gone with child, and I know she would welcome the company."

"Well, Bess is not so far along, your Grace. I have sent her to Berwick for her safety. She does not carry easily, so will give birth there, God willing." He crossed himself, and the other councillors echoed the gesture. "We're thinking Jamie for a lad, Eleanor for a lass."

The other arrival was Richard of Shrewsbury. It had given him nightmares, seeing those three, like evil ghosts out of the past. And worse nightmares knowing what they planned. He had seen the future – himself a puppet king on England's throne, and the traitors free to work what damage they could.

They must not succeed.

Again, he carried the letters he had received, and again the information was priceless.

Richard took it all to Sir William Catesby. "Set your agents on this, Will. We had expected trouble, but God knows I had hoped for some respite. I suppose they took advantage of my absence on the French campaign. We need to know where they are raising their troops, and how they are paying them. I thank God I have the loyalty of men like Rothesay and my nephew. And your Invisible Welshman, Master Bluett..."

Catesby coughed discreetly. "Your Grace, there is more. Rumours."

"There are always rumours, Will. They infest the court like fleas. It was all round Europe that I had done way with my nephews."

"These concern Viscount Lovell, your Grace."

"Well, we know how much credence to give them. That dog won't hunt."

Catesby quirked an eyebrow at the dismissive tone. "I would like to trace the source of these rumours, nonetheless, your Grace."

"As you will. I trust your agents and your own discretion."

"You are a born dissembler, Shrewsbury." Richard congratulated him later.

The youngster stood four-square before him. He was growing into his bones, and would be as tall as his father in a few years. He had the look of Edward as Richard remembered him when his brother had been Edward of March, tall and blond, though the image was spoiled a little by the sulky pout of the mouth. His mother's gift, that. "Do you think they suspected anything?"

"Why would they, sire, when I made a point of sending them such paltry supplies as I could spare, which was little enough – and such vague promises of joining them in the field?" He gave a quirking grin. "Oh, make no doubt, I want to fight. But it'll be on your side, Uncle! They are using my name to rise against you, and I would show that they do not have my support!"

Richard shook his head.

"We will talk more of this, nephew. You have left Warwick in charge of Chepstow?"

"He'll do well there. My seneschal and Master of Arms know my mind, and at the first sign of trouble, they'll lock the castle so tight a mouse would not get in. And they'll rein Eddie in before he can make any mistakes."

Later that evening, Richard summoned the boy to his Privy Chamber. "You understand, Dickon, that I cannot let you fight in this battle." The boy started to protest.

"But Uncle, you fought at Barnet with my father – you led the right wing, and you were no older than me!"

"I do not doubt your battle-skills, nephew. In a few years' time, yes, you will be as fine a warrior as was your lord father. God grant you will not need those skills. I know you would fight at my side. But I have need of you in another aspect. You have knowledge of this country. I would have you use it. Hold the Marches for me, Dickon. And when my son comes of an age to take up his heritage, I would have you act as his guardian and governor. To that end, I am creating you Earl of Pembroke and Lord Warden of the Principality of Wales." The boy gaped at him. "Further, I ask you to aid and protect my queen and my heirs should this fight go against me." *Had not the Portuguese princess prophesied that he would die in battle? Would this be the battle where that would be fulfilled?*

But one did not go into battle expecting defeat.

Shrewsbury went to one knee and bowed his head. "My oath as a Plantagenet, Sire. Though I pray God you are victorious."

*****

There was a thin rain, barely more than a mist, as Norfolk slogged his way to the king's tent. The king and his chosen commanders were studying the map spread over the table. "Blore Heath," Richard said. "My father fought here, and won. There is woodland here, and a stream – my scouts say it runs fast, and there are steep banks to it. Marshy land. I propose to place my artillery here –" He indicated the woodland verge. "There is enough foliage to confuse the enemy. Your command, Jocky. My lord Northumberland, the Cheshire Archers are yours. Use them well. John and I will lead the vanguard. Francis, you and young Rothesay – you hold the rear, and cut off any attempts to flank us." He looked each man in the eye. Good men, and trusted. "Let them come to us. If I know that varlet Jasper, he will want a swift victory. He has the numbers, but the men are untrained and undisciplined. They will not stand fast. I will wager half of them will have deserted before morning. We, on the other hand, have the best army in England."

"And the best commander, Sire," Northumberland rumbled. There were murmurs of agreement.

It was time to prepare for the battle. Young Tom Herriot was holding Pegasus as Richard left the tent – the stallion was fretting at the bit, foam splattering from his jaws. Mounting, Richard settled himself in the saddle, and rode to the front of his army. Grey light gleamed on halberd and helm, the fine rain dewing armour and jack. As he watched, the archers retrieved their bowstrings from under their caps, and fitted the strings to the bent bows. Each face was a mask of determination, of courage. He loved them, every one of them. He was their king, and they were his people. His visor was up, so that they could see his face. He wheeled Pegasus in a tight circle, and looked at his troops. Each of them wore a badge with Richard's blazon, the White Boar Crowned.

"You are the pride of England," he raised his voice to address them. "Those of you who fought with me in France, I know already are the finest warriors this realm has bred. Those new come to fight at my side – from Yorkshire, from Northumberland, from Devon and Cornwall, aye, and from the Marches, from Lincolnshire and Norfolk; from Kent and Sussex – you, all of you, are worthy to stand with the paladins of old. We could drive the heathen Turk from Europe and mayhap we will be spared to do God's will there, but today – today, my friends, we fight for our England against a rebellious rabble! Remember Tewksbury, remember Barnet and Towton! Remember Bosworth!" He spurred Pegasus into a rear. "Now St. Michael and St. George be our strength! Fight this day for our England!"

Norfolk, in his capacity as Earl Marshall, rode out to face the shifting rabble on the far side of the stream, just out of bow-shot. He had a big voice, and it carried. "His Grace King Richard says this. Deliver up the traitors Tudor and Woodville, and enjoy our clemency. Or face us in battle." He waited. Nothing. "So be it." The trumpets blared their challenge. He gave a signal, and the first of the artillery opened up in a blast of fire and choking smoke. Chain-shot scythed through the first ranks, and battle was joined.

Richard felt Pegasus dance under him, held the big destrier back as John of Lincoln joined him. It was like Ambien Hill again… Before closing his visor, he scanned the field – and yes, there was the Red Dragon banner in the centre! And

Jasper, at least, would not be cowering behind a wall of bodyguards.

He closed the visor of his helm, then, and his sight was reduced to that narrow slit. But it seemed that he hardly needed sight. The Royal banner overhead, along with the White Boar Crowned pennant, fluttered and snapped, proclaiming that here, here, was the king! He raised the battle-axe thonged to his wrist over the gauntlet. “Ready, John?”

“Ready, Sire!”

“For England, then!”

“For Richard!” Lincoln shouted, and he heard the men behind him take up the cry. “For Richard! For Richard!” As they had at Bosworth, on Ambien Hill.

This, some small part of his mind said, this is what it means, to be a king.

The axe swept down. He drove his heels into the destrier’s sides. *“For Richard!”*

And Pegasus, like his namesake, might have had wings, save for the thunder of hooves, splashing into the stream, sweeping down to break the front line of the rebels, the whickering of arrow storm above, a deadly hail with men falling, trampled under the weight of his cavalry, and he was among them, axe scything to reap a deadly harvest.

Blood and chaos, terror and wild exhilaration, heart pounding, sweat in his eyes stinging, blinding, so that he was forced to lift his visor.

Blood, as Pegasus trampled the fallen, seized men in his jaws as a hound might, struck out with iron-shod hooves.

Chaos. Blood spraying from severed limbs, the stench of it, the reek of spilt bowels. Clash of sword and axe and spear, screams of men and horses.

But no fear in him, none at all, only a wildfire running through his veins.

Chaos all around him, but there in front of him was the Red Dragon banner, and beside it was the figure of Jasper Tudor. No weakling, he, no coward cowering behind the armoured wall of his bodyguard, but a warrior lord, ready to do battle. “Jasper!” he shouted. “Yield, Tudor, and live!”

He was close enough to see the unvisored face of his foe, see the lips draw back in a feral grin.

“Never!” Jasper howled. “Look to yourself, King Hog!” Raising his sword now, two-handed, and taking a step forward to meet Richard head on, blade clashing on blade. Pegasus screamed a challenge, lunging as he had been trained, to strike with iron-shod hoof, head darting to seize the man as a dog shakes a rat, Tudor ducking to evade the stallion’s jaws and thus exposing himself to the clean downward strike of the axe. It bit with a jolt as it cleaved through mail and flesh, and Jasper was falling, going down without a cry under the hooves, head almost completely cleaved from his shoulders. Richard did not wait to see it, surrounded as he was by rebel soldiers, but it seemed none of them dared face him.

Bereft of their leader, they were breaking, he realised, the rebels turning and running, and he wrenched Pegasus’ head round, fighting the stallion for control, and realised that there was no one around him left to fight. One of his Yorkshire bowmen, grin white in the mud and blood-smeared face, was at his stirrup. “We fettled ’em, Dick-lad! Poxy Welsh bastards! We fettled ’em good!”

“Aye,” he managed to croak. “That we did.” His throat was clogged with dust. He longed for drink, but the stream was so fouled with mud and blood as to be undrinkable, even if he could get to it. The bowman reached up to him, a battered leathern flask in his hand. "Sup up, lad, and welcome!" The contents were sour small ale, but nectar to his parched throat. He handed it back, with a murmur of thanks.

It was over. And he must think now what to do, flogging an exhausted brain to action.

"The day is ours, Sire." Lincoln, armour slimed with blood, knelt before him in the churned mud.

"Now God be thanked." He eased his back in the saddle, wincing. "Your shoulder, John..." Lincoln helped him dismount, supporting him when his legs would have buckled under him. His hands shook with weariness as he raised his arms to lift the crown-encircled sallet helm from his head. The chill of the thin rain was welcome, and he closed his eyes. "The dead?"

"Jasper Tudor's body and that of Edward Woodville are found and identified, Sire. Woodville was taken trying to flee. Got a brace of arrows in the back before he went down and the halberdiers got at him. So we can be sure of those two."

"So. Finally that foul line is ended. Take the heads. Spike them on London Bridge. So perish all traitors."

"Amen to that."

"I will take you to the surgeons first, Sire."

A dishevelled and filthy archer thrust forward, falling to his knees in the mud. "Your Grace, Sir William bids me tell you that his agents have discovered Lord Dorset and the ladies Beaufort and Grey taking shelter in the chapel yonder."

"No doubt wanting to be in at the kill," Richard grunted.

"It is not an accredited place of Sanctuary, sire." Lincoln said. "They will be awaiting word of our defeat."

"Well, they will be disappointed, then. John, do you take a party and arrest them. Bring Dorset to me. The women can wait. I do not think I could be chivalrous towards them..."

Lincoln nodded. "As you will, sire." He swung away, barking commands.

Richard closed his eyes, leaning on Pegasus' flank. Young Tom Herriot, who had fought so valiantly at his side, was worrying at the thong of the battle-axe. "Cut it, Tom. And then go to the surgeons, get yourself attended to."

Richard was beginning to feel the full toll of his own injuries. His right arm and shoulder were solid with pain, his hand, when he pulled the gauntlet off, was swollen almost beyond recognition, near useless.

"Thank you, Tom..."

Then Rob Grant, Lovell's esquire, fell to his knees in the mud. "Your Grace..." His pain and discomfort vanished at the boy's words "Your Grace, Lord King, it is milord Lovell ---"

"Francis?" Last seen in the thick of the fight, his esquire at his side, "Where is he?" He could not even phrase the thought that was poison to his soul.

"They are bringing him to the surgeon's tent, your Grace—"

It was bad, then.

*****

4. Semper Fidelis.

Panting, Dorset thrust his way into the little stone chapel. They were there, kneeling before the altar, hands busy on their beads, heads bent. They did not seem to know he was there. There was no time for prevarication. Lincoln's hounds were on his track.

"Lady Margaret, Lady Mother, we must go. I can get you to a place of safety, and then you can take ship to France. But we must go!"

"No need," Margaret Beaufort said calmly "Even the usurper will hesitate to violate Sanctuary."

"Save this is not an accredited place of Sanctuary, Lady!"

"Nonetheless, God will protect us." She turned her eyes again to the altar. "You have our leave to go, my lord."

Dorset did not argue. He grabbed his mother by the arm and forced her to her feet, ignoring her struggles, hustling her to the door. But too late. As they left the chapel, they were confronted by John of Lincoln and armed men. All bore the marks of the battle, as Dorset clearly did not. Lincoln was still in his harness, filthy with mud and blood. He had the visor pushed up on his helm, shadowing the hard grey eyes, the tight mouth.

"By order of the king, Lord Thomas, you are under arrest. My lady Margaret, Dame Grey, I have orders to bring you before the king also. Had I not, I would have headed you where you stand. The blood of too many good men is on your hands, my ladies."

Margaret stared around her, at the circle of men, and collapsed to her knees with an eldritch wail.

"Where is my son, my Henry?" It came out as a harsh crow. "My boy, my darling, where is he? Be sure he will not see his mother so treated..."

"Your son, madam, is dead." Lincoln said coldly. "He has been dead these many years."

She reached clawed hands to her wimpled head-dress, dragged it off, and began to tear at her dishevelled grey hair, her wailing now guttural. "You lie!" she gibbered. "Foul! You, you are but a cat's-paw for the usurper, you traitor!"

There was foam on her mouth now, and Lincoln took a step back, as if he faced a rabid dog. Her face had twisted, mottled purple. She gibbered again, but incomprehensibly, and then, abruptly seemed to choke, clutching at her throat with a horrible gurgling before falling insensible on the cold stone. She twitched twice and then was still. One of Lincoln's men, at his lord's gesture, moved to examine her.

"She's dead, sir. An apoplexy, looks like."

Elizabeth Woodville stared in mute horror at the body at her feet, then turned terrified eyes to her son. "Tom," she whispered. "Tom, help me!"

Lincoln stepped between them. "He cannot help you, madam. You must ask mercy of the king."

Rob Grant was on Richard's heels as he limped across the churned and muddy field to the tent where the wounded were being attended. It was, as always chaotic, the shambles reek of blood, the cries of men in mortal agony. Hobbes was there working, but it was the Moor who was bending over a figure stretched on a pallet, while a shaking tear-stained esquire was removing blood- and mud-slimed armour, piece by piece. Richard eased him aside. He did not need to be told how bad it was. Francis was chalk-white, and blood was on his mouth where he had bitten through his lip. Heedless of his own injuries, Richard crouched at Francis' side, took his hand. The pain-ravaged gaze wavered, then fixed on him.

"Horse fell on me, Dickon…"

"And that's not all, by your looks. Master Hussey?"

"A crossbow bolt struck the thigh, here, and pierced my lord's armour, at the edge of the right cuisse." The curved plate had been removed, revealing the clotted mouth of the wound, and the stubby shaft of the crossbow bolt protruding obscenely. "I do not know if the bone was touched. The bolt must be extracted. I will know more then." He turned, rinsing his hands in water that was already bloody. "One of your countrymen invented a – tool – for this purpose. John Bradmore, an army surgeon, treated a wound to the young prince Henry."

"I know of it." And he did. He had seen it on more than one battlefield. The wicked little probe to gauge the depth of the wound – the knife to open the torn flesh so that Bradmore's tool could be inserted to grasp and extract the arrowhead, or the bolt, or the arquebus ball, the technique that had saved a prince's life, if not his looks.

It would also be exquisitely painful. Yet Hussey produced a small pin, and traced a line down the thigh before delicately inserting the point into the leg. Francis, already in considerable pain, did not seem to feel it. "There is a plexus, your Grace," he said absently, "a knot of nerves, which if correctly stimulated, can reduce pain… If you have other duties, you may leave your friend safely in my hands. Unless," and he smiled, "you wish to serve as the surgeon's cub?"

Richard did not answer that. He had been dismissed, and knew it. He was not disposed to argue.

Thomas lord Dorset had only seen the full Plantagenet fury once before, when King Edward had vented it on an unlucky courtier. He could not recall the reason, now. He could not even think constructively – he was as helpless as a rabbit facing some venomous serpent or scorpion. The king was seated in the abbot's chair, his face smeared with drying blood, as was the breastplate he still wore. The tabard with the royal colours was a bloodied muddied rag. His eyes were cold grey, glacial, and his mouth a hard line, white-lipped.

"You are accused of high treason, my lord. Of aiding the enemies of this our realm. Have you anything to say before we pass judgement on you?"

Dorset opened his mouth, but no words came. He had been a part – a reluctant part to begin with – of the conspiracy that would have put young Richard of Shrewsbury on the throne, backed by the Beaufort woman, and Jasper Tudor, and – oh God! --his own mother. They had persuaded him that it was possible, that it was necessary to remove the king, to put power back into the hands of Lancaster. They had promised him rich rewards, high status, all that had been his before. It had been a phantasm, a poppy-dream. He was guilty, yes – of being an addled fool, of believing what those witches told him. He had been bewitched, yes, that was it. His half-sister Elizabeth and her husband had tried to warn him. They had probably warned the king, as well.

He dropped to his knees before the unmoving figure in the abbot's chair.

"Mercy, dread sire. I beg you. I was a fool. It was my mother the Dowager---"

"Dame Grey." Richard corrected coldly.

"Her mother before her was accused of witchcraft, your Grace, and I think my own mother must have bewitched me—"

"Enough!" The king was on his feet. "I will hear no more of your babblings, my lord. You have been judged. You will go to the Tower, there to await sentence of execution."

Dorset grovelled at the king's feet, sobbing. "I cry you mercy -- Mercy, Lord King!"

"I wonder what mercy I could have expected at your hands, my Lord." He gestured to the men-at-arms. "The Constable of the Tower will have you in charge. Take him away."

"And Dame Grey?" the Constable asked.

"I will not see her. The Tower, for now, while I decide what to do with her..."

The worst wounded, Francis among them, had been carried into the Abbey precincts. Richard made the rounds, speaking to those who were able to hear him, giving praise where it was due. There were some – too many – who probably would not live out the day.

Master Hussey was seated at Francis' bedside, one brown hand on the slack wrist. Francis lay like one dead, the white of bandaging stark against his skin. The doctor looked up as Richard entered.

"How is he?" He was almost afraid to ask.

"He is strong, your Grace, and if the wound does not mortify, I think he will recover."

"He must." It was not the king who spoke, but the friend. "Whatever he needs, Master Hussey. To the half of my kingdom." He knelt beside the bed. "Francis, hear me," he whispered. "You are my soul-friend, the brother of my heart. Live for me, Francis, for God knoweth, I have need of you." He bent and kissed the pale brow, tasting the sour pain-sweat. *"Live for me, Francis…* Your king commands it."

*****

It was some days before the Moorish doctor pronounced Francis fit to be moved, during which time Hussey was at war with the good brothers of the abbey, whose ideas were not in accordance with his own. "My lord has already lost blood," he announced severely, when they brought the scarifying fleam, the leeches, and the cupping tools to the bedside. "He does not need to be bled." And since this heathen Moor had the favour of the king, the monks withdrew. They could pray for his soul, at the least.

And each day, Master Hussey would change the dressings on the wound, and smell at it for any hint of deadly putrefaction. He would pack the wound with honey and healing herbs, and dose his patient with opiates to ease the pain when he was conscious. And each day the king would demand news of his friend's condition.

"I want to send him to Middleham as soon as he can travel. He will have the best care that the kingdom can provide." He winced, straightening from the bedside, flexing his right hand almost unconsciously. The swelling had diminished considerably, but there was a stiffness that still pained him. He could not make a fist, or hold a quill. Kendall was trying to keep the number of documents to a minimum, knowing that Richard insisted on using his sign-manual on all matters of import. And there were many such matters. Richard had resolved to dig out the conspiracy, root and branch. And this time, the king's clemency would be tempered by the king's justice.

"Another week, perhaps, Lord King. There is an element of low fever, which is to be expected, but the wound seems to be healing cleanly."

Francis tossed in delirium. For all Master Hussey could do, fever ravaged his body.

In the screaming madness of battle, he fought to keep his place beside young Rothesay, except that the face turned to him was that of a grinning skull, and they were both beset by demons that howled and gibbered and shrieked obscenities and the horse under him was a horse of fire that gnawed and stabbed at his thigh. He could not be free of them, the demons, and Rothesay wept for him, tears of blood oozing from empty eye-sockets. I am in Hell, he thought, and it would never be over, ever, and he would suffer for eternity, for his soul was tainted with the blackest of sins, for in loving her, he betrayed his friend and king……

And so the arrangements were made. The horse-litter would travel at an easy pace, with Master Hussey in attendance. It took ten days for the litter and escort to reach their destination. Middleham had been alerted for their arrival by Sir James Tyrell, who had ridden ahead and now led the escort. He knelt to the queen, kissed the hand she extended to him.

"I am to tell your Grace that our forces were victorious, that the king is well, and that he hopes to join you here within the sennight."

"Thank you, Sir James. But now you will rest, yes? And take wine and a void with us."

"Your Grace, I am at your command, but I regret I must instantly to York, on the king's business."

"Return here when you are done, then, and take refreshment before you leave us to return to the king."

"With a good will, madam." He bowed again. A groom had brought a fresh horse, already saddled, and he swung astride, clattering out of the courtyard to continue his errand.

Isabella watched him go, and turned to her ladies. "Now God in his mercy be praised," she said devoutly, signing herself, and they all followed suit. She led them to the chapel, ordered masses of thanksgiving.

The Moorish doctor had seen his patient settled, and sent to ask the queen for the services of Soraya. "For I must sleep, madam, and one should watch."

"Of course, Master Hussey. Whatever you need, you have but to ask."

"Madam." He bowed his head. "There are herbs and other things I will need. I will list them."

"If we don't have them here, then we will send to York, and to the apothecaries there."

"My thanks. And you, madam, how goes the pregnancy? It will soon be time for your confinement. Can you spare Soraya to assist me?"

"I should be going into confinement very shortly, indeed, but I shall do very well with the midwives. Francis is very dear to the king. He must have the best of care."

It was when Sir James returned from his errand in York, and accepted the queen's invitation to dine, that more details of the battle were discovered. Soraya was watching at the patient's bedside, and was not privy to Sir James' news. Hussey, when he returned, sent her to eat. "But before you go, my child, you should know of Lord Dorset."

"My Thomas?" she said faintly. Her eyes stretched wide.

"I know you had a tenderness for him, child. But he had joined with the rebels, and so he has met the fate of all traitors."

"He is dead, then." It was not a question. The physician turned away, back to his patient. And Soraya felt her heart turn to ice, shattering into shards.

*****

February 1492

By the time Francis had recovered from the inevitable wound-fever, and was more aware of his surroundings, the queen had gone into her confinement, and within the day, had given birth to a healthy male child. He was to be christened Edmund. When Richard finally arrived at Middleham, he went first to salute Isabella, finding her sitting among her pillows and suckling his son. "Tomorrow he goes to Betty the wet-nurse. But I wanted him to myself until then."

"Whatever you want, Bel!" She loosened the infant's swaddling, wincing a little as the child reluctantly relinquished her breast. And squirmed in his father's grasp, going red in the face with annoyance at the loss of the teat. "He is a bonny lad, is he not?" she said dotingly.

"Very bonny. You'd better have him back before he screams! Dearling, I rejoice that you are well. But now I must go to see Francis."

"Give him my love, Richard? And send to tell me how he does? And I must talk to you about Soraya."

At the entry of his king, Francis struggled to get up, but Richard pushed him back onto his pillows. The room was one of the best the castle had to offer, hung with tapestry to counter the chill of stone, and the bed was wide and comfortable. But there was a smell of sickness in the air, and the bedside table held a variety of potions and physics. The injured leg was tented with some contraption to keep the weight of the blankets off it. Francis himself was unnervingly pale and gaunt – he had lost flesh during his long inactivity, and the bones of his face were stark under the skin, shadowed by a young beard.

"How goes it, my friend?" Richard asked quietly. He took the bony hand in his, pulled a stool to the bedside.

"Hussey says the wound is clean of infection, and I don't have fever now," he said impatiently "But they won't tell me anything, Dickon! I am mewed up here like a moulting falcon!"

So Richard told him what he wanted to know, and got a grunt of satisfaction at the fates of Jasper Tudor, Edward Woodville and Thomas Dorset. "But sadly, we lost young Rothesay, so Elizabeth is a widow now. Jocky of Norfolk is like to lose an arm -- cannon-shot. There are injuries aplenty, Francis, you are not alone. This rebellion has cost us dear."

"And the Beaufort woman?"

"Dead of an apoplexy, fortunately for her. I'll have her buried with her son. Dame Grey will go into close confinement in Bermondsey after a spell in the Tower. Sir William's agents are on the alert for Morton, should he try to come back from France, and there are orders to arrest him again before he can flee there. If the Council agree, he'll go to the block like the others, loath though I am to head a churchman. Well, the Pope can defrock him first." They sat in silence, each with his own thoughts.

Then Francis said: "How is the queen, Dickon? And the child?"

He saw his friend's face light with pleasure. "A fine boy. Edmund, we thought. I had Tyrell stand proxy for you at the font in the Minster. You should have heard the howls!

Bellowed like a bull calf. He's got a pair of lungs on him like Jocky! I swear Bourchier nearly dropped him..." He went on in this vein, until Francis said impatiently:

"And Isabella? How is she?"

"Blooming Francis, She sent you her love. I really think the air here in the north agrees with her. The roses in her cheeks bear witness to that. And have you seen the new arrival in the nursery? A Spanish dwarf, of all things! The Imp and Nicholas adore him. And he is a merry fellow. He makes Bel laugh with his jests – in Spanish, luckily, for he has a wicked wit!"

Domingo had soon established himself as a vital part of the household. He supervised the boys' riding lessons, and soon led them out to explore the country around Middleham on their ponies, himself riding a small but sturdy cob. He could charm them to sleep with stories – both boys were becoming fluent in Spanish – and he knew innumerable tales of chivalry and adventure, and more songs than a troubadour. He performed 'magic' tricks before their wide eyes, conjuring a coin, a card, a flower. And he was an accomplished dancer and acrobat, to boot, as well as a talented mimic. He won a rare laugh from Richard by mimicking Norfolk drilling his troops. But most of all he appointed himself the Imp's guardian, now that the boy was getting to be beyond his nurses' care.

"It is what my queen sent me here to do, your Grace," he told Richard.

*****

June 1492

The young Prince and his loyal companion roamed the castle freely, with Domingo an unobtrusive guardian, their favoured places being the stable yard and kennels. One of

Richard's favourite harriers, Matilda, had a litter, they were told, and Bevis the Dog-boy allowed them in to see her and the squirming pups. Matilda was a patient beast, and allowed them to handle her babies, under supervision.

"They don't look much like her, do they, Bevis?" Nicholas said, cradling one tan-splotched creature in his arms. It had the smooth coat of its dam, but the big paws showed promise of its sire's size.

"Aye, well, I'm thinking the queen's dog—" he broke off, remembering who he was talking to. "Ah, he's maybe their father." Privately he thought it was more like Hector…

"Do you think so, Bevis?" The prince was enchanted. "I must tell Madam my mother!"

Domingo rolled his eyes. "Of a certainty, my Lord, but after she has heard mass and broken her fast. It is early yet."

"They're all so lovely, don't you think, Nicky? Do you think my Lord Father will let me have one?"

"I think his Grace the king will most like look for an Alaunt for you, my prince. They are kingly dogs."

"Oh. But Nicky could have one of these, couldn't he? I'll ask my Lord Father."

Richard, suppressing a smile, agreed gravely that Nicholas could have one of the cross-bred puppies, and had the satisfaction of seeing the young face bloom with delight. "As soon as they are weaned, Nicholas. Have you chosen a favourite?"

"Yes, your Grace. And I'm going to call him Tiger."

"Why? Is he striped?"

"No, Sire. But Bevis thinks he's son to Leon, then..."

"Son to Leon, eh?" Richard thought of Matilda's size, and the comparative size of Leon, and kept his face straight with difficulty. "Then he'll be a brave dog, and Tiger is a brave name!"

The boys were full of ideas on the training of the pup, deciding that Master Domingo could help teach him tricks. Like maybe walking on his hind legs. The Prince had seen a dog do that when a troupe of jongleurs had come to Middleham. "And he can run beside my horse when we go riding! And sleep by my bed!"

*****

It was late afternoon when Richard rode in through the gateway. His business in York, preparing for the next session of Parliament, had taken too much of his time and he was glad to be home. He tossed his palfrey's reins to the waiting groom, who grinned a greeting as he sketched a bow. "A fine evening, m'lord!"

"It is indeed. Where is the queen, do you know?"

"It'll be her time to visit the nursery, m'lord."

"I should know that, shouldn't I? I'll join her there."

He took the stairs two at a time, and heard peals of childish laughter even as he opened the door.

There, on his knees, was Francis, and there were Nicholas and his own Imp, valiantly battling with wooden swords, while Francis coached and encouraged them, and Domingo looked on and advised and applauded.

The Imp's face lit up at seeing the new arrival. "My lord father!" he cried, and gave a sketchy bow before running to wrap both arms around his father's hips. Nicholas gave an unsteady bow, ducking his head when Richard held out his arms in greeting and knelt to embrace both boys.

"As God sees me, Francis, you are aiming to become Master of the Henchmen? How are you?"

Francis grinned at him. "Well enough, Dickon. I'll be riding again before the month is out."

"And our young warriors?"

"Doughty fighters, to be sure." At which point Nicholas, overcome with excitement, fetched his sire a blow that winded him, and Francis 'died' with appropriate drama at Richard's feet. Laughing, the four of them collapsed on the floor, joined by a small brindle greyhound and a wildly excited puppy, as Isabella's Leon preceded her into the nursery, tail wagging wildly. Hampered by the enthusiastic dogs, it took a moment for the two men to untangle themselves from the boys and dogs.

"Bel, my heart!" Richard saluted her with a kiss. "Come, Imp, where are your manners?"

"Lady Mother," the Imp said, bowing with proper solemnity, giving the lie to dishevelled hair and a large hole in one knee of his hose.

"My lord prince," and Isabella curtseyed to her son before folding him in her arms.

"My sister has a tooth now, father," his son confided.

"And how do you know that?"

"Because she bit me with it. She's really horrid."

“She bit you? It might be an idea not to put a finger in her mouth, yes?”

“And she *smells*.”

Nicholas agreed, backing up his friend, nodding vigorously. The nurse came in then. “It is past your bedtime, your Grace. And you too, Master Nicholas.”

Both looked hopefully at the queen, hoping for reprieve, but Richard nodded, and they turned obediently, the pup at their heels.

“A story, my lord Francis?” the prince begged. Francis got awkwardly to his feet, a little stiffly.

“If it will content you, *hijo mio…*” Isabella took the boys by the hand.

“My lord Francis tells the best stories, Mama,” the boy objected. “Yours are very pretty,” he added, conciliatory, “but my lord tells about battles, and swords, and fire-breathing dragons and lots of blood, and---”

“A true son of York,” Richard said wryly. “Go ahead, Francis. Come, my queen, it is too long since we were – together…” he finished lamely. Isabella smiled at him. She had been churched only days ago, after six weeks of laying in, and Edmund, her third child and second son, was in the charge of the wet-nurse.

Richard took her hand as they climbed the stair to their bedchamber. “I have missed you, Bel, more than you know.”

“And I you, Richard.” He drew her into his arms. “Leave us,” he instructed the waiting ladies. They curtseyed, smiling, and left. “Now I will be your tire-woman,” he said softly, and began to unfasten the laces that held her over-sleeves. The fastenings of her gown and kirtle and petticoat were next, until the rich fabrics were puddled about her feet. She stood at last clad in just her silken shift, and she stepped away from him with a mischievous little smile, raising her arms to unpin and take down her hair. Richard's breath caught in his throat. Her shift joined the rest of her garments. She shook her head. That red-gold glory fell below her waist in a rippling wave. She stood before him naked as Mother Eve. She opened her arms to him.

"Behold, you are fair, my love, behold, you are fair." he murmured. "*Fair as the moon, bright as the sun…*"

He gathered her hair up in both hands, burying his face in the scented silken mass.

*****

Richard, half-asleep, was aware that Isabella was restless. "What is it, lovedy?" he asked drowsily. She snuggled closer.

"It's Soraya," she said. "I am concerned for her, Richard."

"Is she sick, then? Or delinquent in her duty to you?"

"She mourns for Lord Thomas. She loved him truly, though he did not deserve her devotion. She nursed him through his sickness, though Dr.Hussey warned her she should stay apart from him. I wondered if she might be with child by him, but she says not ---"

Richard pushed himself up against the pillows, idly stroking a lock of her hair as it fell across his shoulder. "Dear heart, his death was necessary. He was an undoubted traitor, to me and to England. He abused our trust and deserved his death. I had no choice. A traitor from a family of traitors. And if the Beaufort woman had not died of an apoplexy, I would have headed her too… But these are not matters for our bed, my Bel."

“I know. I am wondering if she will wish to continue in our service.”

“If she does not, then I’ll grant her a pension and she can leave our Court. Though in truth I shall be sorry. She has served you well, and she dotes on our children. Dorset’s treachery was not her fault.” He kissed the lock of hair, smoothed it down, and drew her close. “Accepting him back to Court was a mistake. I was too lenient with him. It is a failing of mine.”

“Not a failing, my dear lord. It is one of the reasons why I love you so.”

“Only one of the reasons?” he teased.

“They are beyond counting, husband!”

He chuckled. “Well, let us talk to Dr.Hussey. She may have confided in him… But that is for the morning.”

“Yes, and I have disturbed your sleep. Forgive me?”

“I am not that tired, dearling. Come here…”

The stringent aroma of the dried rosemary was strong as Soraya’s fingers crumbled it into the mortar. Rosemary, stimulant herb, was sovereign for the memory. She did not need anything to recall her lover to her. The still-room, redolent with the scents of herbs, was her refuge. The good doctor had had her prepare an infusion of rue, that they called Herb of Grace, for the headache she had told him pained her and disturbed her sleep. It was a lie.

She slept and he came to her in her dreams, her lover, so that she wept to wake without him. She did not tell her master of this. He had spoken to her, gently: “The king is most generous, child. If you wish to leave the queen’s service, he will see you well-disposed. Whatever you want – gold, or a position in some other noble house – "

"The king is generous indeed. But I have no desire to do other than serve my lady."

"It is well. The king will know to reward your loyalty. It is his *raison*, loyalty above all."

Loyalty. Tom had trusted her, and she had been loyal to him as he to her. And the king had killed him. Now Tom haunted her rest. *Tom, querido, what can I do?* she cried in her heart as she went about her duties. His answer was whispered with terrible intent.

Avenge me, love! Avenge me!

*****

The household steward came to announce an unexpected visitor – and there in the outer bailey were two men, one burdened with a Swaledale weanling lamb, fleece washed white and fluffy.

"Sire – your Grace, m'lord king, you'll not remember me –"

"Harry Ramsden!" Richard said, descending the stair. "I remember well. How is it with you, Master Ramsden? You're looking better than when I saw you last!"

Ramsden doffed his cap. He was serviceably dressed in what might be his best, a grey woollen tunic with a hooded wadmal cape, and his young companion much the same. No trace now of the starveling outlaw. He beamed at his king.

"Doin' gradely, sire! Gradely! Got us a little cott Malton way, and an 'ansome flock. Got meself wed, m'lord, to a widder-woman – this 'ere's her son Rob." Rob ducked his head, overwhelmed. “Any road, your Grace, I’ve bought thee a gift. A thankee for what you did for us.” Rob divested himself of the lamb, which bleated as it was set down. “The best of the new lambs, sire, and sweeter eating you’ll not find—”

“Papa!” A squeal from the stairs. The Imp broke free of his nursemaid’s hand. “A lamb! Is it for me?”

His father caught him up before he could tumble onto the cobbles, and Richard thought better of telling the child that the creature was most like destined for the kitchens.

“It’s not a pet—” he began, as the Imp squirmed free of his grasp and knelt to embrace the lamb. Master Ramsden looked nonplussed for the moment, then bowed deeply to the queen as she descended.

“A lamb!” she exclaimed. “How kind of you, Master! And such a pretty creature! Now, my prince, remember your manners and say thank you!”

“Thank you,” the Imp parroted, not letting go of his enchanting new pet. “Look, he’s sucking on my hand! Look, Papa! Can I give him some milk? Or does he eat grass yet? Can I keep him? I’ll share with Nicky, I will.”

“I think, Master Ramsden, that the beast will be joining my son’s Middleham menagerie,” Richard said, with resignation, “and I thank you for the gift.”

“Aye, well, it’s like I tell any who asks, go to th’king, I tells ’em, and he’ll see thee right!”

He bowed again to the queen, and to Richard, and then to the child, and with a proud grin ushered his companion out of the courtyard.

February 1493

After his bastard son's death at the Battle of Blore Heath, the Scots king asked for the body to be brought home to Scotland, to lie there with his ancestors. The body, embalmed and encased in lead, was sealed in an elaborate coffin, emblazoned with the late Duke's arms, for its journey north.

Elizabeth, Duchess of Berwick, and now Dowager Duchess of Rothesay, travelled to meet it as soon as was feasible, having been brought to bed of twins shortly after the battle. She met the sad procession at York, where masses were to be said in perpetuity for the soul of the deceased. And Richard escorted her to Middleham to rest before completing the arduous journey back north. He had ordered the Court into mourning, and was clad in purple, a colour that frankly did not suit him.

"Elizabeth, we grieve with you. Your man was a valiant fighter, and he will be sorely missed on both sides of the Border."

She curtseyed to him, her widow's weeds unrelieved black. "Thank you, your Grace." She was no longer the flawless York princess she had been in youth. Childbed had taken its toll on her slenderness, thickening her narrow waist and breasts, dulling the brightness of her hair, but she was handsome still in her new maturity.

"Come now, the queen is anxious to greet you."

Purple did suit Isabella. She raised Elizabeth from her curtsey, giving her the kiss of kindred.

"Sit, sister. Be comfortable. You are recovered from the journey, I trust? And the childbirth?"

"An easy delivery, thanks be to God." She took the offered seat at the hearth beside the queen. "And both bairns are strong and healthy."

"They will never know want while I live," Richard promised. "Nor will you, Bess. Will you take your place here at Court? You will have precedence over all but my queen."

"You are kind, your Grace. But – forgive me – I have come to love my adopted country. It is wild, but beautiful in its wildness. And to be honest, I do not miss the intrigues and protocols of the Court."

"Tell me of the children?" Isabella begged.

"My lassie is Eleanor. She was born first. Her brother is Alexander, for his father. King James has been gracious enough to grant my boy his father's titles and estates."

"It will be our honour to stand sponsor for them at their Christening, Bess."

"I would like that, Uncle." Her eyes glistened with unshed tears. "As soon as may be, I will bring them both to York, to be Christened at the Font in the Minster."

"As always, you will be most welcome, Bess. Now, tell me, how fares your mother?"

Elizabeth grimaced. "She'll never lay eyes on my children. You were too forgiving, Uncle. I know you would not send her to the block, richly though she deserved it. I said I would take responsibility for her, and so I have seen her immured in an Augustinian convent on Inchmahome Island. Oh, she will be cared for, but kept more strictly than at Bermondsey. It is fit punishment. She hates Scotland. She will wish she had suffered the same fate as the Beaufort." A page offered a dish of sugared orange comfits. "I have visited the chantry you established at the Minster. It is very fine! And I would like to see that at St. Alkeda's."

"You must see it before you go back north," Richard told her. "And the school we set up there. If your boy comes to Middleham for his knightly training, he can attend, along with our prince and his fellows." There was a disturbance at the door, and the young prince entered, along with Nicolas, a spotted puppy, and the ubiquitous Domingo. Both boys proffered their best bows.

"My lord father," the prince said, "Sir Francis says the plans for York's sewers are completed!"

Elizabeth raised an eyebrow in query, and Isabella laughed.

"Another of my lord husband's innovations…"

"Yes, well, it will not come this year or even the next, but in the fullness of time, I hope we will have cleaner streets!"

*****

"Dickon, you've frowsted in here long enough! I've had Dragon saddled – it's a fine day for a ride! To Aysgarth and back, perhaps!"

Richard sat back in his chair. It was tempting, indeed. "Get thee behind me," he muttered. The room seemed airless, suddenly. He had left Isabella and Elizabeth playing chess and idly discussing matters to do with children and childbirth in the way of mothers, and he had no part in that. The duchess would be travelling back north on the morrow with the weather set fair. It occurred to him that he had not ridden out for leisure for a week.

The sun was low in a pale-blue cloudless sky, and there was a thin breeze, as there always was on the high moor, to rustle the bare branches of the few hardy trees that managed to live there. The feeble sun had not thawed the hoar-frost from the grass, and it crunched beneath the horses' hooves as their riders guided them down the bank to where water still flowed in the beck under a thin coat of ice. Dragon arched his neck and blew twin plumes of breath like his namesake. He was a bright bay in colour, strong in the quarters, and shaggy of coat since he had not been clipped out in the bitter weather. Francis, on a big dappled grey, followed his king as Richard drew rein, and Dragon stamped, turning his head to lip at his foreleg, then dipped his head to drink from the cold water.

Richard took a deep breath. "This was a good idea of yours, Francis."

Francis grinned at him. "Yes, I thought it was time you emerged from your lair." He eased his back in the saddle, pulling the marten-lined hood closer around his head. "All work and no play, Dickon – it's not good for body or soul."

"Oh, I know you're right. I should delegate more of the kingdom's matters to my ministers. At least we have a measure of peace now. Peace and plenty. We have time, at last, please God. Time to enjoy all the good things of life. Friends, and family."

"You are fortunate in both. Two fine sons and a daughter in the nursery."

"I thank God for them daily, and for her Grace my queen." He clicked his tongue to send Dragon on. Francis urged the grey to his side. "But this I count my greatest treasure, my friend; that my people are content." His gesture encompassed the view before them, the wide expanse of moorland, of hill and dale, where a thin plume of smoke rose from some hidden cott. "This is my Realm, Francis." He drew a deep breath. "This is my England. Not the intrigues of the Court, or the arguments of the lawmakers. This is the true England, my heart land. God's own country, as they say hereabouts, and I will not say they are wrong."

*****

June 1493

Soraya had never acknowledged any God, neither the Christian Jesu nor the Muslim Allah, or the Hebrew Jahweh. She had paid lip-service to all of them over the years, obedient to the demands of her various masters. When they prayed in church or mosque or synagogue, she would mouth the words she had been taught, stood or knelt or abased herself as required, but she knew that no one was listening, no invisible deity to hear the prayers of a slave-girl.

Now, however, she felt an ancient and atavistic need. So, she prayed to whatever god might hear, to the formless djinn of her desert ancestry. She did not know how to address them – if indeed they had names – but opened her wounded heart to them, offering the only thing she possessed, her soul.

Tom haunted her dreams. Her Tom, so tall and fair, Tom, who had taught her to love him, and made that loving so easy. He came to her in the depths of the night. '*Avenge me*,' he whispered from bloodied lips. '*Avenge me…*'

She woke herself sobbing his name. "*I will avenge you, querido. I have a surgeon's skill with a knife.*"

"No. That is too swift a death…"

"Poison, then. I know the uses of them all, of henbane, of hemlock…"

"Too swift, my love. Too swift…"

The king had taken everything from her, leaving her heart a barren wasteland.

"Hurt him, darling. He must suffer lifelong."

"Then I will take from him all that he loves…"

It had been easier than she thought. Dorset had had in her an able and willing pupil. Planting the seed of rumour in hating hearts was not difficult. There were those who still resented the king, resented his friendships, particularly his love for Francis Lovell. She herself had no antipathy for the viscount, but Tom had hated him, envious of his place in the king's heart. People will believe what they wish to believe, she knew. And there had already been talk about the queen's affection for Lord Lovell. She had been regent for her husband, and he her right hand. Easy, then, to embellish the close ties they had developed...

*****

Obsessed with the plans for Master Cabot's new ships, Francis only realised the lateness of the hour when his eyes began to blur with tiredness. He straightened, easing his back against the cramp of bending over the table, and looked at the candle-clock. It was half burned down. Was it that late? Close to midnight... He should get some sleep. Tomorrow he could write out a report for Richard, begin estimating costs.

There was a scratch at the door. He crossed to open it, finding a sleepy page outside, clutching a folded message. "Stephen, is it?" The boy was new to the Household. "You should be abed, boy."

"Yes, m'lord. But I was told to bring you this."

"Do you need to wait for an answer?"

"No, m'lord." And he performed a sketchy bow, spoiled by a yawn.

"Then get you to bed, lad."

"Yes, m'lord. Thankee, m'lord."

"Goodnight, Stephen."

He closed the door, took the folded note to the candle to read it. There was no salutation, and the hand was scrawled, unfamiliar. '*Meet me in the chapel at midnight. There are privy matters we must discuss.'* There was no signature.

Privy matters? Well, the note could only have come from the king, scribbled in haste. What could be amiss? Not another plot?

Moving as quietly as he could, Francis descended the stair. There were always some castle-folk about their duties, whatever the hour. The guards outside the main doors nodded an acknowledgement of his presence, and he passed through the little herb garden outside the chapel. It was shadowy within, lit only by the tall candles and the sanctuary light. Automatically Francis signed himself and genuflected before the altar. The air was still faintly scented with the honey of the beeswax candles, and by the incense of the last mass. He crossed to the Lady Chapel, and knelt there, gazing up into the sweet downturned face of the Virgin, her head crowned with a gilded gem-starred circlet. He thought she looked a little like the late Queen Anne. Maybe Richard had ordered the sculptor to portray her in this fashion...

The candle flames bent and flared in the draft of an opening door. There was a swish of fabric in the rushes, and the clicking nails of Isabella's little dog that was never apart from her.

"Francis?" a questioning whisper. His heart leapt. She was hesitant on the threshold, then the door was silently pulled to behind her, and the slight figure of the Moorish girl was a shadow within shadows. Isabella's hair was loose down her back – the chamber robe she wore over her night shift was crimson damask, furred with sable. The light sparked glimmers in the weave, ran fluid down the folds of the rich fabric, struck fire from the diamond clasp at her throat. He caught the faint elusive perfume of rose water. "Francis?" she said again, and he got to his feet and went to her, taking her hands and kissing them.

"Bel," he said hoarsely. "Bel, why have you come? Is Richard...?"

"Your letter... I had to know," She interrupted him, her voice trembling a little. "Francis, do you hate me?"

"Hate you? God above, Bel, by my hope of heaven, I love you! I have tried, God knows I have tried not to!"

"I thought perhaps... we were friends, Francis," She was hesitant. "But it seemed you changed towards me, and I thought you resented me, because I had the king's love. And I was jealous, I confess it, that there was a part of him that was not, could never be mine. He loves you, Francis, so much."

"We have been friends since we were boys together at Middleham. I would give my life for him, Bel. And I think – I know – he would do as much for me. But I love you, my Bel, my heart, my queen. And I knew I must keep myself apart from you, because I would not betray him, nor would I ask it of you."

"Francis..." There were tears in her eyes. Her breath caught on a sob. "My dear, my very dear. Could you not see that I loved you, too? You are as my brother. My most dearly loved brother."

"Bel, do not weep, I beg you! I am not worth it!"

A tear overflowed, made a gleaming track down her cheek. Seeing it shattered Francis' resolve. Shaken, he raised his hand to touch it, and with a groan took her into his arms. "My love, my heart!"

The candle flames bent and flared again as the chapel door opened. And the king halted on the threshold.

"Francis?" he said. Did he speak aloud?

His world was shifting sand, tilting under his feet, and all his certainties were so much dross, meaningless in the face of this ultimate betrayal. Their faces – so familiar, so beloved – were the faces of strangers, frozen, their eyes fixed on him. His breath caught in his throat.

"Francis."

He was no stranger to pain. No fighting man was. The sharp screaming agony of the piercing blade, the ache of wrenched muscles, the crushing blow that pulped flesh and shattered bone – all of these were intimate memories. As was the constant ever-present pain of his twisted spine.

But nothing, no physical pain, could match this.

He drew a deep shaken breath. And another. His voice did not sound like his, as if it came from far away. "Soraya." he said thinly. "Take the queen to her solar. Piers—" to the goggle-eyed page, "Summon my guard. They are to keep the chapel door. Let no one in."

The little room that comprised sacristy and vestry for Father Dominic was inky dark until Piers lit the candles. Light washed over the sacred vessels, gleaming in silver and gold, and the richly-worked copes that hung there waiting for the next mass. Neither Francis nor Richard noticed. Piers was dismissed with a jerk of the head. And Richard found he could not speak. The pain of this betrayal had him by the throat. "Do you have any explanation?" he managed at last.

Francis dropped to his knees, unable to look him in the eye. "Dickon," he said hoarsely. "Dickon, your note… it said to meet you here, and I thought…what you saw – oh, God have mercy, it was nothing, it was—"

"It was you and my queen in each other's arms," Richard burst out harshly. Both hands were clenched into fists. "Francis, that was not *nothing!* How long have you been cuckolding me? When I was in France? Before that?"

"Cucko –" Francis choked on the word. "Dear God in heaven, can you think that of me? Dickon – your Grace – believe me that I would rather cut my heart out than do you hurt."

"I trusted you, Francis. *Stand up, damn you!"* he commanded. "Of all men, you were my closest and dearest friend." His voice cracked. "And yet you put horns on my head and with her, the one woman I have loved as I loved my Anne."

Francis got to his feet, stumbling a little as he rose to face his king.

"Richard." He had no right, now, to use that affectionate use-name. "Richard, your Grace. My king. You must know – I have to tell you – oh, Jesu, I love her. I do love her. But she knew nothing of how I felt, I swear to you, she is innocent of any wrong doing, in thought or deed."

"But she came here to the chapel to tryst with you. Is that *innocence*?"

"I had word that you wanted to see me. Or so I thought. It was your note…"

"At midnight? What are you talking about? Damn you, you still say she is innocent?"

"Richard, you know your queen. She is kindness itself, she knew that there was something amiss between us. She thought me wroth with her. She wanted to make it right. I had been fighting my feelings for her. Richard, she called me Lancelot. The Ill-made knight. To me, she was –"

"Guinevere? An untrue queen!"

"Not Guinevere. With me she was as chaste as snow. We could never betray you, you who we both love. I loved her, I confess it, and I love her still, and will until I die. If that is sin, then I am guilty." He dropped to one knee, bent his head. "Forgive me. Or if you cannot ---" His voice was a whisper. "If you cannot, then take my life, for without your love it means nothing…"

"Oh, for the love of Christ, Francis, stand up," Richard said wearily. He summoned the guard outside. "Take Lord Lovell back to his rooms. And call the Captain of the Guard…I have to send you away, Francis. You understand? I have no choice."

Francis bent his head in silent acknowledgement.

When he was alone, Richard went to his Privy Chamber, and drafted a letter to Sir Robert Brackenbury. In the morning, he would give the order to his guard, to escort Francis south and hence to the Tower, to be held there at the king's pleasure.

The queen's solar would normally be busy with her ladies about their duties. Now in the still hours of the night, she was alone save for the little dog huddled at her feet. She had been sitting straight-backed in her reading-chair, but there was no book open now on her knees. As the king entered she rose and swept him a perfect curtsey, the chamber robe pooling around her, spread like the petals of a rose. "Richard, husband. Soraya, you have our leave to go."

"Madam my wife," he countered, bending his head in the merest bow. His mind still disordered from his interview with

Francis, his very soul bruised by what he had thought was their betrayal, he hardly knew what to say. "He said you called him your Lancelot, Bel," he blurted at last. "Queen's Champion. Your peerless knight."

"A pretty fantasy we shared. It meant nothing. No, it was not nothing.... I will tell you the truth." She took a deep breath. "For months I had seen him withdrawing himself, as if he could not bear to be near me. We had been used to sing together, to read from the tales of King Arthur. You know, for you were often with us. But then – he changed. I thought I had offended him. I knew how deeply he loved you, Richard. I could not bear that there should be ill-feeling between us. He had always been so kind to me... Even at the beginning, when I was a child, a bride in a country I did not know. He helped me so much – you made me Regent, and he was like my right hand. So, yes, I loved him. Like a brother, like your brother, Richard, like another part of you." She paused, straightened her spine, head high. "And know this. I am a daughter of Spain, of Castile and Aragon, and Princess of Asturias. I hold my honour, the honour of my heritage, unimpeachable. And by no word or deed have I dishonoured you, my king, my love, my husband. This I swear."

"Bel..." he said, choking, and stepped forward, and she came into his arms, trembling. "Oh, my Bel." He buried his face in the silken mass of her hair.

"Entreat me not to leave thee," she whispered," *or to return from following after thee; for whither thou goest, I will go; and where thou lodgest, I will lodge: thy people shall be my people, and thy God, my God."*

They were still for a moment, then Richard drew her closer They did not speak, only clung together. Then she stirred and pulled away. "Soraya brought me a letter, said it was from Lord Francis, and it begged me to meet him, secretly. The chapel, at midnight. I should have known he would not so compromise me, but – I did not think. So I dismissed my ladies, save for her, and – the rest, you know. But I swear on the Holy Cross, my husband, on the relic of Santiago, that Francis is your true, your most loyal friend."

"Yes. But I am sending him away, Bel. I have to. Someone – I don't know who – left me a note in my Book of Hours, suggesting I go to the chapel, that there I would find certain proofs of Francis' treachery. I went because I knew there could be no such proofs. There were rumours," he said slowly. "Catesby hinted at it. Whispers. Saying he was not to be trusted. I dismissed them. I thought – I knew Francis. I did know him. I did not realise he had so many enemies." He sat down on the bed. "When my nephews were thought dead, the rumours ran that I had killed them. My own brother's sons, left in my charge! Dear God, that lie was spread throughout Europe, by my enemies, and I could not tell the truth, that they were safe in Burgundy. Rumours are like a spreading poison, like a creeping infection that taints all that they touch. And now they seek to bring down my friend." He looked at her. "They have succeeded, Bel. I believed them, and so will others. I know the truth, now, but it will change nothing. *I do not know what to do."* He realised he was shaking. "Bel, do you have the letter still?"

"Soraya took it and burned it. I did not think..."

"It does not matter. Let us hope Francis was more wary. Where is Soraya?" He looked about. "What did she know of all this? Or was she merely Dorset's dupe?"

Isabella frowned, puzzled. "She grieved for Lord Dorset, I know. She was quieter than normal, but she went about her tasks as usual. I cannot think she would be part of this..."

*****

Silent in her little kid slippers, Soraya ghosted up the stairs. *I will avenge you, my darling.* The forged letters had done their work. Now it was time to finish the task. She would die for it, she knew. But then she would be with him, with her love, so her death meant little. So, first, the children, Richard's brats.

The guard outside the nursery door nodded to her when she smiled at him, knowing her for the queen's handmaiden, and held the door for her as she slipped inside.

It was dimly lit, only one shielded lamp on a high shelf, and peaceful, with the quiet breathing of the children and their dozing nursemaid.

The cradles holding the little prince and princess were screened from draughts – but they were not her primary target. The two boys, the prince and his companion, were snuggled together like puppies in a basket, fair head and red-gold on the same pillow. She drew the knife, took a step closer – and her foot struck something soft.

Tiger, Nicholas's hound puppy, disturbed from a pleasant dream chasing rabbits, yelped. And at that, another figure rose from the pallet on the other side of the bed – the dwarf.

He took in the threat in an instant; the growling dog, the glint of metal from the upraised blade, and as she struck out at the dog, to silence it, Domingo was there, shielding the boys with his own body.

Soraya snarled, and struck, and he took the blade on his forearm. The boys were awake now, and screaming. Domingo, one arm streaming blood, pulled his own weapons from the sheaths strapped to his wrists, and closed with her.

She cursed him, struggling to reach her victim, but he was faster, and she choked on her own blood as he buried both knives in her throat.

She fell, writhing, and he made sure of her with a blade in her heart. There was chaos, then. The guard was calling the alarm, the nursery maids were screaming, and Nicholas crawled from the bed to where the dog lay.

"I think he's killed, Dickon..." It was a sob. "She killed him...My Tiger..."

"No, young master," Domingo eased him away. He could see the animal was mortally wounded, but was still trying feebly to wag his tail. "But he cannot live. Turn your eyes away, now, and let me do what must be done."

It was the work of a moment, and then the king was there, taking in the gory scene – the dead woman, the dead dog -- and trying to make sense of it.

He had his arm around the queen, who gave a moan and went to her son, babbling endearments. Richard took charge.

"Bet, Nina, take the children into their playroom. Bel, go with them. Now sirrah," This to the dwarf, "What passed here?"

Domingo, wadding up a sheet to bind his wounded arm, told him. Richard listened in silence.

"I did not think she hated me so much," he murmured. To the guard, white with shock and convinced he would be blamed, he said merely, "Get all this cleaned up. Wrap the dog in something and lay it out of sight for now. The woman you can take—" he paused, being about to say she should be taken to the chapel, but that was too raw a memory, "—take her to Master Hussey's surgery. I will decide what is to be done with her later. Master Domingo, that arm needs attention."

"A scratch, sire, merely." The dwarf had retrieved his knives and was cleaning them on a corner of the bloodied sheet.

"Get it seen to."

"As you command, sire." He stood, replacing the knives in their sheaths. "If you would, though, your Grace… Please tell the queen that I am sorry about the dog? I know the boys doted on it."

Richard nodded. "I will tell her. And thank you. Will you go to the children? They will be in distress." He sent one of the guards for Master Hussey, who came immediately.

"My poor child," he murmured, straightening from his examination of the girl's body, closing her eyes. Her loosened hair was clotted with blood. "Yes, bring her to my surgery. I can do what is necessary."

"Why did she do it?" Richard wanted to know. "Had she run mad?" The physician shrugged.

"I cannot say, your grace. It must be that her mind was disordered by the death of her Lord Dorset, and maybe she had some thought of revenge against you."

Revenge, yes. I had taken her lover from her, and so she thought to take all I loved in retaliation. She tried to take the love of my queen, and of my children. And Francis. Dear God, Francis.

"Yes. It is one explanation. If you will, Doctor, hold yourself for questioning. I must know if she acted alone, or if there were others in the plot."

"As your Grace pleases." Hussey gave a short bow. "I am at your command."

"Thank you." Richard left him to do what was needed with the body of his erstwhile apprentice, and went into the day nursery. Lady Dacre was there, with the nurserymaids, and the queen was curled on cushions, both boys clinging to her. She was white as curds, but keeping a semblance of calm for their sakes. He knelt to embrace all three. It was some time before the boys could be put to bed, and it was Lady Dacre who had a sleeping draught prepared.

"I will stay with them, madam," she told the queen.

"As will I, sire." Domingo had spread his pallet beside the bed.

"I am in your debt, Master Domingo," Richard said quietly. "Be sure it will not be forgotten."

Richard led Isabella into his Privy Chamber, sent for wine, and made her drink. She was shaking with shock, her hands icy cold as he helped her hold the cup. He drew her onto his knee, and held her close, and at length, exhausted, she slept. He carried her to the daybed, drew up a fur to cover her, and sat by her side until the webby light of dawn brought remembrance.

It was Domingo who comforted the bereaved Nicholas next day, allowing him to weep in his arms, and when the tears had faltered to hiccupping, telling him of great hero dogs of legend, of Gelert; of Arthur's hound Caval; and of Argo, the faithful dog who awaited his master's return from Troy.

"And for sure, your Tiger runs the fields of heaven in their company, Master Nicholas, for by his bravery he has earned his place among them."

"Do you really think so, Domingo? Do dogs go to heaven?"

The dwarf dried the boy's tears. "I am sure of it, Master Nicholas. Would so loyal and loving creature not be welcomed among the Blessed?"

"Can we bury him properly? There's a patch of ground where the king's dogs are always buried. Bevis will know it. They're never just thrown on the midden. My father the king says that their loyalty is greater than that of any man."

"His Grace values loyalty above all other virtues. He will understand."

Tiger was laid to rest among the many deceased hounds that had belonged to Richard when he was Duke of Gloucester, and lately, king. It seemed appropriate.

If Master Hussey grieved for his erstwhile apprentice, he did not show it. He had concealed her injuries in a linen bandage, and wrapped her in a simple shroud, before having the body loaded onto a pony-cart. Where he buried her, he did not say. "She owned no religion, *la pobrecita,"* he told Isabella when she asked. "So I will not defile your churchyard, your Grace. Alas that she was so deranged as to attempt to kill your son..."

"Love can drive a body mad," Isabella murmured. "I cannot think she was in her right mind. I pray she rests in peace." She signed herself. "Richard, would it be wrong for me to have masses said for her? Although she was not a Christian, for so long she was my dear friend and companion."

"I know, Bel. I will instruct Master Catesby to put in train an investigation that I trust will discover if there were others behind this plot who used her as a catspaw."

In the Great Hall, a week later, Master Domingo knelt before the king, and recited the Oath of Fealty, his hands between the king's. Then the young prince stepped forward, clad in the robes of a Prince of Wales, the coronet bright against his red-gold hair. Domingo bowed his head before him. Richard took the sword from a waiting esquire, and handed it to his son. The boy had perforce to use both hands to lift it. It was unexpectedly heavy, and Richard helped his son with a hand over his.

"For your valiant service rendered to me, your prince, Master Domingo," the Imp said steadily, "I dub thee knight." And with his father's aid, he touched each of the dwarf's shoulders. "I dub thee knight," he repeated, and looked anxiously up at Richard to see if he had done it right, and got a small reassuring smile.

"And for your valiant service in protecting my son, Sir Domingo," Richard said, "What reward would you have from us?"

"Only that I may continue to serve in the prince's household, your Grace," Domingo said smiling, "And, at need, as your Court Fool."

"A wish freely granted! And welcome, Sir Domingo!"

*****

Richard sent for William Catesby, who arrived in York after a five-day journey. He found his king deeply troubled. Richard paced the floor of his Privy Chamber as if unable to sit still. Sir William watched him with sympathy. "Your Grace, please, you are making me dizzy," he said dryly. "You did not summon me to come all the way from London to watch you plough a path through the rushes. You asked me to investigate these latest rumours. Do you remember Miles Bluett?"

"Your spy-master. Yes. Your invisible Welshman."

"Indeed." Miles Bluett was the most nondescript man Richard had ever met. Five minutes after meeting him, it was impossible to remember what he looked like. But at intelligence-gathering, he was a genius, as was the man he reported to. "He worked for me since before Bosworth, and warned against the Stanleys and others. At your orders, I gave him instruction now regarding the rumours that have been circulating."

Richard spat out an expletive. "Yes. The rumours. What has he discovered?"

Catesby produced a thick folder. "It began even before Blore Heath, your Grace. You will recall the sickness that was brought back from France?"

"How can I forget it. I lost a beloved daughter."

"And Lord Dorset was also infected, as you know. But it seems, sire, that at some time during the campaign he met with John Morton."

Richard stared at him, dumbstruck, and the pacing stopped. He dropped into a chair. "Where?"

"In Paris, I understand. He and Dorset between them were the source of the rumours." He extracted a sheaf of pages, handed them to Richard. "It was put about that the reason the Viscount did not go with you was because you did not trust him."

"Would I have left the realm in his care if I did not?"

"Indeed not, sire. But because he was the queen's right hand, then—there is no smoke without fire, they say. It was when Dorset was sick with the fever that he suborned the Moorish wench. They were already lovers, and had been for some time. They acted together to hatch and spread the evil rumours."

"I thought she loved the queen..." Richard whispered.

Catesby shrugged. “As far as we can understand, she did not want harm to come to her mistress. But after Dorset was executed, she was resolved to bring you down.”

“And she knew where to stab at me. My children, and the two I loved more than anything on this earth, accused of such arrant treachery…” Richard shook his head like a horse tormented by flies.

“We have traced the page who brought my lord the letter – which has conveniently disappeared, by the way,” Catesby went on. “As has the page. He was one of Dorset’s household, given employment here after his master’s death. We tracked him down. Or what was left of him. His throat had been cut. He knew too much, you see. Dorset had made sure that his puppets were to be silenced.”

“What an evil tangle…” Richard paused for a moment. “Give me your wise counsel, Will. Forget I am king. Speak to me as a lawyer. What of Francis and the queen?”

Catesby steepled his fingers. “Under the law,” he said dryly, “Their actions can be construed as High Treason.”

“If the accused were guilty. Which Francis and the queen are not,” Richard was quick to say.

“The rumour-mongers have already tried and condemned them, your Grace.”

“As they tried and condemned me over the disappearance of my nephews.”

“Exactly so. Well, let us look at this as if it were a case in the courts. The queen, of course, is untouchable. Even were she guilty of treasonous adultery, she may not be put aside lightly, if at all. She is a daughter of Spain. To accuse her of such a crime… It could mean war.”

“She and Francis are both innocent of those charges,” Richard insisted. “Will, there is no evidence against them. Both Dorset and the Moorish girl are dead.”

“Your Grace,” Catesby said slowly, “I think this may be a case for your Star Chamber.”

Richard looked at him. “‘Justice must not only be done, but must be seen to be done’,” he said slowly.

“Precisely.”

“What are my options?”

“You will not wish for an act of attainder. A judicial review in your Star Chamber. Not a trial in open court. To exculpate the Viscount completely.”

“Members of the Privy Council,” Richard said slowly. “And two judges. Chosen without bias, Will, make certain of that. The world knows what he is to me, and I cannot allow it to be said that I would influence their verdict. God help me, this is like a shadow on the sun. I try to do right, but I am blocked at every turn. My late brother bore the Sunne in Splendour as his banner. My sun is shadowed, Will.”

Catesby nodded. “No matter what you do or say, there are those who will believe the worst anyway. You know as much as I do of the law. And of people, come to that.”

“Understand me, Will, I will not have him condemned unheard. An act of attainder is out of the question. It was bad enough when I had to send him to the Tower. Even though he was to be lodged in the comfort of the Wakefield Tower, still it was confinement.... The queen was distraught...And what of Morton?”

Again, Catesby gave his small smile. “It seems that he had an accident. Of the fatal kind. I understand he had overindulged somewhat, and in a drunken state was wandering the wharfs of Calais when he slipped and fell into the water. The tide being in, he drowned, so my agents tell me." His face had the bland innocence of a child. "By the time he was fished out, he was beyond help. Alas, poor Morton."

"Alas, poor Morton, indeed." Richard agreed. He signed himself automatically. "God pardon him… One bit of good news, anyway. I trust the body was brought back to England? His head can join the others on a spike."

"As you command, sire."

Isabella sorely missed Kati and Soraya both. She still found it hard to believe that her friend could so betray her. And to threaten the children! Lady Dacre was endlessly kind, but she was of a different generation to the queen, and something of youth and gaiety had been lost. Worse, something between the king and herself had changed. He loved her still, she had no doubt, he gave her ample proofs of that. But she knew how he missed Francis. 'My other self', he called him still…

They held festival that Easter, celebrating not only the holy season, but also the six-year anniversary of her arrival in England. There was public thanksgiving for her and the children, and young Richard was formally invested with the heir's title of Prince of Wales in a glittering ceremony at York Minster. He was almost sick with excitement, but carried himself with appropriate dignity, steadied by the presence of Nicholas at his side. Richard had knighted Nicholas along with some others who had served their lords as esquires. It came to him how like Nicholas was to his father – the same ruffled mouse-blond crop, the sprinkling of freckles. How proud Francis would have been, to watch his son receive the accolade…

The boy was part of the Royal procession as king and queen, wearing their royal regalia, walked the streets of York, and he had the honour to serve his king on bended knee at the banquet.

Domingo was at his best, tumbling, dancing, and as a grand finale, 'knighting' Leon with a peacock feather for blade. A giggling Nicholas, as proxy for the dog, promised not to piss on the floor. "For that is not knightly practise," the dwarf explained seriously. Richard, who had seen far worse behaviours, nearly choked on his wine.

*****

Francis

He had been released from the Wakefield Tower after a brief sojourn, and was living quietly at Minster Lovell. Richard consulted the Council, had formulated plans, and had decided to send him to Bristol, to oversee Master Cabot's shipbuilding. Costs had been calculated and agreed. Cabot's small fleet – the Matthew, the Angel, and the Pelican – would be ready within a very few months. There was to be another voyage of exploration to the New World.

Francis could join that. After he was heard in the Star Chamber.

The official summons, in Catesby's hand, required Francis to attend the Star Chamber to be heard, in camera, on the morning of Friday next. There were two letters. He thanked the courier absently, and retired to his privy chamber to read both letters. He skimmed it, the phrases dry and impartial, and it was signed in full by Richard himself, sealed with the Royal Seal. He laid it aside, and opened the other paper.

There was no salutation, but he knew Richard's hand.

Forgive me, Francis, that I cannot be with you. You know why I must stand apart. But if I could, believe me, I would stand at your shoulder and throw their lies in their teeth. Instead, I can only say to you – remind them who you are. And it was signed simply: *Dickon.*

On that Friday, unable to rest, Richard took the stairs to the stable yard in Windsor, outpacing his personal guard. It was raining hard, the dark clouds heavy with it, but it suited his mood.

It was raining still when Francis arrived to appear in the Star Chamber for what Catesby referred to as 'a judicial review'. The weather suited his mood. He had not seen or spoken to the king since the dreadful night in the Chapel. He understood why. He understood also that those who sat in judgement on him could not all be described as his friends. They had sat at the Privy Council meetings with him, had argued and disagreed just out of spite, because they knew he was Richard's friend and had his ear. He had dressed with care. Doublet and hose in unadorned grey velvet. Richard's note had told him 'Remind them who you are'.

Richard ordered Pegasus saddled – the stallion was over-fresh, not having had more than the minimum of exercise over the past few days, and he bugled at the sight of his master, pulling loose from the groom who held him, getting the bit between his teeth. Richard nodded to the groom and swung up into the saddle, not waiting for his guard. Iron-shod hooves struck sparks from the wet stone cobbles of the yard, and then they were out, the track was underfoot, muddy now with the blowing rain. Richard gave Pegasus his head, and the animal went from a jibbing trot that rattled the bone, from a canter into a full-on headlong gallop.

Francis believed that the two common-law judges were impartial, though, being southern gentlemen, one from Wiltshire and one from Sussex, and not courtiers. They sat in front, sombre in their black robes and caps, the only touch of colour their red velvet sleeves. The Privy Councillors emerged from the Robing Room, in their robes of state, crimson faced with ermine, and took their seats. They included the Bishop of Durham, John Shirwood, and Sir Richard Fitzhugh, Richard Salkeld, and Sir Humphrey Talbot.

There was an indrawn breath as he walked out to stand before them in the full panoply of the most ancient Order of Chivalry in the Realm. The dark blue velvet of the cloak, silk lined, bore the Garter Insignia on the breast, with the scarlet shoulder cape, the white silk knots and bullion tassels, the chain of office, all proclaiming louder than speech that here stood the Viscount Lovell, Garter Knight. He took off the velvet cap, with its plume of feathers, handed it to the page that had held his train. The dusty-blond hair, cut now to shoulder-length, was a little disordered. As he raised a hand to push it back, the scarlet sash with the glittering diamonds of the Garter Star was briefly visible. And he knew they all saw it.

Is this reminder enough, Dickon? he thought wryly.

Straight-backed, he moved to stand at the Bar, facing them, the mass of faces, and it was Catesby himself who addressed them. "This, my lords and gentlemen, must be understood to be not a trial but a review. I will ask each of you to consider what you hear, and give an unbiased opinion. And thereto, I will require of you your solemn oaths."

The driven rain seemed hard as hail, soaking man and beast alike. Richard did not allow Pegasus to slacken his pace. He had no idea where he was going, only that he wanted – needed – to get away. He had left his guard far behind.

Francis.

He knew he had done what had to be done, but where Francis had been, ought to be, the absence of him was a gaping wound that bled and bled. Their old comfortable companionship was gone, never to be regained. The leaven that was his friend was gone from the Court, and it was a sadder place without his wit and wisdom to lighten it.

There were, of course, no witnesses to be summoned -- the main witnesses were dead. Dorset had met his end at Tyburn, Soraya was dead also, having failed in her attempt to kill Richard's son. There were no others, save the whisperers, the gossip-spreaders, none of whom had actually witnessed anything, though Catesby's diligent enquiries had unearthed the backstairs pages and maidservants, who were willing to give 'evidence' of what they had heard talked of, of things they had imagined, embellished and had passed on to others… It was like wading in a swamp of lies and half-truths. Listening to it, keeping his face without expression, Francis felt unclean. They had turned something that had been pure and beautiful and fine into something shameful. And he had to listen to it, to hear it being spoken, becoming besmirched and ugly.

Mud splattered up from the flying hooves, but the hard rain had lessened. Pegasus pecked, jolting the rider forward, took a couple of paces, halted. Richard dismounted. The horse was lame on his off-fore, and stood, head down, blowing and shivering. Richard stroked the foam-splattered neck, leaning against it.

"I'm sorry." He did not know if he was speaking to the horse or to his absent friend. "I'm so sorry."

The guard had caught up with him by now, and reined in hard. "Your Grace…"

"He's gone lame. I'll have to walk him back."

"Take my horse, Sire. I'll bring Pegasus after you…"

"No." He shook his head. "Thank you, James, but no." He gathered the reins, stroked the rain-darkened neck and looked around him. "Where are we?"

"Windsor Great Park, Sire."

"Ah. Just so. Go on ahead. I'll follow."

In the end, Catesby asked if Francis had anything to say.

Into the waiting silence, his voice rang clear. "My lords, I can only speak the truth, as I am bound by my oath, sworn before you all. Yes, I loved the queen, I did and do, and shall while I live. I love and faithfully serve his Grace the king, have not broken my oath to my liege-lord, to be truthful and faithful to him – to live and die for him against all manner of folk. This I swore at his Coronation, and as Almighty God is my witness, I have kept that oath."

It was at that moment that the sun came out.

Quite suddenly, the dark clouds broke apart, and the sun came out, spilling dancing diamond light over the grass. But still there were shadows on the sun. There always would be, now.

Catesby came to Richard's Privy Chamber bearing a document heavy with dangling seals, which he laid with due ceremony in front of the king. "As we predicted, Sire," he announced, and Richard dismissed the hovering pages with a gesture. "I have the seals and signs manual of each of the councillors, and of the two judges. Sir Francis has been completely exonerated, as expected."

"There were none to object?"

"None that refused to sign, your Grace." He did not say what he thought, that they all knew what was good for them.

"Does Francis know?"

"I told him myself."

“God be thanked. Will, I want you to consult with Kendal and with the Herald King of Arms. I am creating Francis Earl of Richmond.” Catesby nodded. “It will be ratified in our next Parliament, and I’ll have it announced at the Guildhall. And there’s this.”

The document was waiting, almost completed. Richard took up the quill, signed it with his sign manual. ‘Richardus Rex’. And ‘Loyaulté me lie.’

Richard, Third of that name, by the Grace of God King of England, France, Ireland and Our other realms and territories. To all Lords Spiritual and Temporal and all other Our Subjects whatsoever to whom these Presents shall come, we greet you well. Know that we of our especial Grace to by these Presents advance and create our right trusty and right entirely well-beloved counsellor Francis Viscount Lovell, Earl of Richmond, the dignity and style of Viceroy to serve Us in our new Domains to the West.

Richard sanded the words, watching the sand soak up the ink. He laid the quill down, carefully. Unspeaking, silent, Catesby took the document from his hand, bowed and left the room.

Richard closed his eyes, dropping his head into his hands. He could not help thinking that he was sending Francis to his death.

May God protect you, my Francis. And forgive me that I could not.

It was done, and within the month Francis would be on board the Matthew of Bristol, heading for the unknown west.

*****

Nicholas, my beloved son – forgive me that I cannot give you my farewell in person. I am commanded by his Grace the

King to go on a quest – yes, like the knights of old – though it be not to discover the Grail but to find new lands in the Far West, and perhaps – who knows – to slay dragons there!

I entreat you to be obedient in all things to his Grace the King, who will stand for you in lieu of a father, and to her Grace the Queen, who will be as a mother to you. They I know will raise you up to be a true knight and fit companion to my lord prince, who loves you well.

Above all, love God and serve the King.

Remember me in your prayers, my son.

Francis, Viscount Lovell, Earl of Richmond.

*****

“Tide’s turning, sir. Be time to come aboard.”

Above his head the seagulls were squabbling, diving for the scraps and detritus of a working harbour. A brisk wind was getting up, stirring his hair and catching his cloak. He was reluctant, waiting for he knew not what.

“Sir?” Cabot repeated, more urgently.

Would there be dragons?

A stentorian bellow. “Way! Make way for his Grace.”

Francis turned. The thronging crowds parted to reveal the familiar sight of Pegasus and his cloaked and hooded rider. Francis took a step forward, his breath catching in his throat. The rider dismounted, pushing back his hood. Francis had not seen Richard for months, and for the first time he saw there were grey hairs now among the dark.

"Francis," the rider said. Francis bent the knee to his friend and his king and doffed his cap. "You will be my viceroy in the New World. You carry the letters patent to allow you to act with my authority there."

"I am at your command, your Grace. As always."

"Dickon," corrected Richard softly. "I am still Dickon to you, Francis." He pulled Francis to his feet and into a hard embrace. The king's voice cracked. "Slay dragons for me, Francis."

"Always, Dickon."

Above their heads the seagulls screamed, crying a valedictory. He watched as Francis was rowed out to where the *Matthew* waited. Seamen were busy about the decks, and as he watched the sails filled and bellied overhead. Freed of her tethers, the ship began to nose out into the Bristol Channel, and at last Francis was just another anonymous, distant figure on the deck.

"God speed," the king said softly. "And God keep you, my friend."

END

Author's note

This started off as a simple 'what if...' with the immediate aftermath of Richard's victory at Bosworth. But then the question arose – 'what then?'
It is not history, of course, but as the story unreeled in my head, it developed a life of its own, and just...grew. I wanted to give Richard the happiness that had seemed to evade him, so a young bride who could give him sons was incorporated into the story, and needless to say I could not ignore Francis Lovell and his passionate loyalty to his friend and king.
I plundered actual history with gay abandon, twisting it to serve the story. Whether or not you are an ardent Richardian, I hope you enjoy it.

Terri Beckett is currently living in Wales with her husband and three cats.

- Co-author with Chris Power of historical novel, NETTLEFLOWER

- Co-author with Chris Power of two-part fantasy novel: SUNFIRE and SUNFIRE AND SHADOW

- Author of THE GOD-DANCER (set in pre-Minoan Crete)

- Contributor to RIGHT TRUSTY AND WELL-BELOVED, YORKIST TALES and THE ROAD LESS TRAVELLED.

Printed in Great Britain
by Amazon